When the light cleared, Jack away. They knelt nex words, orders—things I coulc

Beyond them, I saw Jack standing. Beside him was the girl from the water's edge. Water dripped from her clothing and hair. As she held Jack's hand, she looked at me and pointed.

I reached toward Jack and whispered, "Save her."

I saw the terror in Jack's eyes as he stood motionless and stared at me.

"You've got to save the girl," I said again.

Jack looked around, knelt, and whispered in my ear, "There's no girl. It's okay, Caine. I gotcha. There's no girl. You're gonna make it. Just hold tight."

So much, so hard, I wanted to shout, "No. No. That's not it! You don't understand. That girl is the one we need. She's the key to all this!"

But all I could do was cough and buck. I could feel the floor's cold creeping into my body as the pain across my forehead intensified. I was at the point of forgiving everyone that had ever slighted me or anyone that I had mistreated. I thought about Jenna and was sorry about that also. I knew one thing for sure. I was about to die, and I could feel life slipping away. I think the only reassurance I was still alive was the pain. The excruciating pain. Man, getting shot hurts like hell.

Praise for Steven LaBree

COLD WATER CREEK:
"...a gripping and captivating mystery filled with twists and turns...lies, hidden secrets, and revealed truths. Difficult to put down..."

~Jeanne R. Kraus, author of Cory Stories, Annie's Plan, and Get Ready for Jetty.

Cold Water Creek

by

Steven LaBree

Cold Water Creek

Cover Art by *The Wild Rose Press, Inc.*

The Wild Rose Press, Inc.
PO Box 708
Adams Basin, NY 14410-0708
Visit us at www.thewildrosepress.com

Publishing History
First Edition, 2023
Trade Paperback ISBN 978-1-5092-4690-8
Digital ISBN 978-1-5092-4691-5

Published in the United States of America

Dedication

This project results from many people—first, my wife and her unending dedication. We writers are quirky at times, but she has given me constant encouragement. She is my biggest fan and inspiration, along with Will and Claire, for creating great stories.

Chuck Dillaman was my partner in crime. Chuck was one of those people you meet, you feel an immediate connection. We spent many hours chatting about life and things that don't matter. We became good friends, and I will never forget our fireside chats. He, along with Harold, Roger, Miguel, and several others in the Florida Keys, inspire some of my characters.

Many believe a writer works alone. The truth is a story is the collaboration of many people. My publisher, a cover artist, my editor, proofreaders, all the writer's groups I have been part of, and all the beta readers that contributed to the project. My heartfelt thanks to all of you.

I truly hope you, the faithful reader, enjoy this novel. My objective and best intentions are to entertain and deliver a great story. As a reminder, everything I write is true, except for the parts I make up.

Chapter One

Sunrise, Florida—1987

Jefferson Caine stood under the porch at the front door of his parent's home, staring at the green doormat under his muddy boots. The fragrance of roses drifted across the porch from the garden, recalling a memory of him bringing flowers to Sara when he'd hoped to win her favor—as gentlemen often do to impress the one person they love.

What began as a casual conversation, expressing feelings for each other, hoping to talk about their future, escalated into something out of his control.

Rain pounded the porch roof as water rattled the gutters and rushed down the street. His thoughts blurred of Sara and what he had happened. He paused, closing his eyes, took a deep breath, trying to gather his composure.

He considered slipping into the house quietly not to disturb his mother or father. Leaning against the door frame, he wiped the dripping water from his brow, folded one leg over the other, and removed his left boot. It dropped to the floor with a thud.

He thought there would be trouble if he tracked mud inside the house. And then he almost laughed. *How stupid it was to be concerned about something so minor as mud. How would he tell his parents about*

1

Sara? He removed his right boot and set it quietly on the floor.

Reaching into his water-soaked pants for house keys, he realized they were still in the ignition of his van back at the bridge. He cringed as his heart constricted. He thought he heard Sara call his name.

Peering through the glass side panel of the door, he saw his mother, Joanna, under the glow of a tiffany lamp. She sat in his father's brown leather recliner, an open book on her lap, her head angled downward. He tapped lightly on the glass. She glanced at the mantle clock in the curio cabinet, placed her book on the coffee table, and opened the front door.

"Jeff? Where are your keys? You're soaked!"

"It's raining," he said as he stepped past her.

"Where's your van? You're getting water all over my floor. I have towels in the kitchen."

He sat at the kitchen table in the impeccably clean kitchen with spotless linoleum floors. The surface light under the microwave reflected off the pale green walls and a white ceramic tile backsplash aside the Formica countertop. Several towels, fresh from the laundry, sat on the kitchen table, awaiting transport to the back of the house.

With a shiver, Jeff collapsed onto the chair and wrapped a towel over his shoulders. His mother flipped the wall switch, lighting the three hanging pendulum lights above the island area, filled a stainless teapot with water from the sink, and placed it on the burner.

"What's wrong?" she asked as the water heated. "I'm making tea. It should warm you."

"It's nothing, Mom. Nothing." He wanted to tell her but couldn't find the words. He just sighed and looked at her. "I don't want tea."

"No. It's never nothing when a son comes home without his van, and he's soaking wet. And very late, mind you. Obviously, there's a problem. Did you get into a car accident? Are you hurt? How did you get home?"

"Mom. Enough questions, and no, I wasn't in a car accident. I wish it were that simple."

Joanna settled into the chair next to him and placed her hand on his forearm. "Honey. What happened? Tell me." She pulled back, wrung her hands, and then put them between her legs. "Have you been drinking?"

"No, it's not like that."

"Drugs? You can tell me. I won't tell your dad."

"Mom." Jeff pleaded as he tilted his head back and focused on the ceiling. He exhaled. "Drugs or car accidents would be easy. Please. Just leave it."

"Then what happened? You can trust me to keep it between us, and whatever it is, I'm sure it's nothing we can't handle together."

"I'm not sure we can. I've really screwed up."

"There is nothing we can't overcome."

"Nothing we can't overcome?" Fists clenched, he stared at the table. "I don't think so. Not this time."

"Listen, honey. If you can't trust your parents, who can you trust? Just tell me what happened, and we can move on from there."

"My girlfriend is dead," he said without emotion. "How are we going to fix that?"

"Dead? Your girlfriend? How? What do you mean, she's dead?"

"It's not easy to explain," he said. "It was an accident. We argued about the baby."

"The baby? What baby?" Oh my God! Baby?

"Uh. Yeah. I kinda haven't told you guys about all that stuff."

"Jesus!" Joanna said. "You had a baby? With that girl?"

He was silent for a moment and lifted his gaze to meet hers. "Yeah. My girlfriend was pregnant, and she had the baby. What can I say?"

"Why didn't you tell us what was going on? When did you think you would tell us?"

"Mom! Enough," he snapped. "Yeah. We—. You can't do it alone, Mom, and I was going to tell you. I just kept thinking there would be a good time, and then–well–there just wasn't. Besides, didn't you hear what I said? The baby is the easy part of this."

"Sorry, honey. I know. You're right." Joanna pulled her chair closer and reached for his arm. "Talk to me, Jeff. You know you can." She guided his wet hair behind his ears and gently brushed her hand across his shoulder, adjusting the towel. Jeff hung his head and sobbed. "It's okay," she said. "Let it out."

Jeff knew this was a mother's unconditional love. His mom's kindness he had felt every day of his life. This situation was no different; he knew he could trust her with his darkest secrets. He sat back, inhaled deeply, and through an exhale, he said, "Okay."

"You good?" she said.

"Yeah. I got it," he said, adjusting his posture. "So Sara got pregnant and wanted to keep it quiet. I swear you could hardly even tell she was pregnant the whole time. Then he was born, and we needed to decide what to do. Long story short, she wanted to keep the baby. That's what she said last week. But tonight, she said she would put him up for adoption. I told her that was stupid. We could raise him. But then she said she could raise him herself and didn't need me. We argued all night about it."

"Whoa. Hang on a minute. You at the girl's house?"

"No. We were hanging at the bridge with the gang."

"Arguing?" she asked. "Couldn't the others hear you?"

Jeff sighed. "Well, not exactly. Everyone else was asleep under the bridge after escaping the storm."

"Why were they asleep?"

"Passed out mostly from the beer and pot."

"Oh, Lord. You were smoking pot?"

"No. Not me. The other guys did. I got there late because I had to pick up Sara from work. We stayed in the van because it was raining."

"We could have helped you."

"I know, Mom. I tried to tell her that, but she wouldn't listen. She told me that the baby wasn't ours. I knew he was our baby. I knew there wasn't someone else."

"So, what happened? You said you think she's dead?"

"I dunno. The conversation really heated up, and she got out of the van. It was still raining like crazy. She continued to argue after I got out and tried to convince her to go back inside. She pulled her arm out of my hand as I pulled her toward me. I said something—I don't remember exactly—but then she swung at me. She came at me again and I pushed her away. I was only trying to stop her and calm her down."

His mother nodded. "That's what you should do."

"Yeah, except when she jerked her arm from me, she tripped, slipped, or something. Anyhow, she fell backward and hit the ground, I thought. I tried to get her up, but she wouldn't move. I couldn't even tell if she was breathing. I figured she was unconscious, so I tried to pick her up. The rain was coming down hard, and my hands were wet, but when I pulled my hands away from her head, blood was all over them, and I saw it in her hair. She was lifeless. I tried to get her up again, but she was limp like a doll. That's when I saw the pipe thing that jutted out of the ground. I realized she'd hit her head on that."

"But not dead?" she whispered.

"I didn't think so. I dunno, Mom," he said as tears spilled over and ran down his face. "I carried her to the van, but I still couldn't get her to wake up."

"So, what happened then?"

"I don't remember. Honest. The next thing I know, I'm standing at our front door."

"Okay. I think you're in shock and are not making rational decisions. I'd ask your father, but that would make it worse. Let me think." She looked at him for a long moment, then stood. "Okay. We have to go. Come on."

"Go? Go where?"

"To the bridge, Jefferson. We need to check on your girlfriend. I realize decisions are tough for you right now, but we can't waste any more time. I am hoping she's alive and we can get an ambulance. God. Let's pray she is."

"I think she's dead, Mom," he cried, dropping his head into his hands. "What can we do?"

"If Sara is dead, we have a bigger problem. Besides, she's in your van, and if someone finds her before us, there will be a lot of explaining. You don't want that. Let's get over there. *Now*."

****

The drive to the bridge was less than a mile. Joanna turned to her son. "I didn't ask before with all the confusion. What's the baby's name?"

Jeff gave a sad chuckle. "That was the problem. Sara couldn't decide on a name."

"But you do that at the hospital when the baby is born."

"You're assuming the baby was born at a hospital."

"Wasn't he? I mean, how else?"

"It's a long story, and we can talk about it later. I don't really feel like discussing it right now."

The rain had slowed to a drizzle. A light fog lay across the grassy field. Around the bridge was visible. Jefferson looked beyond the dash and checked out the dark area around the bridge for any activity. He swallowed hard but stayed silent.

Joanna opened her car door and stepped out. "Where are the others?"

"Over there. Under the bridge. You can't see anyone. It's too dark, but they're there. Don't worry— everyone is out like a light."

"Where's the girl?"

"She has a name, Mom. Sara. She would be in my van unless she left."

He could only hope he'd been wrong, and she'd woken and gone home to their baby, somehow. They got out of the car and walked to his van.

Jefferson watched as Joanna opened the side door

of the van. Peering over her shoulder, he saw Sara's lifeless body. It almost looked like she was sleeping. Jeff pushed his mother aside and climbed in. Then he held Sara's hand. It was cold. He looked back at his mother through his tears. "See, Mom? Nothing."

His mother climbed into the van, touched Sara's neck and wrist. She pressed her ear against Sara's chest. Jefferson remained quiet, his cheeks wet as he watched, unsure who his mother had become.

"Follow me," she said and stepped out of the van.

Trembling, Jeff placed Sara's hands on her stomach, then swiped his arm across his face. He stepped out of the van and slid the door shut.

They stood at the front of the van. "Let me think for a moment." Joanna lit a cigarette as the rain started again. The wind increased, and the rain pelted them with big drops. The flashes of lightning brightened the dark sky.

"We don't have a choice," she said at last.

"What in hell are you saying?" Jefferson growled.

"I am saying your girlfriend is dead, and you will not go to jail for being stupid."

He looked at her. "Okay, but what does that mean? What do we do? I mean, we can't leave her here."

"Push it in," she said evenly.

"What? Push it *in the water?* The van?"

"Jefferson, you are not hard of hearing. Push the van down the embankment and into the water."

"The water? Are you out of your mind? What the hell?"

She reached out and touched his arm. "Listen to me. What's the alternative? Push the van into the canal and bury this problem before anyone sees us. There's nothing we can do for Sara. She's dead. Do it. Now!" she hissed as she flicked her cigarette butt away.

"You mean leave her in the van and walk away? Just like that?"

"Jefferson. This is not science. Yes. In the water, walk away, and hope this goes away. We don't have a choice as I see it. What would you tell the police? You accidentally killed your girlfriend because she had your baby? I'm pretty sure that wouldn't work, would it? You'd spend the rest of your life in jail and destroy all of our lives. You already told me her father doesn't care where she is; her mother is dead. She has no one else that cares about her but you. Everyone will think she ran away. Now help me do this before your idiot friends wake up. Go on! Move it."

Jefferson reluctantly agreed with a nod. "Fine. Gimme a minute." He climbed back into the van and held Sara once more. He kissed her lightly, said goodbye, and again told her he was sorry.

He slid through the front seats, placed the transmission into neutral, and then walked to the vehicle's back. He looked at his mother, who waited, her hands bracing against the van's back doors.

"Ready?" she said.

"Not really."

"Push, Jefferson. You can grieve later. We're running out of time."

The van moved slowly toward the embankment. Their feet slipped in the mud as they pushed, and Joanna stumbled to her knees. Jefferson continued to push until he was almost waist-deep into the water.

Joanna got to her feet again, wiping the mud from her knees. Her son stopped as the van floated. As water seeped into the vehicle, it tilted and bobbled. He watched as his van descended into the depths of Cold Water Creek.

The top of the van disappeared below the surface, replaced by a large plume of bubbles. As if on cue, the rain stopped. The waters flattened into black silence.

Jefferson continued to stare. Nothing remained but silence as lightning streaked across a western sky.

Joanna tried to remove some of the mud from her hands and wiped them on her blouse. Her whisper was harsh. "What the hell are you doing? Get out of the water and let's go!"

Jefferson turned and trudged to his mother's car. He looked back to the shoreline. Pulling the car door open, he got into the passenger seat. "Sorry."

"No time for sorry. We need to get out of here before your friends see us."

"It's not that. I just—."

"Just what? Second thoughts? Too late for that, son." She started the car, leaving the headlights off. She drove the car onto the street.

"No. It's just as I stood there watching. I just, I thought I heard something."

"What does that mean? You had better hope it wasn't one of your friends."

"No. I mean from my van when it was sinking. There was a noise I heard. I dunno. Maybe it was the water pressure collapsing the metal. It was something. A noise. A bump. Probably the thunder."

Jeff stared out the passenger window and occasionally sighed. Joanna turned into the driveway. "The lights are on in the kitchen. That's not a good sign. Your father is awake."

"Shit," Jeff responded.

"Watch your mouth, young man, especially with your father. It's early, and he will not be in a good mood."

Quietly, his mother opened the front door, and they entered. Light from the kitchen shadowed the living room floor, and the aroma of fresh coffee filled the room. William, his father, sat at the head of the kitchen table, dressed in shorts and a T-shirt facing the kitchen doorway. Jeff followed his mother.

"Where have you two been? Is everything okay?"

Joanna placed her purse on the kitchen island. "The, uh, the van broke down."

"Yeah. The van," Jefferson echoed.

William placed his coffee mug on the table and pointed to the clock on the wall. "Let's start again. What's going on? You're covered in mud and if the van had broken down, you would've got me up."

Jefferson stood in the doorway with his head down. "I don't know how to say this, Dad. I fucked up bad."

"Your mother is in the room, so watch your language. My suggestion would be that you start at the beginning and get to the end of the story before I lose my patience."

Jefferson paced the length of the kitchen and explained the story, avoiding eye contact with either parent. Once he felt he'd clarified everything, he sat at the far end of the kitchen table.

"So, let me get this straight. You hooked up with this girl from your school, got her pregnant, and now she's dead," William said.

Joanna interrupted. "We didn't have a choice with the girl, Bill. I know it was wrong, but what were the options? It wasn't like we were bringing her back to life. She was most definitely dead. I couldn't let Jefferson take the blame for this. You know they would put him away for murder."

William rubbed his forehead. "Joanna, if this comes back to haunt us, we *all* go to prison."

She touched the tissue to her eyes. "We will have to take that chance. My son–Our son will not go to jail."

"I get that, but my gut tells me to arrest him."

"Are you nuts? You can't arrest your son!"

"Of course I can. And I wouldn't be the first law enforcement officer to do that. But I said my *gut*, not my conscience. As parents, we need to protect him, but I also know what could be ahead. The courts will not be kind, and he'll be tried as an adult. Still, you need to understand what this means to this family, and to be honest, we either hide it to the grave or come clean right now and face the consequences."

Joanna stood. "Our son is not going to jail."

"What do we do then?" William pondered. "I guess the truth is both of you have rung the bell, so there's no going back now. I have a plan, but if it fails, we're doomed, destroying everything we've built." After a deep breath, he said, "But if you're determined, then we'll have to chance it." He stood from the table and walked to the window overlooking the garden in the backyard. "I have an idea. There is something I can do."

Perplexed, Jefferson looked at his father for the first time during the conversation. "Do?"

"Yes. That's what I said. Do. I have a plan, but I'll have to cross over to the dirty side to get what you need. There's an informant that I have used from time to time. We have a good relationship, and he is a lawyer of sorts. Shady as hell, but he can get what we need. I'll talk with him, but it's going to cost us. Anyhow, you said there's a baby. That will complicate things, but it's a priority."

"Yeah, there is. At her house," Jefferson said. "You're not planning on harming him, are you?"

"Not a chance," William said. "You mentioned the girl lived with her father and has no other family, right?"

"True. And that guy is a drunk and doesn't care about Sara or the baby."

"Okay. I haven't figured out that part yet, but you should ensure the baby is okay. Your next move will be tricky and certainly not what I'd want for you, but it might save your ass. I make no guarantees, but from what I see, we don't have much choice if we're not coming clean." William sat and adjusted his chair to face Jefferson. "The first thing to do is to check on the baby. Make it look like you're going by to see your girlfriend. Make it as if nothing has happened. You're just there for a visit. Do you understand me?"

Jefferson nodded. "Actually, that should be easy," he said. "My guess is her father is drunk or passed out. Either way, he won't know what's going on."

"What about her mother?" William asked.

"Her mother died a long time ago. No one will be at Sara's, but her father."

"Okay. That makes it easier. You and your mother go. I'll wait here. Make sure the baby is clean, fed, and such. Then both of you get back here. I will work on what's next and one more thing. If you see someone or the father is awake, deny everything. Don't say a word about anything."

****

After a change of clothes, Jeff and Joanna drove to Sara's house. It was seven o'clock in the morning, and the streets were quiet. Jeff approached the front door. He could hear the baby crying. He knocked, but no one answered. He knocked again, harder, then called Sara's name. He took a deep breath.

The door was ajar, and he pushed it open. Her father, unconscious, with a bottle of whiskey at his feet. Moving quietly, he stepped into the baby's room, picked up the infant, and comforted him. "Shhh, little one," Jeff whispered while he stuffed diapers and baby things into a bag.

He checked on Sara's father who was still snoring. He closed the door behind him and headed toward the street.

Joanna jumped from the car. "What are you doing with the baby?"

"What do you expect me to do?" Jeff asked evenly. "Leave him here? With that drunk ass? Mom, the old man is passed out on the couch, and Sara's not coming back. Without us, this baby won't survive. What else am I to do?"

Joanna rubbed her hands through her hair. "I get it, but oh boy, I don't think this is what your father had in mind. Come on. Get in the car before someone sees us."

Jeff got into the backseat of the car, carefully holding the baby snuggly against his chest. "We'll figure it out, Mom. We gotta figure this out. For his sake."

****

Jefferson stepped into his house with the baby in his arms. His father stepped from the kitchen. "You brought it home?"

"What were we supposed to do, William?" Joanna asked. "This child has no one."

"Yeah, Dad," Jefferson chimed in. "I didn't have a choice."

William threw his hands in the air. "Let's not get started on you and your choices. This one isn't one of your better ones, either." He glanced at his wife. "You two have no idea how complicated this makes things. I suppose we'll need to remedy this too, somehow."

"You're right, but how?" she said.

"The lawyer I mentioned earlier can fix this. He owes me a favor. This process will not be easy or cheap, but we can navigate it."

Jefferson paced the room. "So, what now? What do I do?" He stared down into his son's face, who was now quiet in his arms.

"All I know at this point is that our lives have just changed forever. This can be fixed, but there will be some significant changes. I'll make some phone calls." William looked over at his son. "Go pack your belongings. You won't be coming back."

"Where am I going?" Jeff asked.

"I have the same question," Joanna chimed in.

"Listen—both of you. We need to act quickly; less than twenty-four hours. There's a guy I know, Howard Devoit. He's a piece of shit lawyer and keeps a low profile. The courts revoked his license to practice several years back. Anyhow, it seems he couldn't get past a nice bottle of bourbon, which got him involved with some questionable characters, leading to some shit we don't have time to discuss, but it was inappropriate for attorneys. He moved on and found his niche, so sometimes missteps can disguise themselves and become blessings. In this case, he carved out a profitable operation while keeping it under the radar to certain clients with money to remove their history. So, pack your bags, and we can head over there."

****

The building was a non-descript block-style square with a few windows at the end of the street off the main highway. Jeff remained quiet as they walked into the faded gray entry door. The office area was bleak and worn except for a neglected plant in the corner that was dying from dehydration. A fluorescent light fixture flickered above their heads. They approached a frosted glass window at the counter, and William slid it open.

A small woman sitting behind a computer monitor looked up from a solitary desk. "How can I help you?"

"I'm looking for the office," William replied. If someone was looking to do business with Devoit, they asked for the office. No one used the words lawyer, Howard, or Mr. Devoit. Subtle and under the radar was what Devoit demanded.

When she stood, William noticed her casual attire; blue jeans and a blue top. Her hair pulled into a ponytail. She pressed a button on the wall. A door to their left buzzed. They followed her down a long, unadorned hallway past the factory floor of humming machines and workers. They turned right through another door and opened a large wooden door leading to a reception area.

"Sit here. I'll be right back," she said and exited through a door at the opposite end of the room.

"This is kinda scary," Jefferson said.

William nodded, his arms folded across his broad chest. "The truth is, you should be scared. Let's hope this works. If it does, you may have a chance at a somewhat normal life."

"What about the baby?" Jefferson asked, looking at the wall.

"Your mom and I will take good care of him."

Jefferson shook his head. "I can take him with me and raise him myself."

William's laugh was harsh. "Yeah. That won't cause any suspicion, will it? A young boy shows up alone in a new town with a baby. Yeah. That's not going to work."

"It could."

William's cheeks flushed as he shifted his posture toward his son. "Really? How's that smart guy? How are you going to get a job? Create a new life? Along with worrying about how to raise a child?"

"I guess you're right," Jeff said.

"Damn skippy I'm right."

****

Jefferson was about to speak again, but the woman came out of the office. "You can go in now."

William and Jefferson walked in to see Howard Devoit standing behind an elaborate wooden desk. He was dressed casually in a striped button-down shirt, black slacks, and a precisely coifed comb over. The office was bare except for a table with a computer, a camera, and a printer.

"Marshal Caine. Good to see you again," Devoit said as he rose from behind the desk.

"Good morning, Devoit. This meeting is an

unofficial visit, so no calling me 'Marshal,' please."

"Got it. What can I do for you, and who is this fine-looking young man with you?"

"This is my son, Jeff, and we need your services."

Jack sat behind his desk. "Sit, sit," he said. "To the point, as always, eh Bill? Onward and upward as they say."

"Yeah, great. Let's cut to the chase. I'll need your full cooperation and advice."

"Bill. We have quite a history, don't we? You know I can help you, but this sounds personal. Am I right about that?"

"You could say it's personal, but it needs to be completely confidential."

"Okay. Let's have it," Jack said, ready to listen to what his newest client needed.

"I need my son to disappear," Bill said. "Everyone, and I mean everyone, must believe he just ran away, left town."

Devoit leaned back in his high-backed leather chair and sighed. "Hmm. So, you want the full package. Erased. And then everything a new person will require moving on?"

"That's what I am thinking. Remember the Schilling case?"

"The one where we created an entirely new persona? You know no one has ever found that man," Devoit said. "What's it been? Twenty years?"

"I know, and that's a good thing. That's what I need, but there is something else I need, too," Bill said.

Jack sat forward in his chair and looked him in the eye. "Sounds complicated."

"It could be. There's a baby involved. He wasn't

born in a hospital, so there's no official birth record. These foolish kids thought it would just be their little secret," Bill said through a clenched jaw.

"Okay," Jack said, interlacing his fingers and placing his hands on the desk. "The Florida Department of Health has no birth record."

"That is correct. The baby doesn't technically exist."

"That makes it easier. I have a contact in that office. How do you want the records to read?"

"We need to have the document show it's our child. My wife, Joanne, and I."

"That's easy to do on paper. The neighbors might be a different story." He smiled at his humor. "So, Jeff needs a new identification?" He glanced at the boy. "How about his girlfriend?"

Jefferson's gaze stayed fixed on the floor. "She's already gone," William said evenly. "His new ID must be real, not the bullshit you give others. If you catch my drift, social security number, driver's license, the whole nine."

"I get it," Devoit said, getting to his feet. "Let me explain how I do this. Fake IDs are one thing; kids need them to get into bars and such, but those are flimsy and won't hold up. They work for bar bouncers and store clerks, but a cop will see faked a mile away."

"I need something solid," William said.

"I get that, so let me explain. Everything requires a social security number, so that's where we start."

"Like from someone that's died about the same age?" William asked.

"No. Not at all. That will get you caught, and I am a professional. When a person dies, so does the number if associated. We use real people that no longer need a number."

"Try me again on that. I don't understand."

"Mostly, our clients are homeless drug addicts and need money." Devoit shrugged. "They will end up dead on the streets, so I give them a decent fake ID and cash. They turn over their actual information, and I use it for *my* clients. When the cops find them dead, they have an ID, so no one questions it. Of course, no one comes forward either, so the social security number we swapped remains good."

"The shit we are doing for you. You'd better make your fresh start work. Damned good thing I retire next month."

"Dad–" Jefferson started.

William cut him off with a wave of his index finger. "Don't say a word. Let's just get this done."

Marshal William Caine reached for his wallet. "Retainer, I am assuming? Cash, of course."

Chapter Two

Fort Lauderdale, Florida—March 2017

Jenna and I met in college, and other than the first couple of years, it's been downhill ever since. I tried to make the best of balancing police work with marriage, and I gave her space. Most of the time, she gave me mine. Looking back, I can see that was no way for us to have a long and happy marriage. Hindsight is perfect vision, right?

The real turning point was a Saturday morning, the weekend before I got shot, which only substantiated her claim.

The evening meteorologist predicted a great day for surfing was coming up. Jimmy and I wanted to take advantage, and it was a chance to escape reality. I was thinking of a couple of beers and chilling because, to be honest, surfing isn't a real sport in South Florida.

The coming weeks were going to be hectic with my latest assignment with my partner Jack. A van found at the bottom of Cold Water Creek. I needed a distraction before the new week started, and it seemed the weather was helping me move in that direction. Some surfing would do well to clear my head.

I was up early and kept quiet because I didn't wish to wake Jenna. With board shorts and a favorite T-shirt, I grabbed a mug of coffee from the pot on the kitchen counter and headed outside.

Ducking under the garage door, it creaked open, reminding me to oil the hinges. I pulled my surfboard off the rack. It was all planned; pick up Jimmy, head to the beach, hit a couple of bombs, a nug or two, and then lay back with some cold beers in the afternoon. I slid my surfboard into the back of the Jeep.

That's when I heard Jenna. The creaking had attracted her attention. In my mind, I told myself a little squirt of oil would have saved the day. I wouldn't have heard the door or her. I thought about what Jimmy would say. "Shoulda, woulda, fucking coulda."

She stood in the doorway of our house, door wide open, in a pink cotton housecoat, matching faux feather pink slip-on bed slippers. "Carter! What are you doing?" she shouted loud enough to tell the whole neighborhood. "I told you I need you here today."

I looked over and cringed. With what Jenna was wearing, I hoped she'd get back into the house before our "conversation" became more of a spectacle than it was. I also figured that if ignored long enough, she would get bored and go away, and I could keep loading the Jeep.

As if.

I hung my head in defeat, knowing what was coming next. There was no choice at that point but to respond to her antics. If nothing else, perhaps I could appease her need for attention and get her to quiet down.

"I hire out that stuff, and you know that," I said. As the words left my mouth, I knew that was the wrong response. "Ya rang the bell," Jimmy would say every time I did something like that.

I shrugged it off because I didn't consider myself the problem. As well, I did not like conflict. It was not my strong suit, but I always stood up to her bullying manipulation. But it always ended the same way with me realizing what I'd done wrong. I turned back to my Jeep, knowing I was about to lose this argument.

All my days were getting harder to get through, always filled with the same drama. Jenna would have one hand on her hip, her foot tapping restlessly, and the other hand wagging in the air. She'd harp on me about what I'd done or not done.

Anyway, on that Saturday morning, the only thing I heard was fuckity, fuck fuck fuck. I did my best to ignore the ranting. I buried my head deep into the Jeep's interior and pretended to be busy. I hoped for the best outcome and prayed she'd step back into the house. She didn't. Of course.

"Yeah. Well, Carter," she shouted, "I have an appointment at the spa, and I told you last week. I scheduled the painters to start today on the house. Not next week, not next month. *Today.* I told you that three days ago, and I also told you I don't want them to be here unsupervised. Someone, and that someone is *you*, will need to be here because that *someone* is not going to be me."

"Well, butter my butt and call me a biscuit," I said under my breath, then removed my head from the back of the Jeep. "I told you about this exact thing during a conversation last week. It was well before you scheduled any painters. I told you, Jimmy and I were planning to surf this weekend if the weather was right. I specifically asked that you *not* schedule painters for this weekend. As usual, you ignored what I said and did

23

exactly what you wanted."

My retort got me the total sum of nothing.

She looked at me with her head cocked sideways, hand on the hip, and said, "My nail appointment is at nine." She flipped her nose to the air, turned, and shuffled back into the house. Being Jenna, before the door could close, she turned around and said, "You're too old for this crap, Carter. Surfing is for the younger crowd. When are you going to grow up?"

I had honestly tried, during our marriage, to be a good husband. Whether I fought it, gave in, or tried to reason or compromise with her, I was wrong. I sat on the tailgate and dialed up Jimmy's cellphone to give him the latest update.

Unpacking the surfboard, I recalled when Jenna was a lot of fun. Back in college, she was a different person, someone I loved to be around. Married life had seemed to dampen every reason we married in the first place.

To the most casual of observers, it was clear this weekend was now over. My only choice was to move forward with what I expected to be a shitty and uneventful day designed by Jenna.

There was nothing left to do but make another pot of coffee and wait for the painters to arrive. My day couldn't get any worse, I thought. But then, of course, it got worse.

It always did.

****

The morning passed; the painters didn't show. It felt like I had consumed enough coffee to fill a fuel tanker. Of course, as if I could read minds, I already knew Jenna would blame me. I gave the painters a couple of more hours, just in case. By noon, I decided the painters weren't coming and tried to salvage the rest of the day.

I called Jimmy to see what was up, but he had made other plans. My nerves were jittery from all the caffeine, so I decided on a run to help calm them. I kept the T-shirt on and grabbed my running shoes and shorts.

Running was salvation and helped me get to that point where I could relax. The pounding rhythm of the shoes against the pavement helped me keep time with the music in my head.

At the end of the run, my heart was about to jump out of my chest. Worse, I was edgy, electricity crawling through my pores. The gym wasn't far from the house, so I kept running. Then I jogged home, showered, sat by the lake behind the house, and finished the day with a cold beer.

One beer turned into a few, but a few wasn't enough. A bottle of gin and a touch of tonic water fit the bill. That was the last I remember about that day, except for the Anvil Crawler. The lightning danced across the western sky, signaling me to go inside.

I awoke sometime later in a sweat. Through burning and bloodshot eyes, I saw the ceiling fan wasn't spinning. The power was out. My head pounded. My eyes were on fire, and other than a dim light coming in the windows, I had no idea of the time. That didn't surprise me, considering the pounding thunder before I blacked out. It felt early in the morning, but I didn't think I'd slept.

Most of the time, liquor or not, I sleep like a rock, and I hadn't dreamed in what seemed to be forever, but now, the dream was back. Not only a dream, but a story I'd thought was over. It had haunted me since I was a young child; I always had the same dream, and I always woke at the same time. I didn't like it. There was nothing I could have done to stop it.

Maybe it was the liquor or the thunder. It could have been Jenna who had torqued me up for screwing up my weekend or a combination of all three. Regardless, I awoke knowing one thing, without a doubt. It didn't matter what had called it to life again. The dream was back, and it was about the little girl.

As far back as I can recall, she visited me at night when I was alone. Like clockwork, she woke me and tried to tell me something. When I was a kid, I tried to explain the dream to my parents, but they said it was my imagination. They thought she was one of those pretend friend things since I had only a few friends and no siblings.

But somehow, it felt too real to be my imagination. The dreams continued into my twenties. In that endearing way of hers, Jenna had always said to quit eating too many burritos for lunch.

Knowing what I know now, I wish friends, siblings, or even bad burritos had been the explanation.

Something always tells you the answer in the back of your mind, but you must listen. I learned that lesson the hard way. After what I discovered, I realized there wasn't any other way to understand the why behind the puzzle.

Regardless of the weekend and the drinking, I knew enough to know I was in my bed, and it was earlier than usual. Staring at the ceiling I was thinking, too early for work, but I couldn't stay there.

It surprised me to find Jenna asleep next to me. I hadn't heard her come in. Usually, after I'd had a drinking binge, she would sleep at the other end of the house, in a spare bedroom she created specifically for those occasions.

Her sleeping in our bed was confusing and not like her. I had no recollection of the night. I knew I could be a pain, but I tried to make it work. I believed I was sensitive and caring and couldn't understand why Jenna didn't see that. She stirred as if she could tell I was watching her, so I lifted the sheet and slid out.

Downstairs, I made coffee, then sat on the back-porch bench overlooking the lake where we lived. I thought about the days and nights. I thought about Jenna and what to do. The moon's light still shimmered on the water like a line of diamonds, making a peaceful setting. I wanted to enjoy the quiet moments. They were few and far between. My gut also told me things were about to change.

The disagreements with Jenna had become the norm. I accepted that. I believed the dreams had ended, but they hadn't. They were back, and that created an additional concern.

I knew, in the past, that when I felt things were going my way, it would all go south. With everything that had happened over the weekend, I was still at ease. I couldn't explain it, but it was like someone had removed a significant obstacle from my path. I should have known this was a sign. It seemed whenever life was good; everything would soon be upside down.

I'd left Jenna in bed, hoping she would sleep longer. But no, that would have been a different dream. She was up by seven. We passed in the hallway as I was leaving for work.

"I'm not making breakfast," she said. "Fend for yourself, and don't get killed today."

I didn't respond. I wasn't the bad guy here. I knew I didn't cancel the painters. I'd just wanted a day to spend hanging with Jimmy that didn't work out, and things got carried away afterward. So, I had a bit to drink. *So what?*

I grunted because her comment didn't deserve a response. Rather than start the day with a fight, I kept quiet. My mind would not.

Nice, I thought. *She has such a way with words.* I grabbed a breakfast bar and headed to the office to pick up Jack.

Chapter Three

I watched her die a thousand times.

A life cut short by the ember of fear prowling within all of us. The errors in judgment and the stupidity of our actions as fear controls emotions. It takes only a moment for evil to come alive. It takes a lifetime to forget what you did at that moment. In the end, I discovered that with love, like fear, you can do anything, including murder.

The truth revealed; my answers were always there. Every clue was in front of my face, even if I couldn't see them. My shrink called it denial; you know the truth but don't believe it. You can't. Things like that don't happen to good people. Instead, you go through your life blind and trust that everything is fine. Your life is ordinary.

My name is Carter Caine, and the story I'm about to tell you happened to me. Otherwise, I never would have believed it. You've heard the line before: at the request of the survivors, we've changed the names. Then again, by the time we finish this story, there won't be many survivors.

I suppose my life is like a baseball game. Bases loaded, two outs. Your team needs a point to win. Just *one* point, and there is a chance for three. But the guy at bat has the worst average in the league. The pitcher has the best curveball in the league. So what do you do?

You pray and hope the dumbass at home hits the ball speeding towards him at somewhere around 100 mph, or maybe you get really lucky, and he'll get walked. Ya gotta have hope but you know none of that will happen. Your gut tells you, game over. But you hold on to your happy ass and hope for the best. You watch the pitcher. He winds up. The ball leaves his hand. And you lose all hope. You know it's game over. But as if some angel came down and blessed the hitter's bat, he swings and nails the damn ball in the sweet spot. And there is hope. The ball soars across the pitcher's mound just out of reach and directly into the shortstop's glove. Yup. Game over. Welcome to my life. Fucking shortstop.

Working as a detective can be a sedentary job. You sit at your desk and question people. There are days you talk to news reporters and do the general desk and investigative work. Often the job is routine. Crime happens, we find the bad guy, and the bad guy goes to jail.

My captain decides which detective best fits a case and assigns the workflow. My partner and I manage anything from petty theft to burglary, murder, and rape. Mostly, there's little to do but investigate something that's happened in the past. Once you've resolved a case, you tackle the next one. Of course, there is *always* another one.

The years of police work shaped my mind and my thought process. I also learned that people could surprise me. They never seem to be who they appear to be. The average citizen—often witnesses—seem to believe there's something special about killers. They think they can pick one out of a lineup based on looks alone.

They've said things like "he's scruffy," or "he has shifty eyes," or my favorite, "he looks suspicious." Even before my training and experience, I somehow sensed it was much more complicated than that.

The average citizen believes they would see the look of a murderer. That specific look about them telling you I could kill.

To the untrained citizen, murderers look like murderers—crazy looks like crazy. Yet, I knew that was far from the real world. I learned a lot over the years about murder, crime, and how people think, but with our recent case, my gut said it would be different this time. This investigation would change everything I had ever believed—every fact, detail, and everything I knew as a cop or a human being.

Some people say life ends at death–the eyes close, and everything goes black. It's all over; there's no afterlife, there's no heaven. You dig a hole, toss dirt on the coffin, and that's the end.

Sure, we've all heard stories about a bright light or maybe your body floating overhead and looking down at a seemingly lifeless body—yours of course. That one makes me chuckle.

Some folks say the soul stays around to watch and protect the people we love. Me? I figured all that was bullshit except for the dead-is-dead-thing, since none of the people retelling stories about *being* dead are *actually* dead.

Other than that, I didn't have answers or preconceived notions about death. I had never died before. But sometimes, thoughts about dying consumed me. My conclusion was a combination of all those things. I thought I had it all figured out at one point in my life. My story proves that anything can happen; anything can be real, and just about anyone can kill you. Even with all that, I am not so sure about how life *or* death works. I know this. I left Jenna sitting in our kitchen as I left for work, thinking it would be a typical day. Nothing has ever been the same since. Fucking shortstop.

****

Everything that you'll read after this is the story of my life—my second one. If I'd begun with the story of my *first* life, you wouldn't understand my second life. Confused? Think about how I feel about that.

I discovered one truth after I recovered from the gunshot. In the end, truth floats to the surface through all the crud and crap called life. Sometimes, it's dumb luck. Sometimes, it's good police work. Sometimes, the dead walk right back into your fucked-up life and tell you everything, whether you want to hear it or not.

Oh, and there's one more thing I know about killers: they look just like you and me.

****

The workday started as it always did, for the most part. Sure, it'd been a tough weekend between me and my wife, Jenna, but that wasn't groundbreaking news. I mean, our marriage started like gangbusters right out of college, then a few years passed, and the everyday set in. She came from a wealthy family, and I got the feeling she didn't want me to be a cop.

The problem was, I am a cop. A real cop. I live and breathe it every day like it was my destiny to be what I am. The best news was that my partner Jack, and I had a new assignment, and I could bury my feelings in my work, and the weekend was now a faded memory.

"Looks pretty open and shut. How much more of a waste of time could we get?" I asked Jack.

He shrugged and handed me the summary, so I leaned back in my chair and gave it a quick read-through.

"Go see Captain Daniels when you finish," Jack said, then walked down the hallway.

A city maintenance crew assigned to clearing city property had discovered a van in a Florida canal. My experience and my *mind* said it wouldn't amount to much. My *gut* told me something else. Hell, we found vehicles at the bottom of canals in Florida all the time. We often find it's some citizen trying to claim an insurance loss or a teenager on a joy ride with their friends looking to hide the evidence.

The teenagers would steal a car and joy ride around town. It was a rite of passage I didn't experience, not with a US Marshal for a father. Anyway, they'd stop to get a pizza or convince some sucker to buy them beer at the local convenience store. After a night of the usual stupid teenager antics, they'd dump the car in a canal so the police or their parents wouldn't find out. I hated those cases, but it had been a slow month. I assumed my captain thought it was something to keep me and my partner busy.

In that I am a homicide detective, my first thought was the case belonged to Auto Theft. *Was this my captain's way of paying me back for being, well, me?* As I sat in front of his large, battered desk, with three paper coffee cups of a brown liquid filled to different levels, many considerations crossed my mind.

"You gonna drink those?" I motioned toward the cups.

"They get cold, and I don't like cold coffee."

"So, you're keeping them for who?"

Captain Daniels nudged his head toward Rick Taylor, the head of our Auto Theft and Recovery Unit. "Shut it, Carter, and listen up. They need some help, and you guys are doing a lot of nothing lately."

I sat there thinking, *those guys were a bunch of numbskull losers in my book. This case is ridiculous and insulting.*

That was my thought until Daniels shared the complete story. "You can wipe that annoyed look off your face, Caine. It's not only about a van in the water."

I felt that same familiar pang in my gut. "But that's what you said, right?"

"Looks like you had another rough weekend."

"Let's say it was interesting and leave it at that."

"Let me guess. Jenna wanted you to do something, and you fucked up. She got mad. You had a few too many—."

"That's enough, Captain. I get it."

"Do you? I mean, you've gotta get your shit together before it affects your job."

"It's not and it won't. So, why the Auto Theft case?"

"That was my point. You missed the part in the summary about the remains."

"Remains?"

"Yeah. Seeing if you were paying attention. There are remains."

"No shit. Well. That changes it up."

"Yeah, and with that, you get my point. You are a brilliant detective and need to stop letting your personal life interfere with things."

"Got it. Priority one."

"Anyhow, it appears it *was* a body. Only bones right now. To ID the victim, the initial challenge will be the timeline," he said. "The van was at the bottom of Cold Water Creek a very long time."

"How long is long?"

"Unknown. Twenty-plus years? Maybe thirty. We know that much."

"How do you know that already?"

"The van pulled from the water is an older Dodge van. It's in terrible shape, meaning it's been there for a while. There aren't too many of those left on the road, and there haven't been for a while. I'm guessing somewhere around twenty-five to thirty years. We'll know more soon. Should be a VIN on the block."

"Gotcha. I'll grab Jack and keep you posted."

****

I wasn't thinking about the case other than as a distraction from my wife. After the last weekend with her tantrums, the case would keep my mind occupied, at least.

Jack told me it looked like a bullshit case and wanted to be rid of it as soon as possible.

"What's your rush?" I asked.

"I got a fishing tournament this weekend in Islamorada with friends," he said. "It's for a good cause, and I wanna be there."

"Me too," I said. "Let's bury this thing and do it."

As the words left my mouth, I got that gut reaction again. Jack must have seen me cringe. "You good?"

I winced. "Yeah. I'll be fine." I said it, but I didn't believe it. The case wouldn't be easy to solve. Something was missing, and something in the back of my mind was poking me.

I'd seen thousands of faces in my years as a cop. Over those years, I discovered I had a natural gift. I could identify trouble long before it happened, pick out a suspect, or have a good idea of the suspect's identity. It was like my school days when I just "knew" stuff I had no way of knowing.

Of course, some of my abilities probably came from working with the criminal element. Eventually, a cop develops a propensity for spotting the characters. We meet them all the time, and it seems the same type of person finds themselves in trouble with the law. Of course, that was my theory, and everyone who met me knew I had a mind of my own.

My first thought was that the victim was driving the van and ran it off the embankment. It just so happened there was a canal in the way. The victim drowned, making it a simple case of accidental death in a van pulled from the water.

The Auto Theft team would get busy with the specific steps for evidence gathering and processing the incident. Of course, with the crime scene being at least thirty or more years old, there wouldn't be much of a scene to investigate.

For this investigation, the forensics team would identify the van. The Medical Examiner would identify the body. They'd tell us who it was that died in the accident, and we notify loved ones. If there are any, that is. Simple as it gets. The case would get closed, and we'd be onto the next case. I shook my head. There was nothing simple or easy about my life.

Jack looked at me. "So, what's the plan?"

I shrugged. "Usual. Let's go chat with the ME and

see if he has anything."

"I have never liked the Medical Examiner's office," he said.

"Fine. You can sit in the car while I go in."

****

The van, the remains, and all the clues were at the Medical Examiner's Office. Dr. Artemis Rite was the head of forensics and the prime investigator. Most of the time, he was temperamental and demanding. That day was no different.

Everyone knew the city was planning on developing the Cold Water Creek area. They had grand plans to make it a friendly park for everyone to enjoy, including a small pier and a new boat ramp. There was always a makeshift ramp, nothing more than sloping dirt into the water for small boats and kayaks. The waterway was a popular place for kids back in the day. I considered how curious it was that the police discovered a death as the city planned a new family park. Go figure.

The investigation, what we knew so far, rolled around my head during the drive. There were no leads, but the case was new, and Jack and I hadn't dug into the details. I was hoping to see if the ME had discovered any specific evidence that might tell me where to start.

Jack's stomach growled, loud enough to remind me I'd missed breakfast. After the less than a spectacular weekend and the squabble with Jenna about me surfing and canceling the painters when I didn't, her Monday morning instruction to me was, "I'm not making breakfast, so fend for yourself and try not to get killed today." Yeah. Welcome to my life.

Before lunch could happen, the morning lent itself to a homicide and autopsy details. Then we'd go about the business of investigating leads, then head for lunch as usual.

"Before we head over to Rite, how about a quick stop for some Cuban?" I asked.

"Cuban?" Jack asked.

"Yeah. Sorry, Cuban coffee."

"Gotcha. Like Espresso! Sounds perfect."

"Sort of," I said, grasping that Jack's New York taste buds didn't have my South Florida appreciation.

The Versailles Cuban Bakery sat amid iconic Little Havana in Miami, and most days, a stop there was part of my morning routine. But it was new to my partner, Jack Nelson. I thought he'd enjoy it.

I liked to get Café Con Leche and a pastelito, a small, baked, sweet pastry. Whenever we had an active case, I had a routine that seldom faltered: a quick visit to the bakery and then on to the Dade County Medical Examiner's office on northwest 9th Avenue in Miami. Of course, Jack preferred his black espresso with no sugar, so I had to explain that to the young woman behind the counter.

My pastry was just a memory, and my coffee down a quarter of a cup, we headed for the morgue. On an earlier call, Doctor Artemis Rite told me the evidence wasn't notable. I hoped he'd discovered something else to help us solve this case.

Jack got the car keys after I pulled into a parking space. "I probably won't be long, but you may need the AC. Don't go anywhere without me, partner."

The ME's office has a low-key exterior. It's a white building with one sign that reads in small letters.

If you're not paying attention, you'll pass it. I think it's by design because who wants to know where they store the dead bodies? Once inside, it's easy to navigate. Then again, I had been there before. I scanned my access card, and the airlock doors opened. I walked to the fourth doorway on the left.

Doctor Rite wore a white smock, a plaid button-down shirt, and a royal blue bow tie. His eyeglasses rested at the end of his nose, and he hunched over a long metal examination table. He peered through a giant magnifying glass attached to an extended arm. The formaldehyde aroma assaulted me as I pushed open the examination room doors. I placed a handkerchief over my nose as I moved beside the ME. Rite guided the magnifying glass above the table to scan the skeletal remains.

Without looking up, he said, "Can't handle the smell, Caine?"

"It's not that."

He just nodded. "Is that right? Where's Jack?"

"Dude. It stinks in here," I said. "How do you work like this? Jack is in the car."

"Like what?" Rite said.

"Whatever. You look like my mom when she's at the jewelry store."

"What's that mean?" he said, not amused but continued. "You know, one day, Jack will have to come inside the building. It's inevitable."

"Yeah. I got that. What I meant was, you know, standing at the counter looking for the latest timepiece or bracelet for her collection. Smoking your pipe and looking all debonair."

Rite didn't look impressed. "So, this is all we

have?" he asked, using his pipe tight in his grip as a pointer.

I crossed my arms, hoping to ward off the room's cold. Standing at Doctor Rite's left shoulder, I examined the bones, which looked like brown sticks. They were strewn haphazardly on the metal table.

He nodded. "That's all we have, at least, so far," he said. "Forensics is continuing to dig through the van."

I paused for a moment, thinking I should say something else, and that I always felt less than adequate around Rite didn't help my comfort level any. "There's a lot of scum and crap in there."

He turned and looked at my shirt. "Speaking of scum and crap, what did you spill on your shirt?"

I looked down. "Oh, that. Jack and I stopped for a coffee at Versailles on the way over."

"And mine is where?" he asked, one brow arched high.

"Oh. Sorry. I was so desperate this morning I didn't think," I said and made a mental note never to forget again.

"Let's try this," Doctor Rite said. "Let's arrange the bones to simulate a human skeleton as best we can. We must take into consideration it's all we have."

"Sounds like a plan," I said. "May be tough with so few bones."

Rite looked up and said, "Oh. That's not a problem. I have plenty of extras here and about. We can use them as fillers."

I stared at him, but I wasn't sure he was kidding. Then I saw him chuckle. "Just a joke, kid. Relax."

"At least, it seems, she didn't drown," I said.

"What do you mean by that? I never said she did or

didn't, and, perhaps you've forgotten, I am the guy that determines the cause of death."

"Uh. Sorry. You're right. I was assuming."

Rite continued to place the bones in what he believed were their most likely locations. He paused and scratched his head, adjusted his eyeglasses, and sighed. "Let me explain," as he turned toward me, "There was a cranial impact, but it doesn't seem serious enough to cause death. More likely, the victim had a condition referred to as catalepsy brought on by blunt trauma to her skull. I am not saying she was alive, but I can't say she was dead. Honestly, my assumption would be the impact, whatever caused it, was enough to make the victim unconscious."

"But not dead?"

"It's a tough call. If we had the internal organs, that's one thing. We don't. We have bones, and all I have to go on is a cranial impact, so my report will read the cause of death as blunt trauma because that is the only diagnosis I can provide accurately. We also need to classify this to know how to handle the case."

"So like accidental, murder, self-inflicted?"

"Exactly. I am going to assign this as a murder investigation."

"Agreed."

"Thanks for your input. As I said, murder. I want to ensure we cover everything. For example, she could have drowned because the van went into the canal."

"Got that, but it would be an accidental death."

"Right. But we have evidence of blunt trauma to the back of her head. So, I deduce a hit on the cranial region and dumped into the van."

"I can see that."

"But what you don't see is the severity of the blunt trauma. It didn't break through the skull; it cracked it. That's what leads me to the theory of catalepsy."

"Are you saying she wasn't dead when the van entered the water?"

"Thanks for keeping up. That's exactly what I am saying. Theory, of course, but backed by science and fact. There was a case in Mexico. They prepped the man for autopsy, marked, and everything. The weird part of it is that three doctors said he was dead. He wasn't and woke up on the table awaiting autopsy."

"Good thing he did."

"That's what I'm saying. But that's not a mistake we can make here since there's nothing but bones. So, like I started to say, not much to go on, but at least I can determine she's a she."

"How's that?" I asked.

"Simple. See this bony ridge above the eye? It's sharper in females than males. Females also have rounder or more pointed lower jaws than males, whose jaws tend to be squarer. Either way, most of the rest of the bones are missing. Is there anything else coming?"

"I don't believe there is anything else. It seems the forensics team collected only fifty-two bones along with a skull. That's what you have, right?" I asked.

"That's it," Rite said as he clenched his pipe between his teeth. "We are a bit short of bone structure, and I don't expect all the bones, but something closer to two-hundred would be helpful."

"Can we identify anything?" I asked.

"Not much," said Rite, "but at least we have the skull, which means my forensic artist will create a clay replica to give us a better idea. I'll shoot you a picture of it as soon as we're done. Also DNA might match something if she is in the system. Still, with the contamination of the water and the evidence being this old, that's a slim chance. There is one other thing I found that might interest you."

"Really? What is it?"

"In the slime, after cleaning all the debris from the skeleton, I uncovered a high school class ring, a thin gold chain, and what appears to be a plastic hair clamp."

"Now that's a positive lead," I said. "Anything else?"

"Other than young, female, and dead?" Rite asked. "No."

"That's her ring, you think?"

"I'm about ninety-nine percent sure on the dead part, but a hundred percent sure that's not her ring," Rite said.

"Sorry. What?"

"Too big. It's a male's ring."

"Got it. It's a start, at least. Anything else?"

"Well, Detective Caine. The mentioned class ring, about the only solid confirmation we have, shows the evidence is around thirty years old, so there's that. There is not much more to talk about until the forensics team returns with information on the vehicle."

"Is there anything else you tell me about the ring?"

Rite looked up from the table as if I had said something stupid. "Rather obvious, don't you think? Either it is a male's ring, or the victim had huge hands. I doubt that because the rest of her basic structure leads me to estimate she was about five feet tall," Rite said. "That being the case, most kids get rings in their sophomore to junior year. Take that into consideration. Not that it means anything. After all, I am only a doctor, and you are the detective."

I shook my head. "Yeah. I got all that, Doc. So, this is a thirty-year-old case. Back then, it was popular to wear the boyfriend's high school ring on a chain around the neck. We'll start checking for unsolved missing persons in that time frame."

"Good thinking, Carter. It's like you're a genius or something. Now you only need a name, and you're done. Then you can go home."

"Funny, Doc. If you can clean the ring, perhaps we can determine the name of the high school. And sometimes, there are inscriptions inside those rings. Then, since there was a ring, the boy was about seventeen or eighteen years old, so the girl was probably about the same age. That's where I was going with this."

"As I said, Carter. It's like you're a genius or something. Let me get right on that and scrub that ring for you," he said as he moved the examination glass out of his way.

"Smartass."

"Not this guy. Call me later."

"Tell you what, Doc. Do what you can. Me and Jack will grab some lunch and then talk to some folks. I'll call you this afternoon."

Rite waved me off, turning his attention to the table. He reached for the microphone hanging from the ceiling to turn on the voice recorder. He rattled off details as if he were making a grocery list. "Female. Approximately five feet zero inches. Skeletal remains only–bone count fifty-two, including a skull. Severe water damage is not remarkable. Cranial fracture evident unknown origin. Don't forget to scrub the ring for Carter." His voice faded as the examining room door closed.

I walked back to the sedan. As I opened the door, Jack asked, "Anything?"

"Well, we didn't start well," I said.

"What happened?"

"First off, we ticked him because we didn't bring him a coffee, but other than that, he was okay. He offered no evidence to speak of at this point. Well, some minor stuff, but nothing to go very far on. We know the victim is a girl, and the van has been in the water for about thirty years. We've got some research to do. You ready to hit lunch?"

"Yeah. I'm starving, and I can't wait to dig into something Italian today," Jack said.

"Okay, yeah, me too. I'm thinking of a big bowl of pasta, but first, the ATM."

Jack frowned. His grumpiness wasn't unusual. Today, he seemed worse than expected from the summer heat and an assignment that appeared impossible to solve. I shut the car door and headed to the ATM. My mind reeled with details and what-if scenarios. *Thirty years*, I thought. *Rust, sludge and old bones pulled from the canal's depths were the only evidence.*

The DNA, if there was any, might shine a light. It was our only hope at this point. Rite said tests could take months or longer. More evidence or identification could surface, but what could it provide? Even then, the evidence would be sketchy.

Then there was the vehicle's identity and the call

our captain had received from the FBI that said they believed this could be part of a serial killer they were tracking. They mentioned they would like us to keep them informed of the progress and offered assistance in tracking the vehicle. It was their way of involving themselves without taking over the case. The problem was the FBI always took their time researching, and this was a thirty-year-old cold case rust bucket. No worries, I thought. It's our job to solve cases, and we will keep moving forward.

Lost in thought, I realized I was staring at a dead ATM. Perfect, I thought. *Is this how my whole day is going to go*?

I looked over to my partner sitting in the car and pointed to the bank doors. The look on his face showed his impatience. He was hungry.

He turned his attention to the hot dog vendor cart. Shaded by a blue and yellow umbrella advertising New York Style hotdog, it was tempting. He waved me off, and I saw his lips move. "Speed it up." He tapped his watch for emphasis.

The pastelito breakfast didn't last long, and lunch was high on the list of priorities. It wouldn't work without cash, and I knew Jack wasn't the type to buy lunch for anyone. All I needed to do was get some money from the teller, get through the day, get back home, have a couple of beers, and watch the game. A simple process if you think about it, but we are talking about my life. Nothing is ever simple with Carter Caine.

Jack stepped out of the car, deciding to grab a hotdog while he waited. No surprise there.

I started for the doors at a jog.

Chapter Four

Once inside the bank, I saw that several teller lanes were open. Helen Kowalski was at the last line, and I liked her. She also had the shortest line, and experience had taught me Helen was always efficient. I knew she would get me out of there quickly. We made eye contact, and she gave me a nod. Knowing Jack's impatient nature, I checked my watch and figured it wouldn't take long to get my cash.

It was eleven fifty-five in the morning, and my stomach grumbled, reminding me what the wife said about not getting myself killed today as she shooed me out the door. *Thanks, honey*, I thought again. Of course, not getting killed was always high on my priority list.

I scanned across the people milling around within the bank, a habit of mine. When my eyes stopped scanning, I noted the characteristics of each one and moved to the next. That's when I noticed a squirmy little guy. He wore a Red Sox ball cap and charged through the front doors like he owned the bank. I knew he didn't.

"Sonovabitch," I mumbled as I felt a spasm in my stomach, and it wasn't from a lack of food or the fact the punk wore a Red Sox ball cap in south Florida.

It was that feeling again. I can only describe it as standing on the edge of a cliff or a tall building. You look over; you believe you will not fall to your death, but you could. As if you fell off that cliff, you have a twinge in your gut. Not butterflies, but as if something sucked the air from your insides. It was that twinge or reverberation deep inside my body.

The feeling alerted me when something was going wrong, or usually more than wrong. Whatever was going to happen was going to be big and most likely ruin my day. I'm sure it had a name but calling it 'the thing' seemed to fit, so I kept it at that. I wished 'the thing' would give me a little more warning. I had only seconds to respond.

Throughout my police career, 'the thing' was with me and had saved my life a few times. Now I stood in line at the bank, and it was starting again, and I knew this day would not end well. I braced myself for the inevitable.

I knew by the way this guy moved toward the bank counter that there was about to be trouble. It was in his eyes, his expression. He had one goal, and that was to get the money and get the hell outta the bank, fast.

He was a squirmy little turd, and he bounded past me to the front of the line and moved directly toward the bank teller counter. He looked like a hawk after a rabbit. Preparing for the encounter, I reached inside my blazer and rested my hand on my service revolver. I gave her a little pat for reassurance.

The perp wore an oversized Black Sabbath T-shirt large enough to hide his handgun. There was no room for a mistake, and I had been in this situation before. I released the grip on my service gun. It was a sure bet Squirmy had a weapon.

He flung his ball cap to the floor and pulled a laced stocking over his head. *Excellent timing, dumbass. Wait until you're under the camera to cover your face.*

As predicted, he pulled up his shirt to show a cheap .38 caliber handgun. Any police confrontation now would only ensure someone getting hurt. I also knew this could cause a hostage situation or something worse.

I thought of Jimmy and knew he would tell me, "This ain't your first rodeo, buddy. Cool your jets for a minute."

Jimmy was right, and all hell was about to break loose.

"Freeze!" Squirmy yelled. "Everybody on the ground. *Now!*"

He pulled the gun from his waistband and waved it around. He fired one round into the ceiling. Everyone dropped to the floor, hid under a desk, or tried to scatter. The action would play out. I didn't think Squirmy looked smart enough to know a 2-1-1 meant armed robbery, but I also understood that the sound of a police dispatcher would spoil the fun.

I reached for the radio's volume and silenced it. As I knelt on the floor, Squirmy moved closer to the teller. He switched his glance from the counter to the others in the room. He pointed his weapon as a warning. I figured Jack would hear the radio call from the silent bank alarm, and I hoped he wasn't in the mood to play hero and burst into the bank to save the day.

Squirmy needed to finish his task and head for the door. I figured Jack would wait outside to apprehend him. I believed the incident would be quick and dirty, and we would be on our way, letting the uniforms handle the details.

Squirmy sprung to the counter. He bounced around like a ball, still shaking from his withdrawals and nerves. He smacked his hand on the marble countertop. "Gimme the money! Gimme the fuckin' money!" he screamed. He tossed his backpack over the counter, hitting Helen square in the chest.

Helen stands about four feet eight inches and was almost as wide, so she was a big landing spot. She reached to catch the bag in her arms. *Oh! Ladies and Gentlemen. The wide receiver has fumbled a perfectly thrown pass.*

I watched as the black backpack bounced off her breasts and onto the floor. Her mouth gaped open, and her eyes were wide as she bent to pick up the bag. Otherwise, she stayed calm and stuffed the bag with the bills from her cash drawer and a parting gift. Her chubby cheeks were as red as her lipstick, and her tears drew black lines on her face from melting mascara.

She never took her eyes off Squirmy as he repeatedly slapped his left hand on the counter and yelled, "Faster, lady, faster."

Like Helen could have moved any faster.

I worked on the plan in my head. I knew what he needed. Let Squirmy finish with his demands, grab the cash, and then I could make the arrest when his arms were full.

As predicted, she pushed the cash-filled bag across the counter. Squirmy, with wide-open arms, grabbed the bag. His eyes bulged at the bounty before him.

He grinned, showing a partial grill of decayed yellow and brown teeth. He turned, pointed his weapon at the ceiling, and fired two shots. Everyone hunkered down. Helen placed her hands over her ears and ran screaming to the back of the bank.

Squirmy hugged the bag like a baby and ran toward

the front doors. He stopped and looked over at the crowd, then lowered his weapon. I wasn't going to react, but he pulled the hammer back. I couldn't take any chances.

I jumped to my feet, drew my revolver, and yelled, "Police Officer. Freeze. Drop your weapon."

He froze, stuck his hands up, and kneeled on the floor. "Alright, alright, ya got me. I'm doing it."

That response did not feel right. It was too easy, and every cell in my body said so. I knew something was about to happen, and it didn't take long. I noticed a turn of Squirmy's head, and his eyes shifted to the right. There was a slight grin, and that's when I knew trouble was around the corner. I had missed Squirmy's partner, who had, it seems, entered the bank before I'd walked in. *Well planned.*

He stood across the room, acting like a customer, and stepped around the deposit table. As the song goes, he was a man just released from indenture and no stranger to weapons handling. He and approached me with a steady, confident gait, a weapon aimed at my head—an enormous weapon.

I saw the barrel of a 460 Magnum revolver and knew one shot anywhere on me would be deadly. There is no surviving this weapon, and from the deafening sound of his first shot, he had it loaded with 460 Fusion ammunition—*boom*—first shot. I couldn't help but think why this guy would bring a cannon to a dove hunt. People were going to die. At that moment, Jenna's comment wasn't such a big deal, and I hoped for a Mulligan, but there was a bigger problem—a much bigger problem; a man coming at me with no desire to return to prison.

I turned with my weapon pointed at him but couldn't get a clear shot with everyone running through the lobby trying to get out of the way. He fired his gun again—*boom*—like a mortar exploding. Every window in the building shook as the sounds reverberated off the walls. That weapon is so powerful that you can't fire it without massive recoil, and this shot flew across the bank and slammed into a concrete wall. Rubble exploded across the lobby. Number three—*boom*—goes through the bank's front window, showering glass and sounding like thunder. I was sure that shot got Jack's attention. As he approached, number four—*boom*—his aim was better and hit the teller line marble counter, but thankfully missed me. I get one shot off during all the commotion, but I miss. *Boom*—number five ricochets off the floor next to me. His aim is getting better, but no shots left. He was so close to me with the last shot I could see the flame in his barrel, but, lucky me, shot five, and I had a chance. I thought.

I hollered for him to stop, but he kept coming, pulling a smaller handgun from his waistband and firing. It all felt like it was slow motion, and all I remember is that it was a *pop* and not a *boom,* but it burned as if a hot coal rod had wrapped across the top of my head. He had five more shots in that handgun. My head slammed onto the counter after I stumbled back.

Squirmy held the money bag while I heard him cackle. The partner continued to march toward me, his arm extended, weapon still firing. *Pop, Pop, Pop, Pop.* Number five hit my leg, and damn, did that burn like fire. One bullet left in his chamber, and he was close now—less than ten feet away—there was no way he was going to miss number six. I was very confident of one thing; I was about to die.

I rolled onto my side and returned fire. It was blind firing, but sometimes fate intervenes because, to this day, I can't explain how it happened. I hit the partner with a kill shot in the forehead. The surprised look on his face was satisfying. He dropped to his knees and fell forward with a thud. I thought about that shortstop catching the fly ball and hoped it wasn't game over.

I felt a hot slug in my thigh, blood covering my face, and a screaming hot burning above my right eye, but I had to fire on Squirmy. I raised my service revolver but melted back to the floor; everything faded fast—*at least one lucky shot.*

I watched as Squirmy gaped at his dead partner sprawled across the floor. He screamed like a little girl and fumbled for his weapon. The backpack exploded with Helen's parting gift, leaving a plume of red. I guess he realized I had destroyed his plan. He dropped the bag and his gun and ran toward the front door.

The security guard found his courage and jumped to his feet, tossing his Billy club at knee height toward Squirmy. The club crossed through Squirmy's legs. He tripped all over himself and slid headfirst through the glass door. He stayed face down, bloody and twitching. I tried to stand again but melted back onto the floor like a big puddle. With every ounce of strength left, I pulled my body toward Squirmy. I felt my body shutting down. There was blood spreading, people screaming, smoke, and chaos everywhere.

A burning pain thundered across my forehead and down my arm. I rolled onto my back as another pain shot through my body like a bolt of lightning. I stared at the ceiling of the First National Bank and wondered if I would make it home ever again. Hell. I just wanted lunch.

All I could think of at that point was Jenna, our last conversation, and the damned breakfast bar. I accepted this day would be my last day, whispering a prayer, knowing there would be no tomorrow.

As usual, Jenna was right.

****

Jack slapped his handcuffs on Squirmy, then ran over to me. Blood streamed from my thigh like a fountain. The gash from the near-miss of the bullet was bleeding into my eyes.

Jack knelt beside me, trying to get me to calm down. I knew it was over for me. I had a head wound and a shot through an artery in my leg. When I was a rookie, one of my colleagues was a leg shot at a gas station robbery. I tried to stop the bleeding, but it hit his thigh straight through the femoral artery. I couldn't stop the bleeding, and he died within minutes. Even with Jack's help, I knew it would only be minutes.

"Help's coming. Hold on, pal," he said while pressing his hand against the wound as the dark red blood pulsed through his fingers.

His words echoed inside my head. I knew this was it and the fear of every cop. Death had arrived, and it was my time. The room spun like a carousel, and it was so cold. Jack held the pressure.

The room darkened. The water screamed through cracks in the bank walls. I was going to drown. The water overtook me as I felt the water rise above my neck.

My entire perspective changed when I grabbed for

Jack. The robbery was a distant memory; I was in a dream, alone, sitting on the edge of a canal bank. A teenage girl sat cross-legged across from me. A low fog surrounded her. She stared at me without expression as she ran her fingers around a dainty gold chain hanging around her neck. I could see it held a golden ring.

Her hair was black and matted, her skin ashen white, and her eyes glowed like red embers. She beckoned for me with her free hand. Instinctively, I knew I needed to save her and reached out. But as much as I stretched, the distance between us grew. She faded, and I crawled to her. I pulled my body through the mud. I saw she was begging me, crying, still reaching out, but something pulled her away. It felt like a maelstrom sucking us down a long tunnel. Just before she disappeared into the darkness, she raised a finger and pointed toward the sky.

A bolt of lightning filled my vision, blinding everything, and everything went black and silent.

When the light cleared, I saw the paramedics kneel alongside Jack. They rattled names, words, orders— things I couldn't understand.

Beyond them, I saw the girl from the water's edge. Water dripped from her clothing and hair. She had a hand on Jack's shoulder but looking at me. Her arm extended, and she pointed.

I reached toward Jack and managed a whisper. "Save her."

I saw the terror in his eyes as he stared at me.

"You've got to save the girl." I tried to speak louder through garbled words.

Jack looked around then leaned down to whisper in my ear, "There's no girl. It's okay, Caine. I gotcha.

There's no girl. You're gonna make it. Just hold tight."

So much, so hard, I wanted to shout, "No. No. That's not it! You don't understand. That girl is the one we need. She's the key to all this!"

But all I could do was cough and buck. The cold of the floor crept into my body as a gripping pain across my forehead intensified. I was at the point of forgiving everyone that had ever slighted me or anyone that I had mistreated. I thought about Jenna. I was sorry about that also; the way I treated her. For sure, I knew one thing. I was about to die, and I could feel life slipping away. I think the only reassurance of life was the pain. That excruciating pain that told me I was still alive. I mean, dead feels like nothing, right?

Jack had kept the compression tight on my thigh, saying, "Take a breath, kid. Just fucking breathe."

The paramedics pushed him aside and rushed me out of the doorway on a stretcher. "We got it, Jack," one of them said. "You can ride in the back with us."

Jack followed as they called out the process and placed me into the ambulance. He never left my side.

I felt as if I were floating deep inside the hull of a large boat. Echoes of sounds and faces faded in and out; sirens blared, voices shouted, and bright lights flashed in and out before my eyes. My long-dead father stood by, watching me. He was smiling, and then there was a more brilliant light, and everything was white. I felt life draining, and I couldn't hold on any longer.

Through it all, the little girl never left my side and kept calling my name *Carter, Carter, Carter,* in an echoed whisper. Water started flowing inside the ambulance walls. From the depths of my body, I pulled every ounce of strength that I had. I tried to move.

I grabbed Jack's hand one more time. "Save—her. She—knows."

"Save who?" Jack said as the ambulance pulled into the ER bay. "Save who?"

Everything faded to black, and when I opened my eyes, I saw myself standing at the door of the ambulance. The Fire and Rescue guys pushed the gurney into the truck, shut the door, and drove off with me in the back. A crowd had gathered, and the department had taped off the area.

Next, I saw the paramedics wheel me into the Emergency Room. I turned to see an escort of motorcycle police flank the drive of the Emergency Room entry. A team of physicians and nurses waited at the curb and helped remove me from the back of the ambulance.

I heard a paramedic say, "Hurry up boys, we're running out of time."

Chapter Five

Several hours passed. Jack, Jenna, the captain, and others waited. While lying on the surgical table, it felt like I was floating above the action in the waiting room and overhearing what others said.

At one point, Jenna turned to Jack. "Will he be okay?"

"We have the best working on him," Jack said and slid an arm around her shoulder. "This is a great hospital. He's gonna make it."

Captain Daniels walked over to update Jack on the perpetrators. "The guy who grabbed the money was Joseph Barnard, a small-time thief who's been around a while."

"Sounds familiar," Jack said. "I think we've busted this guy before. Just minor crap, though."

"You're correct. It was petty theft and such," Daniels said. "Nothing like this."

"The other guy?" Jack asked.

"Carter got off an excellent shot. His name was Joe Dinkins, new to our fair town. He had an armed robbery conviction and got out about three weeks ago from Oklahoma."

Jack shook his head. "Won't be a problem now."

Jenna stood as a pair of men dressed in ugly green scrubs and wrinkled white lab coats entered the room. One of the white-coated men walked over to the group.

"He's good and, let me add, lucky. The trauma team pulled him into surgery immediately. The only reason your partner didn't die was that one of you put a tourniquet around the leg in time."

Daniels nodded. "Thanks, doc. Anything else we should know right now?"

"We stopped the bleeding and repair the artery, which was our biggest concern. The head wound was a grazing. Serious, but not as serious as the leg."

"Grazing?" Jenna asked.

The surgeon turned to address her and made a gesture with the side of his hand across his brow. "It wasn't a direct, penetrating hit, which is why I said Detective Caine was lucky. We don't believe there'll be any permanent damage other than a scar. We'll continue to track the situation."

Jack was pacing. That didn't surprise me. He'd missed lunch, destroyed his clothes, and his partner was almost dead. Almost. He paused and raised a hand; the surgeon nodded to acknowledge the motion but continued. "The bad news is he has not regained consciousness, which is a concern. Fortunately, he is breathing on his own, so there's no need to intubate him. We'll take care of his nutrition needs if needed via a tube in his gut."

Jenna made a whimpering sound and grabbed for Jack's arm. He squeezed her hand.

The second surgeon spoke up. "The consensus is his coma state is probably due to head trauma. We'll ship him to Intensive Care for observation."

"We'd like to know how long he'll be in a coma?" Jack asked.

"Hard to tell," said the second surgeon. "It could

last an hour, a week. There's no set time for things like this. He should come around when the brain is ready. As the swelling reduces, we'll know more. We will monitor his vitals, keep him comfortable and hydrated, and ensure there's no infection."

Jenna walked to the nearest sofa and collapsed with a loud wail. Jack followed and sat next to her. "We're gonna make it through this," he said. "I know Carter, and he will make this work."

The doctor added, "In due time, we'll move him to the Unit from the Recovery Room. Once they get him settled, you can see him." He looked closely at the group, making sure they heard what he was saying. "In ICU, it's two at a time. That's the rule. Got me?"

****

I saw myself in my bed. Orderlies wheeled me to a room, and nurses attended to me. The lights were bright, and I heard voices. It was cold. My throat felt as if it was on fire. Getting something to quench my thirst was the only thing I wanted.

The room seemed to hum. I heard machines as if they were all around me. The rain fell against the window. I thought, *"This doesn't make any sense."*

In bed, I faced a doorway. I saw everything in the room. The last thing I remembered was standing at an ATM. *What was that all about?*

I tried to recall what had happened, but everything was fuzzy. I heard mumbled voices from the doorway, but not clear enough to understand what they were saying. An antiseptic odor hung over the cold air along with the ceaseless beeping, beeping. The sound was constant, and then I thought: *hospital? That's where I am? Why the hell would I be in a hospital?*

I felt restricted, as if heavy blankets covered my body. I couldn't move. I thought about Gulliver's Travels, where the little people had tied Gulliver down with strings. I remembered a strange dream: I was in an ER at the hospital, and everyone was talking about me. No one noticed me. I was standing behind them, watching. It was strange, and I couldn't explain it. Then I was floating.

A voice drifted from the corner of the room. I turned my head and, under the reflection of a small lamp, watched Jenna carry on a deep but calm conversation on her cell phone

"No," she said. "I'm still waiting for the results from the doctor. You'd think they would know something by now. You're right. They don't allow cell phones in ICU because it could muck up the monitors, but what the hell. I saw it was you and wanted to share this."

She had a solemn tone to her voice, which was unusual. It was low and firm and almost a whisper. I felt like I was watching from afar, as if detached from my body. Her words echoed, and fog hovered around her.

Is this part of a dream? If it were a dream, I wouldn't be asking myself a question. Or would I?

Then I realized the scene was real-time and immediately understood she was talking about me. And then I realized she said she could screw up the monitors keeping me alive, but she had to share the news? WTF!

"*I am in the hospital?*" I asked. I was sure the words came out of my mouth, but Jenna didn't respond.

Confused, I tried to process the information and thought I could have one of those near-death experiences I had read about in magazines. I thought it was way cool until I remembered that sometimes an NDE might not mean *near* anything, and I was dead or soon to be. That spoiled the moment, but I figured, fuck it, and roll the dice. Let's see where this ride goes.

"He looks awful," Jenna said. "His head is all wrapped up in bandages, and there are tubes and needles and things stuck in his arms. It isn't pleasant. The doctor said he would have a feeding tube through his stomach. Gross right? No. No intubation, since he is breathing fine on his own. Ugh. It's like I'm in some horror movie. No. He doesn't know I'm here. No. He hasn't moved since they brought him in. Not a word. They said he's in a coma. At least he doesn't need life support."

"*Now I remember*," I said.

I recalled the bank robbery, Helen, the hotdog kiosk outside the bank. Oh yeah, Squirmy, and the sound of gunfire. Then I chuckled at how comical Helen Kowalski looked with her makeup streaming down her face. I'm betting she was pretty damned terrified.

I remembered Jack's expression as he hovered over me. Sweat across his brow, his face red as he yelled, "Hold on, pal! Help's coming!"

My attention turned to Jenna. She spoke in a cold, calculated voice as if acting in a play. I felt something differed from usual. Something was missing.

Something.

"No. Carter doesn't know if I'm here or in Milwaukee," she said. "He mumbled something that sounded like Lilliputian, but I have no idea what that meant. Good grief, Marcia. No, I'm not going to

Milwaukee. It's a figure of speech."

"*Marcia? I don't like that woman. And why in the hell are you talking to her? Oh, wait. You had to share. Jesus! What in the hell is wrong with you? And I am here, and you can see me because I can see you sitting there, flipping your leg back and forth like you always do when you're impatient. Please come over here?*"

My throat felt like a gravel road, and I could hardly swallow. "*How about getting me something to drink?*" I said.

With her phone propped between her shoulder and ear, Jenna continued to talk. She flipped through a magazine and kept talking and talking. I watched her ignore me, legs crossed. Her foot bounced, and blah, blah, blah. *Marcia.*

"*Hey. Jenna. Come on,*" I said. "*How about some water? Can you talk with Marcia later?*"

I wondered if she could hear anything above her voice and self-consuming thought. Nothing new because that was Jenna at her usual; wrapped up in her world, calling and talking to everyone she could think of calling.

I asked again, and this time, I raised my voice. "*Water. For God's sake, can I have a glass of water?*"

I watched her again for any reaction. Nothing changed, and Jenna kept flipping and talking. She also kept ignoring me without the slightest acknowledgment. *Good grief,* I thought. *What, is she deaf? She's sitting there like it's Sunday morning on the beach, and everything is beautiful.*

I listened as she made plans for lunch with Marcia. The doctor entered the room, and she cut Marcia short. She put the phone in her bag as the doctor walked in.

They greeted each other, and I watched them approach my bed.

I spoke again. *"Finally, I'll get some answers. And something to drink."*

The doctor was a round little man with a mustache and a friendly disposition. He examined me and checked the beeping machine behind the bed. Besides annoying me with the constant beeping, I had no idea what the machine did.

The doctor talked to Jenna about a Glasgow Coma Scale. I noted the earnest look on her face as she nodded, acting like she understood.

"Your husband has suffered a debilitating head injury," he said with a serious look. "The projectile grazed the cranium deeper than we had originally thought. Although there doesn't appear to be serious damage, we will continue to watch this. He should recover just fine with time. Our challenge is getting him out of this coma. The implication is that it could be more serious the longer he remains in this coma. From the MRI, his cognitive functions appear intact. The other tests showed neurotransmitter process anomalies. We will have to observe those anomalies and continue to run tests. Still, one can never tell the full impact of an injury like this. He should recover, but I can say there will be a hard road and rehabilitation. Rest assured; we are doing everything we can to make him comfortable."

"Does that mean he will live through all this?" Jenna asked. "His leg will heal, and he'll be normal again?"

"I'm not concerned about his leg wound," the doctor said. "It will heal in time, though he will need physical therapy. He'll probably have a limp, but that should also improve with patience and hard work."

"What about his head?"

"That's an interesting question," the doctor said. "The brain is a fascinating organ. You've heard the stories of people that would speak another language? Play a musical instrument after a traumatic brain injury? Well, the brain is resilient and can rewire itself after damage."

"He has brain damage?" Jenna asked.

"It's not like the usual damage you would see. We refer to it as blunt trauma damage, but it is serious. The point is, Mr. Caine's brain can rewire, and who knows? You could have a genius on your hands when he recovers."

Jenna crossed her arms and cocked her head to one side as if trying to absorb the doctor's words. That stance was all too familiar; I'd seen it before.

There was a time I came home late one night. I had tried to explain the situation to Jenna. It was an error in judgment, and I was going along with the guys from work, and I didn't realize it was a strip bar until it was too late. I didn't mean to spend all my money. She didn't believe a word of what I said. Now I saw the same look on her face with the arms crossed and the head cocked. Her actions told me she didn't believe a damn word of what the doctor said, either.

Jenna then turned toward me and leaned over the bed. She reached out and squeezed my hand. It was at that moment everything became clear.

What happened next, I can't explain. I didn't understand how or what was happening. Still, everything was there, in my mind, like a movie. There was a shock and then a flash, and my gut turned, and I saw every memory she'd ever had as if they were mine. From the day we met until that moment—every single thought. Her entire life before me and changing before my eyes. I couldn't explain it, but I realized I saw and heard everything around me. I could hear and feel and smell. It was all real. I realized it was me in the bed, and I didn't look good. I stopped and regrouped. Being a cop is what I did best. I assessed the situation.

There was a list in my mind. A tube in the nose, left leg throbbing, head burning but memory intact. The room was chilly. The doctor was chattering, and Jenna had cold eyes and a touch that told me everything in a flash.

When she touched my hand, a thunderous bolt of lightning streaked through my mind. I felt it and heard it as if she had yelled the words in my ear—as if there was a giant billboard flashing in front of me. I knew what she was thinking. *"You think I'm already dead, a goner—for nada—zippo de gonzo baby."* As if seeing inside her without eyes wasn't strange enough, I felt her mind and emotions.

My entire body, as she held my hand, became her body. It was as if she absorbed me inside her, now looking out and feeling what she was feeling. Something was happening. Jenna had changed. Her thoughts played in my head like a weird movie. *What a freaking mess she had in there*, I thought. *Her every idea, her every dream and desire. Everything she had ever known was strewn about the room like dirty clothes on washday*. Then, as quickly as the thoughts rushed through my mind, they vanished.

"It felt like he squeezed back," she mentioned as she released my hand.

She turned to the doctor. I then felt a massive jolt of indifference. Cold and unfeeling emotion screamed through me. It was like she had played an actor in a movie waiting for the curtain to fall—my curtain.

I could tell she had felt something too when we touched, as she stared at my closed eyes. The doctor touched her shoulder and interrupted her thoughts. "We can't tell the future," he said, "but we are hopeful he should come around. It will take some time."

"Oh—is he—it just seems; I thought he would speak or…" Shaken by the experience, Jenna's voice trailed off. She took a deep breath. "Earlier, before you came in, he moaned several times. Is he in pain?" she said. "And just now, it felt like he squeezed my hand."

Excellent play, honey. Let the doctor think you are a caring wife.

"No," the doctor said, "with an injury like this, there is a lot of bruising in the cranial area. I'm sure you understand. The brain is where dreams are. The neurotransmitter anomalies we observed could affect serotonin levels. What you see are reactions of the nerve endings. The moaning is nothing more than Mr. Caine talking in his sleep, and I can assure you there is no pain. We have him on medication through the IV; he doesn't even know we're in the room."

"*Oh really? What the hell do you mean I don't know you guys are in the room,*" I shouted. "*You idiots are standing right here in front of me! Can't you see I'm trying to talk to you? For the love of God, all of you keep talking like I'm some kind of vegetable. Like I am not even here.*"

"His vital signs are good, but he needs rest now," the doctor said.

"*I need something to drink, moron,*" I injected into the conversation.

Having spent a fair amount of time hanging around the Medical Examiner's office, I knew what he meant when he described the layers covering the meninges of the brain, the dura, arachnoid, and pia maters. It was true; it was interesting but lost on Jenna. I said, "*You might want to try some plain English to the wife, doc… something like they shot him in the head. She can understand that.*"

"Keep it simple, is what Jimmy says," I repeated, but of course, the doctor couldn't hear me. Jenna couldn't hear a word from me.

No one could hear me.

Chapter Six

Time passed, and everything faded as I found comfort in my hospital bed. There was no pain, no sound, no light. It was quiet, and I felt a fog roll across my room as the day ended. As darkness crept in and overtook my thoughts, I saw a shadowed, shimmering shape.

She was back, the young olive-skinned woman who stood maybe five feet. She wore what looked like hospital scrubs, but two sizes too big. At first, I thought she was a nurse, but then I recognized she was young, a teenager maybe, and her body was almost transparent. She stood at the foot of my hospital bed, arms reaching toward me; her long black hair hung across her youthful face.

She spoke in a whisper that seemed to seep into my every cell. *"You'll be fine. Don't worry. I need you to be fine."*

All I knew was I felt good when she spoke, as if wrapped in a warm blanket. Somehow, I felt everything was going to be okay.

The visits were frequent; my ghostly visitor became more animated. She seemed to shout something I couldn't hear but was trying to make an important point. I didn't put it together at the time and assumed it was the morphine drip in my arm more than reality. Getting back to work was more of a worry for me.

I also had to get back to Jenna. We'd left the day on a sour note, and I thought about how she might feel. Did she wish we'd had breakfast? Did she regret her last words?

I lamented how our marriage was not much of a union anymore. But then, Jenna was Jenna. By that, I mean she'd survive because my wife knew how to get whatever she needed. As I lay there, I analyzed the situation. I thought about the Cold Water Creek case Jack and I had started working on and how we, or should I say I, had left it hanging.

Since I like to associate things, because my theory is that all things are related, I realized the dreams that I'd always had become more intense after the van was discovered. The case only needed a few loose ends tied up. I believed Jack and I were on the path of discovery when I walked into the robbery.

I thought about what Jenna said about not coming home from work. It seemed we'd fought about everything lately, and we were in constant disagreement. Those differences became a wedge, driving us apart. I recalled the vision I'd seen in my mind when she touched my hand and what I now knew about her. I finally understood why she always wore that perfume when she arrived at my bedside. I now knew her efforts weren't for me–and hadn't been for a long time. I hadn't even bought that scent for her. I never paid attention to the signs right in front of me. Some kind of detective, right?

I was a vegetable, as far as she was concerned, an actual piece of squash. My life had changed. I knew there was not much chance of my ever leaving the hospital alive. If by some miracle I did, I would spend the rest of my life laying in a bed with only my thoughts, surrounded by nurses and doctors, or worse, nurses' aides. I'm betting they wouldn't even know my name. I'd spend all day talking to them, and they could not hear a word. I surrendered to the idea that Jenna would leave, and we would not be together for much longer. What worried me more was that I wouldn't be a cop anymore, and whatever the young girl told me would die with me.

Jenna complained to the doctor that she'd been coming to the hospital "forever." Her words, of course. She wanted to know if my situation would ever improve.

The doctor explained, "As long as there is brain activity, we consider him alive. He breathes on his own, and there's no artificial life support. At this point, we watch and wait. We expect he will recover, but we never know about these things for sure."

****

Several weeks passed. At least, I think it was several weeks. It could have been months. It's not like I had a watch. Everything ran together, and I kept thinking about living in a bed for the rest of my life. Oddly, I felt at peace with the idea. A transitional dichotomy, Jimmy would say later when I described my experience. Still, there was no need to worry. There was nothing I could do about my situation. Time was the only thing I had left. Time to think and reflect on how my life had become so foul. I thought about Jenna. How could we have gone so wrong?

Right in the middle of my pity party, the doctor arrived, flanked by two orderlies. He instructed them to move my bed to a new room. The first thing I noticed was these voices were different.

I still couldn't move, but I noticed the words had changed to more normal sounds, without the echo. They didn't sound so far away. I understood my coma and saw things without my eyes opening. It was odd that my hearing had never faltered. The outside world didn't know that, but I did.

I'd learned that talking to anyone was a futile attempt at communication. The words I thought I was speaking never really left my head. The experience of a heightened sensory perception was surprising to me. My ability to read the thoughts of those around me was frightening as well as enlightening. As a cop, who wouldn't want to do that? I also discovered hospitals were crazy places, and not all the patients were in beds.

The nurse was an interesting character. She had slept with one orderly and was at least fifteen years his senior. They didn't see each other anymore, but that affection was still alive. Every morning, she'd arrive and first adjust my bedding, fiddle with the machines, and last, write things on a clipboard. She always hummed the Battle Hymn of the Republic. That made me smile. At least it felt like I was smiling.

Jenna arrived each day, and the doctor would rush into the room as if he was late getting somewhere. The room was like a revolving door. All the people came and went, my mother, Jimmy, Jack, and even my captain.

As they came in, I greeted each one, but they couldn't hear me. Mom didn't do much other than wring her hands, say a prayer, and pat me on the head.

Jimmy loved to tell me jokes, figuring that if I could hear them, it would help. I could, but he didn't know that, and I had no way to let him know.

Jack always ended the conversation with, "Well, that's it, pal. Get out of that bed and get back to work."

He didn't know how much I wanted that to happen.

My doctor loved cats. He owned more than he could count, living far out of the city in the Everglades. The house was on twenty-two acres, with barns and outlying buildings, overrun with feral cats. The doctor had named each one after cartoon characters.

At night, the maintenance guy came around. He cleaned floors and pretended he was a superhero spy. He would hum the Mission Impossible theme in his head as he mopped. For the past twenty years, he brought a ham and provolone cheese sandwich on white bread for his lunch every day. I knew those things as well as I knew my name.

I thought the incidental "trash thinking" would drive me completely mad because it was useless to me or anyone else. What good is a secret when you can't use it? Being unconscious served no purpose.

I knew everyone thought I was some kind of vegetable, taking up space. No one could hear me, yet I could hear everything they said, or thought. I knew everything that was going on around me.

Now that I knew I was alive, my biggest fear was that I would die before I could get back into my life. Jenna was hoping for a chance to pull the plug on me, but she'd have to wait until I was on life support. She had thought about it more than once. I knew that much.

As orderlies prepared the bed for the move to my new location, I had become preoccupied with death. After all, if I wasn't up and around and having conversations with people, I considered I was already dead, right? Maybe not biologically, but in every other way.

Wasn't that what being in hell was all about? It was all so confusing to be stuck between the now and there. My body felt paralyzed, and they taped my eyes shut to keep them from drying out and developing an infection, but today seemed different.

At least today, the sounds sounded normal, and it felt like something was happening. I had hope for the first time since I'd been in that bed. I might survive, but I could sense that my ordeal was far from over. Once in my new room, I thought about all the conversations I'd heard. But for how long? Days, weeks, months, years? I had no idea.

I thought about the conversation the doctor had with Jenna just before the move to the new room. I was lying there like a slice of zucchini. She asked about when to stop life-sustaining measures if I never regained consciousness. The doctor reminded her I was still alive, just asleep. They discussed what to do if my brain stopped sending electronic signals. The last thing I remembered that day was the smell of the floor cleaning chemicals. The maintenance guy was down the hall. Then I drifted off into sleep.

The only explanation for what happened next would be like you are sleeping, then your eyes open, and you're awake. That was it and that simple. The nurse walked in, humming as usual, and opened the blackout curtains. As bright sunlight streamed across the room, I felt the brilliant warmth from the rays.

"Well, I'll be damned," I muttered.

I felt my vocal cords move, though there was pain. The words were raspy, and I cleared my throat. That hurt, too. The words were there, and my voice felt real. There was no response. The nurse hummed, tucked, tugged, checked, and wrote things down on the clipboard.

"Good morning," I whispered, feeling my voice in my throat again.

Her hands stopped pulling the sheets, and she slowly raised her head. Her eyes grew wide. She jumped back as if somebody tazed her.

"You're awake! Oh, my sweet God! Be still. Let me get the doctor." She rushed out of the room as if I had set her little butt on fire.

"Well. That didn't feel like a dream," I said aloud and heard the words hang in the surrounding air.

The doctor arrived shortly after that. He checked a few things, rattled off some orders—all in medical jargon—to the nurse, and asked her to call Jenna. She hurried out of the room again as the doctor examined me.

"This is the miracle we've been waiting for, Mr. Caine," he said as he removed the bandages from my head. "And everything looks excellent."

"It seems like it's been quite a while," I said, still a little dizzy and my throat was dry.

"I'll have the nurse moisten your throat before you take fluids. And it hasn't been as long as you think it has." He glanced over at the medical chart. "Let's see. It's been just over eight days. That's quite remarkable. When you are in a coma, time stands still. Of course, there will be a long course of recovery, so don't expect to go dancing tomorrow."

"You're reading my mind, doc. I was planning on dancing tomorrow."

"Well, you have a sense of humor. That will help in your recovery. Also, the vision in your right eye will be a little blurry. But full sight should return in time."

He examined the rest of my body. The leg was healing. "You know, you are very fortunate."

"You think?"

"If that bullet had been a quarter of an inch off its mark, we wouldn't be having this conversation."

I was going to explain how luck didn't play into my life when the nurse returned to the room. "I got a hold of your wife; she was getting her nails done, and she'll be here soon."

Big surprise. It's always something, with her nails, pedicure, hair, car, shopping, or other ways to spend money. She had a real knack for spending, but not so much for saving. I guess that happens when you marry the daughter of one of the wealthiest men in town.

I looked down at my hands and arms. Blue, greenish, and yellow marks covered me from elbow to fingertips. It felt good to see with my eyes again, and the vision in my right eye was a little blurry, as the doctor had said. I confirmed it for him, and he placed a patch over my head and settled it over the eye.

"The focus will clear up as time passes, but you'll have severe headaches without the patch."

"Worse than the one I have right now?"

"The headache and the widespread pain are normal effects considering the injuries you've had. After all, you had quite the head trauma and a major wound to your leg. No worries," he chirped. "Before you leave, I'll give you a prescription for pain medication."

He handed me a mirror to view my new eye patch. A crimson scar ran from my hairline back to the crown of my head. "I could be a pirate." I tried to manage a smile, but my face wouldn't cooperate. It battered me for sure, but not dead. Not dead was good.

"The scar color will fade in time, and when your hair grows, it will cover most of it. You'll return to the same Detective Carter Caine you were before the accident."

I managed a *yup* but honestly just wanted to sleep.

The doctor continued to chatter about something. My nurse, who wasn't humming now, arrived bedside with a pan of warm water, towels, and a washcloth. I closed my eyes and rested my head back on the pillow. The warm water felt great on my face and bruised arms.

She wrestled me into a fresh hospital gown, and the doctor asked if I had questions. Sure, a million, I thought, but asked the most important one. "When can I go home?"

"Just give us a few days to get you up and moving without the risk of falling—you've been in bed a long time. And you need to eat on your own, too. We'll start a liquid diet today. Tomorrow, you'll be on your way if you do well with solid food."

With a grin and a wave, he left the room. The nurse was right behind him, now humming.

I sighed. I felt lucky to be alive and glad to be awake, but almost wished I'd died. The reality of the mess of my life overcame me as it became clear the situation was actual. And I could still see things with my mind.

I had survived within an inch of my life; well, a quarter of an inch, according to the doctor. I considered how Jenna would feel when she heard the news. Boy, would she be disappointed. I knew that answer. As the widow of a cop killed in the line of duty, she would have been the beneficiary of a decent payout—at least that's what she thought.

When we started having problems, I knew it would be only a matter of time before we went our separate ways. I changed my work insurance and named my mother as beneficiary. I knew Jenna wouldn't take care of Mom if I were gone. Since Jenna didn't need the money, it was a straightforward choice.

She'd also demanded that I take out a million-dollar term life policy. I bought a policy, but I changed the beneficiary on that one, too. I often thought about that and understood I could have sold my soul instead. I could have made a good living working for Jenna's family. I could have taken the easy way, but I would have to be crazy to work for Jenna's control-freak father every day. Living with Jenna's demands could drive a man to a slow death, and who knew that better than I did?

At the end of the day, I knew she would have fought to stop all life support if it were up to her. Good for me, the time hadn't run out soon enough, and all my worry was for nothing.

Well, a surprise to the bastards. I have survived. Now they'll have to deal with it.

Chapter Seven

April 2017

A few days had passed since I rejoined the living. All I knew was I wanted to be out of the hospital. It took some creative thinking, but I convinced the doctors to release me and receive PT at home. Insurance covered it so that I could be out of here. They agreed and set it up. Jimmy and Jack were so excited I was getting out that they wanted to throw me a party, but I declined. I figured I had a way to go before I was partying. Or surfing. Or I was even walking. And going back to work was out of the question until I could shed the pain and the pills.

The service aide wore blue scrubs and a high and tight crew cut. When he walked into the room, he was pushing an empty wheelchair. "Good morning, Mr. Caine. I'm Scotty."

I noted the toothy grin. "That go-cart for me?"

"Yes, sir. It looks like homeward bound for you."

I expected he would end his sentence with a hah-yuck laugh. "You gonna push me there?" I wondered since I hadn't heard from Jenna.

"I don't think so," he said, as if pondering the thought.

"Just kidding, buddy. I guess someone called my wife?"

"I suppose, sir. I'm gonna wheel you to the waiting area, and when she arrives, she'll come in and get you."

Ten minutes later, I was sitting in the Patient Pick Up area. CNN played on the overhead TV. A couple of other patients waited for their rides, too.

As promised, the doctor had arranged for physical therapy because of the head wound and leg injury. He also said I'd need a walker, so I didn't put pressure on my legs for a while. He called it muscle atrophy, and the therapist would help me improve my balance and strength.

The good news was that coordination, strength, and balance would return, and the blurry vision would improve. Of course, I'd need to learn a few things all over again. I dozed off while the buzz of the news droned on.

Some time passed. I couldn't tell if it was an hour, a day, or ten minutes, but Jenna touched my shoulder and woke me from a deep slumber. "You ready?"

I thought about saying no. I was enjoying the place, but I grunted, "Sure."

She was unusually quiet about the whole situation. I also knew this attitude wasn't the approach I usually experienced. Arriving home, I noted she'd set up in the front bedroom, saying she didn't want to disturb me— also not a Jenna move. I felt the indifference and tension about her, as if she wanted to say something but didn't. It didn't take long, but she came around. Let's say that her coming around wasn't a surprise. I had felt her mental state in an earlier confrontation, so I knew what was on her mind. I needed to let her work it out because she would only deny everything if I had brought it up.

The doctor called surviving the bank robbery and my wounds a miracle. It thrilled him I recognized Jenna and could name the current President. I remembered sensing the truth with such clarity back when Jenna first walked into the room on the day of the shooting. She'd leaned over the rail of the bed with one of her half-smiles and her painted-on makeup. She kissed my cheek. The message was loud and clear: "I hate you, but if I don't give a show, the doctor and you will suspect something."

Well, I understood what that something was, and it had a name. She'd already decided to leave me. I *felt* that recovering in the hospital and *knew* it after waking up.

I was popping Vicodin like candy. I could hardly stand, much less pee, without getting it all around the toilet. Jenna became outraged about the mess and yelled that I should sit when I peed. I would've fallen asleep on the toilet if I'd done that. Then what would she have done?

An occupational therapist came to the house every morning. We'd sit there in the living room while she asked me questions. Sometimes, I read to her from a book. After a walk up and down the street, she'd massage my limbs into unnatural positions. I'd moan and groan. It was painful, but I knew I would soon be in la-la land. Two more Vicodin, and I'd drift off into a dead sleep.

The pain across the scar on my head was better. The dream, or the vision about the young girl, came more often, and it was more explicit. I was learning to live with it, as weird as it was.

I could make it around the house on my own with

the help of a cane. To Jenna's delight, I peed without hitting the floor. The therapist said I needed to keep exercising my mind and body and could be a hundred percent in no time. She said the exercise would help me sleep. I told her Vicodin helped me sleep.

I'd returned to my bed and drifted to dreamland after the therapist left the house. Jenna came in and drop her bombshell. She announced she wanted a horse.

With half-open eyes and a very unclear vision of her standing before me, I said, "Sure, honey. You can get a horse."

Through a blur, she stood at the foot of my bed, hands on her hips, and glared at me. "It's clover, Carter. It's clover. Do you understand I am asking for a horse?"

I didn't understand what clover had to do with a horse or why she was so angry. It all made perfect sense once the drugs had kicked in again. She wanted a horse and to keep it in a field of clover.

The following morning, still trying to process Jenna's request for a horse, I made it downstairs independently. I hobbled into the kitchen. She had every light on, the window shades up, with the sun blinding through the bay window. Jenna sat on the kitchen island high-back chair while drinking coffee with Marcia.

Not a good way to start my morning. I shaded my eyes with my hand.

Decked out with her usual flair, Marcia wore a sleeveless floral blouse with white slacks. She also wore a huge, wide-brimmed hat that made her head look small. I found that amusing. Her perfume of choice was horrible. Unfortunately for me, she believed more was better. She also knew I hated that scent, which was why she wore plenty of it. She gave me a head-to-toe look as I leaned against the granite countertop. "You look like you've just died, and they forgot to bury you," she drawled.

I nodded and smiled. "Thanks. You too, Marcia. And you certainly have a fragrance about you today."

Jenna's girlfriend didn't like my retort, so she stood and grabbed up her fancy high-end handbag and car keys. "Jenna. I'll see you this afternoon. There seems to be some tension here, and I'm not about to stick around for this abuse."

Marcia toddled past me as if a store clerk just yelled fifty percent off on everything in aisle three as I reached for my coffee cup. I held the mug with both hands and strained to set it on the counter, controlling a slight weave in my stance. I tried to recall what I would typically put into my coffee.

Jenna watched me as she sat, crossed her legs, and placed her fist under her chin. "You take it black. And did you think about what I said yesterday?"

"What? Yeah. I did. You said you wanted a horse. Where did that come from?"

"A horse? You're an idiot. I said *divorce*. I'm seeing the lawyer today."

"Well, that's quite different, although not much of a surprise. You're seeing 'the lawyer' today? I'm thinking you mean your brother will represent you?" At that point, I glanced at the calendar on the refrigerator; April 1st. "Oh, wait. April Fool's, right?"

"Just shut the hell up and drink your coffee, Carter."

For a long minute, I looked at her. Then I shrugged

and raised my mug in a mock salute. I wasn't surprised or alarmed at how the morning unfolded. I'd seen it all in the hospital when she'd held my hand. Only now, all that echo and confusion I saw in her head made sense.

I could still see what was going on in her head, but it didn't matter, so I shut it down. A lot of stuff didn't matter anymore. I had survived, and I would live with or without her. It didn't bother me one way or the other.

Of course, I didn't think the pain medication had worn off, and I wasn't about to let it. I found the prescription bottle and popped a couple more.

After Jenna left the room in a huff, I sat and drank my coffee. What else was I going to do? She'd decided, and when Jenna makes her choice, I'd learned there was no changing it. At least there were no kids involved.

I smiled into my coffee. I *could* say something to her about Edward, her new boyfriend. Like, ask her how he was doing, or I saw him in your head when you touched me in the hospital. Then I realized if I told her about my mind reading while in the coma, she'd think I was nuts and have me put away. I thought it best to keep quiet, but I knew Edward had encouraged her to pull the plug on our relationship.

But nobody could make Jenna do anything. Well, maybe her father, but then maybe not. I figured she had to be serious and meant what she'd said, and I realized people deal with things at their level. Not everyone can manage their husband almost dying.

It had been a long time coming, and as Jimmy always said, what goes around comes around. I figured I was lucky to be alive, and Jenna would always get what she wanted. She'd get what she deserved if she tried hard enough.

As she walked back through the kitchen, she smelled nice. It was my favorite fragrance, but I told myself she wore it to aggravate me.

"I'll be late," she said. I saw tears running down her face, and she tried to smile, but it was a fake. Even though I knew her new boyfriend would be her penultimate stop, I still appreciated it.

I wanted to tell her I wouldn't have left her if she were in the same predicament. I would have lived through the blood, pain, and piss around the toilet. I should've tried, but all I could muster was, "Yeah. See you tonight if you make it back. You smell nice."

"You just don't understand," she said, looking directly at me without trying to hide her face.

"I understand more than you know."

"No, Carter. You don't. I can't live with your nightmares, the bullets, and the everyday fear of you coming home dead."

I sat there thinking about what she said. It didn't make sense, especially the coming home dead part. She kept saying she loved me. I knew that was a lie. Now she was going to leave me because she loved me. She can no longer think of me getting killed on the job, and she wants a divorce, so I will be out of her life.

Oh, wait. Maybe it makes sense. Me not rich like daddy's girl. Me not sexy like your boyfriend. Yeah, that makes sense.

"Okay. Whatever you need, Jenna. Whatever works inside that fucked up head of yours."

"You just don't get it, do you, Carter?"

"I get plenty."

"We can't have a conversation without you going off the deep end and screaming at me or coming up with some smart-assed remark. And it's getting worse every day. And now, your attitude isn't getting better with the drugs you're taking. Honestly, I can't trust that you won't just kill yourself."

Jenna walked out of the kitchen without looking back. The next thing I heard was the front door closing and her fancy sports car roaring to life. I got up and took a couple more Vicodin, forgetting I had just taken two. I needed to forget many things: Jenna, her father, her family. Her trust account, her new boyfriend that she didn't think I knew about, and at this point, my life seemed was spinning out of control.

Jimmy says, "It's better than a kick in the ass with a frozen boot." He was right.

I was tired of all the fighting and wished it would all end. I wished the bullet would have hit me square in the head—right between the eyes.

I wanted to be dead, but it seemed someone needed me alive.

Chapter Eight

May 2017

The week had not passed before Jenna moved out of the house. I'd like to think she'd figured I had recovered well enough to be on my own, but that would be my medication talking.

Several weeks later, I was still stumbling around the house but making it through the day. The biggest challenge was that every turn reminded me of Jenna, and sometimes I missed her. The medication helped with the pain, but I missed having a cold beer or a couple of whiskey shots, although I admit I slipped once or twice.

On good days, I looked for places to rent. I figured if I got away and had a change of scenery, I could clear my head a little easier. It would still be some time before I could drive on my own, so I needed a place close to the bus line and the beach. As usual, Jimmy came through with a plan. A month after Jenna left, he'd found me a place near the beach. Not too far from the main strip of Las Olas Boulevard.

I trust Jimmy. Before I became what I am today, my life was different before all these things happened. My world was ordinary, and I had friends like James Warner. Of course, no one called Jimmy, James, Jim, or anything else. It was always Jimmy. The name fit him for whatever reason. He was the happiest person I've ever met and always up for a great time. We met in gym class in our first year of high school.

I was standing in line at the urinal behind Robert Sheckler, the school tough guy. I think every school has one. Robert thought I bumped him, so he was "going to kick my ass." His exact words. I wasn't the big guy on campus. I was the well-behaved skinny kid that teachers liked.

Either way, when I look back, I realize why Robert thought I was a threat. A girl named Linda Bishop sat next to me in one of my classes. I heard later that she had mentioned to Robert that I was cute. Of course, Robert said nothing to me, but I suppose he figured that if he "kicked my ass" as he promised, I wouldn't be so cute for the girl of his interest.

That day, Jimmy was standing behind me, in line for the urinal. Best day of my life because Jimmy was the tallest kid in school, had long black hair and piercing green eyes, and carried a naturally muscular physique. His stride was long, and he had natural confidence that simply said, 'don't screw with me.' As I have learned from my experiences, looks are deceiving, and Jimmy had no violence in him. In fact, he was a very kind person who wasn't afraid of some tumbling around the ground either. As it was that day, he was my hero when he stepped between Robert and me. He stared Robert dead in the eyes while clenching his fists and said, "Go through me first." At that point, Robert chuckled and said, "Dude! I was kidding. Only kidding."

In the summer of 2009, Jimmy and I finished college. Armed with new degrees, we needed some time to decompress. We packed my Jeep Cherokee, surfboards, and not much of anything else other than surfing the coastline for the following year.

Here we are eight years later, with me needing some decompression time from the recent divorce, and Jimmy comes through again. He tells me he has a friend needing someone to house-sit his mansion for a couple of months. I wasn't going anywhere soon, and it seemed the perfect solution. Las Olas Boulevard wasn't far from the beach or the shops, and the neighborhood was secure.

I watched the reflection of our car in the storefront windows as we drove past through the shaded downtown street that would lead us to the residential areas and toward the beaches. I noted the outside dining restaurants, bars, pubs, art stores, and other places. A French café caught my attention, and I made a mental note to visit once I had settled into the house. We turned off Las Olas Boulevard onto a private road leading to a small bridge. I knew there was no way I could afford a home like this, but Jimmy's friend needed a sitter, and I qualified. I say residential, but the truth was the area had some of the most expensive homes in Fort Lauderdale; giant mansions against the backdrop of the Intracoastal waterway, yachts, expensive cars, and lots of gated entries.

Jimmy turned into a driveway with a small guardhouse. "Hey, Max," he said to the enormous man inside the small building.

"Hey, Jimmy," he said and bent over to look inside the car. "You must be Carter."

I nodded and said hello. Max welcomed us and opened the main gate.

We drove to the end of the road and onto a long driveway with a large decorative entrance. Jimmy pushed a button on the remote attached to the visor. The gate opened, and we entered a circular drive. The house sat on an acre of land with a view of the Intracoastal Waterway.

"How am I supposed to keep this place up?" I asked.

"No worries," Jimmy said. "This guy will take care of everything: maid, yard, pool, even the boat on the dock has a captain and crew to take care of it."

"Boat on the dock?"

"Yeah, well, the owner has a yacht parked out there. He uses it to travel back and forth to his place in Bimini when he has the time. Otherwise, he flies."

"Who *is* this guy?"

"Not your worry, Carter. He's an old family friend and will be in Europe next year. He said the house was mine to do whatever I wished. I told him about you, and he thought it a great idea to have someone here to watch over the place."

"Yeah, tell him I said thank you, but there seems to be plenty of security for that."

"There is, and that will ensure you're safe while here. It's a pleasant neighborhood, although the neighbors aren't what you would call next door."

"Yeah. I won't be popping in to borrow a cup of sugar."

Jimmy helped unload my few belongings, and we sat by the pool with a cooler and beer. He tried to give me advice. "You probably want to save the house. At least sell it and split the money."

"Sure. Like it means something to me? It doesn't

anymore. I would prefer a clean slate. Make this experience the end of this chapter of my life. For all I care, Jenna can have the entire thing."

****

After settling into my new digs, I explored the house and gardens for the first week. There were fifteen bedrooms and twenty-eight bathrooms, and the primary suite was more significant than my entire house. Although I could have lived in any part of the house, I stayed in the guest cottage, which is an understatement, considering the place was the size of the house I just vacated. It was next to the pool with a perfect view of the Intracoastal Waterway. My only job was to be there and monitor the place.

After a month of torture by my physical therapist, she gave me a clean bill of health and pushed me out the door. My limp had improved to almost unnoticeable, but I kept a cane handy, just in case. I could stop the damned pain pills, get on with life, and maybe have that cold beer I'd been missing. I could also drive again, and since I was still on paid leave, I had the money to find a new place to live. I liked the big house, but it was time to get something I could call my own and get my life back on track. I knew rebuilding my life wasn't overnight, so I took it slow. It came back faster than I thought it would.

After a bit of searching, I found a 1975 Jeep International to replace the one I'd lost in the divorce. Jimmy was right. Jenna got everything. I named my new vehicle Mahalo but anglicized to Molly. The word is Hawaiian for thanks or gratitude. The name seemed to fit and pay homage to my situation. Jimmy suggested one of those personalized license plates. I did.

Molly was in excellent condition and restored with deep blue paint and a great top rack for surfboards. It felt good to be behind the wheel and not rely on taxis and bus routes.

Finally, I called my captain to talk about getting back to work. I reminded him it had been about ninety days since the incident, and I felt great. He said it was time to work on my head.

"Nothing personal," he said. "Any of us involved in a shooting altercation must go through this. It's part of the process to ensure you're okay to come back to work."

"I'm fine," I said.

"You don't sound fine."

"It was a pain in the ass to go through this and the divorce at the same time."

"That's the point, Caine. Suck it up, get this over with, and pay your dues. The department needs to know they can trust your judgment before putting you back on the street. It's not only for you, but for the public."

The captain scheduled me for a meeting with the department psychologist. I knew enough to keep the details of my marriage and divorce out of the conversation. I was also worried about revealing the dream and the visions. Doctor Reginald Sparkman didn't need to know.

My visions about the young girl were coming more often, and I felt there would be a day of reckoning. Out of my control, but it was part of my life. If I thought Jenna's nagging was bothersome, the ghost-girl kept at it like a dog on a bone. I wished she would just come out and tell me what she had to say, but it seemed she wanted me to figure it out.

I arrived late for my appointment with Dr. Sparkman. There was a barrage of forms to complete. After completing all the information requested, I sat back on the stiff couch. The office seemed normal enough. There were cheap paintings on the wall, a plastic palm tree, and uncomfortable chairs. I waited for the doctor to call me in.

At least I was alone and didn't have to sit with other patients and wonder why *they* were there. The wait was killing me—the endless tick of the clock on the wall kept time with a blurred TV infomercial.

I tried to focus on the mission at hand, closed my eyes, and took deep breaths. The anxiety in my chest made me feel worse than I had the day I read Jenna's mind in the hospital. I felt like a cat's tail under the rocking chair. I believed I could lose my job and everything I had worked for as a law officer. I was drowning in a wave of impending doom, the pit in my stomach turning and twisting like I was on a roller coaster. The doctor opened the door and startled me.

Doctor Sparkman seemed to be a nice enough fellow. A stout man with a gray beard and a balding head, he wore a white smock over a dark blue suit; friendly and offered his hand like we were old friends. He invited me through the doorway and led the way to his office. "Sit where you wish."

I chose the leather chair in the corner. The doctor started the session with small talk and asked me about my sleep habits.

"I don't sleep well," I admitted.

He nodded. "How do you feel about the incident at the bank?"

I shrugged. "I don't feel much of anything about it.

Stuff like that is part of the job. I mean, not every cop goes through a robbery or getting shot, but we prepare for both at the academy. Does that make sense?"

He nodded. "Go ahead."

"No cop *likes* to pull his weapon." I leaned forward, rested my elbows on my knees, and then looked at him. "We all know the consequence of those actions."

"What consequence is that, Carter?"

"Killing someone. No one wants to kill someone unless there's no choice or there's something wrong with the person."

"What do you mean by wrong with them?"

"I dunno. It's like a normal person, like me. I don't want to shoot someone. I want to give them every chance to surrender. And I did, but there was no choice. His partner came at me, guns blazing. There was no time to be polite. Cops have to ask themselves many questions in a split second. Is the person crazy? Are they troubled somehow? Mentally ill? No sense of right or wrong? We have to make those choices in seconds without a lot of time to analyze the situation."

"Do you believe you're normal, Carter? Like most people?"

"Well. Yeah. I mean, I'm just a regular guy with a regular life. Right?"

The doctor smiled. "You tell me. Is a police officer a regular guy?"

"Most of the officers I know are regular. Normal," I said.

"Do you have friends other than police officers?" he asked.

I nodded. "I do. Some great ones."

"Are they like you? Is their normal the same as yours?"

I looked at him and thought of Jimmy. There weren't many others. "Yeah, they are. We like a beer; we have hobbies, we bet on football; win some, and lose some."

"Do you justify your actions in the bank that day?" the doctor asked.

"Of course they were. I mean, I didn't draw my weapon to make a point or to dish out my justice. I drew my gun to protect the people in the bank."

"So, you justifiably responded in your heart and mind?"

"Of course."

It was his turn to be silent for a long minute. "So, what's troubling you?"

"Troubled? I'm not." I leaned back in the chair and observed the doctor, who sat quietly without looking up. He tapped his pen softly on his notepad for what seemed like an eternity. He stirred and then stroked his chin pensively.

"Tell me why I don't believe you."

"I don't know. But I'm not asking you to believe me. I'm just saying I'm not troubled."

"Hmm. Okay," the doctor replied. "But you aren't sleeping well. That usually means we're troubled about something."

"Fine," I said.

"Fine?" the doctor repeated. "What's fine? Sleep is important."

"I think sometimes life outside work can cause friction, but that doesn't always carry over into work."

"How do you mean?"

I rolled my eyes. "Take that morning, the morning of the bank robbery. Jenna and I were engaged in our usual antagonizing style of relationship."

"Okay. Go on."

"It was probably leftover weekend stuff when we argued about the painters."

"What about the painters?" he asked.

"She scheduled them. I had plans to go surfing with Jimmy. Those two things kinda clashed."

"What happened?"

"She left for her spa day, and I stayed. The painters never showed."

"And that caused the argument?"

"No. Not exactly. The result of all that occurred and what I did afterward, and not getting the house painted, created the argument."

"Tell me about your day after she left for the spa.

"I spent the day waiting for the painters and drank way too much coffee with that. The coffee wired me up by early afternoon, so I went to the gym. That didn't help. I got home, had a few beers, then continued until I had too much and passed out in bed."

"I see," he said.

"No. You don't. Then I had the dream again. Jenna was still fuming the next day because the painters didn't show, which she was sure was my fault. Everything was my fault. It just went on and on.

"You said you had a dream," Sparkman said. "What kind of dream? About the shooting? Do you blame yourself?"

"No. Nothing like that. The dreams started way before the bank robbery." I realized my tongue had slipped, and I mentioned exactly what I didn't want to explain. I tried to move the conversation back. "Besides, I know it was a justified shooting. I'm not losing sleep about the dirtbag or his partner."

"I'm not understanding. If you're not bothered by the incident, then what is it? Your divorce, perhaps?"

"No. Not at all. Jenna and I separated as amicably as we could. She ended up with everything, and I got my freedom. Of course, there were the normal discomforts of a crumbling marriage. Also, the disagreements were as much my fault as they were hers. I hold no grudges, and to be honest, I rarely think about her."

"Sounds like you've moved on from all that."

"I have."

"So, then what? What are your dreams about?"

I sighed. Sparkman would not let it go. "I have, or should say, I've had the same dream about a little girl."

"That's Freudian," he said.

"Not that kind of dream, Doc."

"I know," he said with a short laugh. "I just wanted to see if you were paying attention. Did you have these dreams before the shooting?"

"Oh, hell yeah. I have had this dream my entire life. Or, I should say, at least as far back as I can remember. As a child, they were vague; I suppose I just thought that was how it was since I was young. But they've always been sort of vague."

"Well, dreams are normal regardless of age, but are you saying they're no longer vague?"

"Somewhat vague, but they seem to reveal more each time. I get deeper into the story she wants me to know. At first, my thoughts were brief visions and nothing more. But as time passed, I believed she was trying to talk to me. Now the dream comes more often, and there's a little more each time. I see things more clearly. Honestly, they're getting a little spooky."

"Well. Most dreams mean nothing, and you shouldn't worry," Sparkman said. "There are many dreams: wealth, vacations on sunny beaches, you're naked in front of strangers, or perhaps flying like a bird."

The doctor's job was to assess my ability to continue as a police detective, regardless of what I had to say. I understood that. I had always dealt with police matters and not the kind of craziness the doctor was exposing. I thought back to when the word "dream" came out of my mouth. I wanted to un-ring that bell. That's when I knew whatever was going to happen was going to happen.

I quit listening and sat back, crossing my legs. I stared at the painting behind Sparkman and began thinking about what I would rather be doing. I knew we wouldn't accomplish anything regarding the dream even if I listened. I knew the rest of what he said would be clinical mumbo jumbo, and I didn't want to hear anymore.

I closed my eyes and felt like I was floating. The doctor's rambling monotone voice became an echo in the background. As he'd mentioned, "silly dreams are common, and you just wake up."

I felt my face heat; my body felt rigid. "Does your dream jolt you awake in the dark of night and feel like someone ripped your heart from your chest?" I asked. Sparkman mumbled something. "I'm trying to explain to you if you will just listen, that I wake up screaming, sometimes crying; sometimes, the sweat is dripping off my skin. I just wish I could forget about them—I wish they would stop, and it would be like they never happened. These fucking dreams keep coming and coming, saying nothing, making me guess, wake me up; my heart feels like it will jump out of my throat. I can't get a decent night's sleep. Do you understand that? Do you?"

That's when I realized I wasn't sitting in the leather chair in the corner. My eyes were not closed, and I was leaning over Doctor Sparkman. The look on his face said everything.

"I'm sorry," I said and sat back in the chair. "Oh my God. I'm so sorry."

"Does this happen often?" he asked, slightly less frightened than a minute ago.

"You mean the outburst and me looking like I have lost my mind? Not really. No. Not like that. I'm so sorry."

My scar was burning. She was trying to speak to me. I ignored it and moved on. I wanted to tell him how it was while I was in the hospital but decided I had talked too much already. I stood and extended my hand. As the doctor politely grasped back, it happened again—that bolt of lightning and the shock through my body. Then the burning of the crimson scar on my forehead became fiercer.

In the flash of a second that felt like hours, I saw myself standing away and watching the doctor. It was his life in front of me, like a movie. His secrets were gone, and I knew everything about him—everything he'd done before this day. Everyone he'd seen and even what he had for dinner last night.

"Are you okay, Carter?"

I smiled. "Yes. Yes, I'm good. Thanks for the session."

"I think you need a little more time."

"Probably right," I answered. "But I don't think that time is the answer."

"You may be correct. It seems you have some demons to work out, but from a stability standpoint, you will pull through as a police detective."

"You're saying I'm not a danger to myself or others. Right?"

"Let's say I'm comfortable with your moving forward but in a limited capacity—a desk job at this point and away from the pressure of police cases. I will also prescribe something that will help you remain calm. It's a benzodiazepine and essentially reduces brain activity. It also helps with nightmares, so perhaps your dreams will lessen. Let's try it for thirty days and talk again.

****

I left the building and didn't recall much of the drive back home but thought about giving Jimmy a call as I pulled into the driveway. A couple of beers at Nick's Bar were in order. I called Jimmy, but his line was busy.

I settled for a couple of shots of Jack Daniels, and the patio beckoned to me in the cool of the evening. I watched the boats meander through the Intracoastal as the day filtered away. I replayed my psych session, thinking of what the shrink had said, and wished my life were that simple.

But, thanks to my new abilities, I also knew life for the doctor wasn't so simple, either. The handshake told me his marriage was in shambles. His kids hated him, and he was two steps from broke because of a gambling habit. I found a quiet comfort knowing the doctor was as fucked up as me.

Before I realized it, the bottle of Jack was empty. I stumbled into bed and stared into the shadows of the darkness, taunting thoughts poking around a sleepless mind. It had come to where all I had to do was close my eyes, and I saw the girl's fear, the questions unanswered.

In corners, I could almost see her secrets. I could practically see someone standing there. When I turned my head to see them, they were gone. It felt as if I knew what was hiding behind the eyes of her killer.

My gut said I knew who did this, and I knew the answers were there. I only needed to put the puzzle pieces together, and I could solve this.

Chapter Nine

Mid-June 2017

Although there were several more visits to the shrink for further evaluation, Dr. Sparkman finally gave me a positive recommendation. At least, it was sort of positive. I knew it would be a stretch for him to say I could return to the street. I hoped for, at minimum, a desk job. According to Captain Daniels, the doctor reported that I wasn't entirely ready for duty, which didn't come as much of a surprise. But the doctor recommended a slow introduction back into the workplace and showed that he thought something administrative might work until I could handle the pressure easier.

Hell, that made me happy. At least I was back. The doctor felt I needed to continue psychoanalysis. With some structure and purpose back in my life, I complied with Dr. Sparkman's recommendations and continued treatments, along with the medication. I moved forward with my life regardless of what Jenna had left me or, should I say, what she hadn't left me. I have to say, though, that it was my choice to leave everything behind.

As always, my surfing-fishing-wise man, Jimmy, gave me sage advice. "You got a clean slate to work with."

I knew it was time for my life to change for the better, and there was plenty to keep me busy. It was time to rebuild Carter Caine. I'd been given a second chance but didn't know where to start or where the essential pieces of my life should fit. I suspected I had an arduous task ahead.

A week had passed when the captain called my cell phone. He said he'd heard from Doctor Sparkman and spoke with our Human Resources team. They agreed to allow me back in at a desk. The situation would require a review in thirty days. It pleased me with that decision.

It had been months since the discovery of the van, the bank robbery and the injury, the hospital, my wife leaving me—how much more could I take? I was ready to get back to work, even a desk job.

The following Monday, I arrived at my desk. Jack looked up from his morning newspaper. "Did you bring coffee?"

****

For the next several days, I reviewed old cases and sorted possible follow-up leads or if they were dead ends. That voice inside me kept saying, *this is not what you need to be doing,* and I could feel the heat against my scar. I knew there was more, and I had to get back to work on the case.

What did I have to lose? All he could say was no. I spoke with the captain and made a deal with him. I needed to continue the Cold Water Creek case before he assigned it to someone else. I knew he thought there was no rush at this point; the case was thirty years old; everyone was dead, and it couldn't come under too much pressure by outside forces to solve it. After I explained all that to him, plus the fact that Jack supported the idea, Daniels agreed.

I jumped back into the case, ending the week with nothing more than what we had started with other than a skeleton. We hadn't created a witness list because we didn't have a lot of evidence pointing anywhere, but that was next on our list.

At the start of the next week, I passed the captain's office. He was on the phone. I kept moving, but he called out as soon as he saw me. "Hey, Caine. Hold up! I need an update on the case."

I walked back to his office and sat across from him.

"Welcome back," he said. "I think I said that already, but I don't remember. Either way, it's good to have you back. How's the head feel?"

"Better," I said. "The doctor told me the headaches and the scar should fade. But I'm good most days."

"How's the case going? I ask because the State Attorney's office called. They seemed interested since we found a body."

"I wouldn't get too excited about that," I explained. "Jack and I have just started back with the details. I spoke with Rite, and we have some bones and not much else. He said they are still trying to match some DNA to see if that turns up anything, but there's not much hope. The FBI gave it up since there was so little to go on and told me it was our case to figure out."

Daniels grunted. "That sounds like them. Pass the buck with anything that won't make them look good."

Back at work and at least semi-functioning, I felt a lot better. After leaving the station one afternoon, I stopped by my mom's house to give her a progress report.

"I just made some tea. Would you like it hot or

cold?" she asked.

"Hot sounds great, thanks."

"How's work?"

"It's slow getting back into the grind, but I'm handling it."

"I know, but old habits are hard to break. Like riding a bicycle, right? How's Jenna?"

The comment puzzled me because she knew about that, and the divorce was final quite a while back. I noticed confusion in her look, but I passed it off as age-related. "We're divorced, Mom."

She diverted the conversation. "When your dad would come home from work, we'd always have coffee before dinner, and I would ask him about his day."

"What did he tell you?"

"He'd always say it was good. I made it home."

I smiled. It sounded just like him. "He was a man of few words, eh?"

"That was about the extent of our conversation."

"I get that," I said. "Captain Daniels has allowed me to get back. I'm on the desk but will be on the street soon enough. He said he wasn't going to rush it."

"What about your cases?" she asked as the teapot whistled.

"I guess the good part of this is that I only had one. It's an interesting one. The city was clearing a lot by the bridge. They dredged the canal and found a van at the bottom."

"Oh?" Mom answered. "Where was that?

"Cold Water Creek. Close to here, maybe a mile or so. You know that place."

She nodded, but her face told me she'd gone far away again. "Why would you investigate a van in a canal?"

"That's exactly what I said to the boss but come to find out they discovered a skeleton inside. It happened probably thirty years ago and they just found it. It's not going anywhere, so the captain said I could take my time with it. It would be easier to work on that than on a fresh case. Who knew it would turn into a murder investigation? Oh. And I found a new place to live."

"What about that big house you were living in?"

"Time to move on, Mom. The new place is nice. It's a condominium and still near the beach."

"Good. Maybe I can see it over the weekend. Is it nice?"

"Yeah. Anytime is fine, and I'll make dinner. And yes, it's nice. My place is on the 12th floor overlooking the New River waterway. A great balcony with an amazing view. The person who lived there retired and moved north. He didn't like south Florida. Good for me. Oh! And it has a concierge at the entry; it's near Las Olas and the beach, so it's perfect."

She placed a mug of tea in front of me. "I'm happy for you. Maybe after all this, you can get your life together again without Jenna."

"I will. I've closed that chapter of my life."

"You'll be fine. Someone out there needs you, and I'm positive you'll find the right person, or they will find you."

I sipped at my tea and stayed quiet.

That gnawing feeling in my gut never left me. I thought the emptiness I felt could be as simple as living alone. Jenna and I married young. She was the only woman in my life, and now I had no one. That's sometimes hard to accept. You get accustomed to someone being there when you come home or sitting with you across from the dining table. I felt that someone was out there and we would match, or maybe someone out there was looking for someone like me. Wouldn't that be something?

In the end, Mom was right; someone out there needed me, and I would find the right person. Who could have predicted they would be people I would have never suspected.

On this day, however, it was that feeling of someone following you on a dark street. Each time you stop walking, they stop walking. You know they're there. You hear the echo of their footsteps, the click of their heels on the pavement, as the sound bounces off the buildings surrounding you. In the end, you usually find out it was only the echo. All that other junk only happens in movies and in your imagination. I hoped the dream was just my imagination, but my scar was burning. I knew it meant something was coming. Imagination would not only have made my life easier but also left me with my sanity and life as it was now.

As I continued to sip my tea, I knew it wasn't just a thought in the back of my mind. I knew it was real. I have imagination, but not one can make up what happened in the hospital. Not an imagination that can conjure a vision of a young child calling my name. My experiences while in the hospital caused me to question everything around me. As I look back, I was terrified. I would have forgotten if it had been a dream because no one remembers a dream after waking. I knew it was real, and I knew there was a reason behind it all, and I could remember *everything* as if it had happened yesterday.

As part of the deal with Daniels about my return to the office, I agreed to spend several weeks visiting Dolly. She was a physical therapist and had the most oversized hands I had ever seen. I worked hard. I stayed focused. After six more weeks of therapy, my body healed, and I could walk with a little shuffle. Dr. Sparkman suggested that maybe my limp was psychosomatic, and I should toss the walking cane and learn to walk on my own, to trust myself. Running again would be great. It was a regular part of my pre-injury routine. So, I worked on the psychosomatic limp, as the doctor mentioned.

The one thing that was with me for good was my scar. Each time I shaved, the crimson groove on the crown of my skull was a reminder of my attempt at heroism at the bank. I'd grown to appreciate my new "companion" in that it served as an early warning system. I could tell when my friend–the girl in the dream–wanted to talk. Sometimes, while in bed waiting for sleep to come, my scar would burn as I drifted off. Pulsate like a heartbeat.

Ba-bump, ba-bump, ba-bump, ba-bump. That's when I knew she was coming.

She arrived one night; it had been a grueling day with the investigation. As my head hit the pillow, I experienced a sharp pain through my scar as if it were her way of pressing the doorbell button and telling me to let her in. Rather than falling asleep, I was standing and looking into an abyss. I heard the pounding of her fists as they synchronized with her heartbeat; *ba-bump, ba-bump, ba-bump, ba-bump*. I saw her through a haze; she was on her knees. Tears poured down her reddened cheeks, and her lips moved as if forming words like she was screaming *No, No, No!* But I couldn't hear anything above the loud thuds of her fists. *Ba-bump, ba-bump, ba-bump, ba-bump.*

Her eyes reflected the terror she was experiencing as the constant pounding continued. I couldn't see what she was hitting. A wall? A door? The pounding became so loud that my ears rang from the echoes. *Ba-bump, ba-bump, ba-bump, ba-bump.*

And then, silence; the kind that screams in your ears with a high-pitched screech of pain.

Gasping for air, I rocketed back into my bed. I stared at the ceiling. My sheets soaked. My eyes were wide open. It felt as if she'd left a small piece of herself with me.

I understood her a little better.

It became unmistakably clear to me; she was the girl standing next to Jack at the bank. She was the girl in the ambulance, and *she* was the one hovering near me while I was in the hospital, trapped in my coma. But why?

It was all true, and it was all real. She was as real as Jimmy. And the oddest thing? I knew her but couldn't place her. I knew I'd seen her, but felt it was long ago. Above all, I knew she needed my help; she was dying, and there was no one to save her but me.

****

My days became routine—I went through the same drill; coffee, toast, and hanging out on the patio until the sun came up. I'd head to my office, shuffle papers, talk with Jack, and research old cases. To change it up, I'd go to the gym for a couple of hours rather than lunch. Working my body into exhaustion was the only way I could sleep since I didn't need the Vicodin any longer. Plus, Doctor Sparkman had taken me off the benzodiazepine. The good news was I was improving.

After a day in the office, I'd hobble to the beach in the afternoons, find the first open bench, open my journal, and write. Doctor Sparkman said writing could be good medicine and thought I should write whatever came to mind. He said to put the words on paper and release the thoughts held in my subconscious–let the words flow.

He called it free writing or stream of consciousness writing. I had to look it up: put the pen in your hand and write the first things that come to mind–whatever came to mind. I figured I'd at least try it. How much effort would it take? A pen, some paper, a few words. That's pretty much where my journey got interesting.

I sat with my eyes closed, trying to ignore the surrounding sounds—my consciousness drifting. I practiced a Zen breathing method that Jimmy taught me.

It took a few weeks to understand the rhythm needed. Once I had it, it calmed me, and I could open my eyes and begin writing. Sometimes for minutes. Sometimes for hours. Sometimes late into the night, and before I knew it, I'd journaled pages upon pages of thoughts.

When I read it back, it was often like someone else talking. I couldn't explain it; the thoughts, ideas, and things I couldn't remember when awake seemed to fall in front of me. My brain felt jumbled up like Grandma's yarn ball if I didn't write.

But each day, writing became more straightforward. One evening, I relaxed on my couch after a long meditation session. I drifted off to sleep.

That's when the dream changed.

I floated on a cloud, then descended onto the soft ground. A slight mist lay above the surface, and there was a light in the distance. It came and went, flash and go dark. As if a car was driving through a hilly area: up, down, left, right.

Then faces came forward and then faded out. There was a constant murmur of voices in the background, and then rain, rain, rain. The raindrops started small and then grew larger and larger. I saw a body of water—a waterway or canal with trees on each bank. Branches hung low with Spanish moss. The moss looked like an old man's gray beard. The mist laid across the water, and the sky flashed in the distance. And I saw a light hovering through the tree branches reflecting across the water. I turned and looked down and saw myself in a long rectangular hole dug into the ground. It felt like a burial site, and the rain turned torrential, pouring downsides of this hole.

The hole filled, and I tried to climb through the mud, sliding down. The sides became softer, and then I saw my dad above me. He was reaching his hand toward me, but I slid farther down; his arm was stretching but remained just out of reach.

There was a repeated flashing of light; white, blue, red, white. She was there, standing next to me. A heartbeat was getting louder and louder–*ba-bump, ba-bump, ba-bump, ba-bump*.

She rushed at me and pushed hard. I flew upwards to what felt like the eye of a tornado far above the hole. Looking down, I saw her. Arms stretched wide. My dad was standing next to the hole and pointed down at her. She screamed my name, *Carter,* but it came out like *thunder.*

Spinning around me were cars, sheets of water, and faces of people I knew. Then a thunderous crack of sound, and the earth opened below me. I fell and spun, then I felt like I hit the ground like a rock from the sky, and everything was black and silent.

That's when she started talking to me.

At first, the words formed in my head were choppy and noisy, like an old radio transmission. Over time, I could make out single words: *water, help, cold,* but nothing else. It was the voice of a teenage female, scared.

She said, *"Locked,"* and, *"Are you going to help me?"*

I didn't know what she meant, and the words stuck in my head. The comments I'd written before were only feelings, but this felt real. With those words, images would pop into my head: my childhood, family, a story about me and Jimmy. Bits and pieces of the puzzle, but it was there. And then, as easy as it was to drift off, I was back.

I awoke with a pen and a journal on my lap. I looked down to see I had scrawled one word across the page: VAN.

Chapter Ten

Mid-July 2017

I arrived at my office on Monday morning, and as I stepped off the elevator, I looked across the bureau floor. The area is just a dozen desks in the middle of the room with enclosed offices along the walls. One belongs to my captain and today his office was empty. That was odd—until I realized he was sitting at my desk.

"Hey, boss. All good?"

"Yeah. We're good. Can we talk in my office?"

I looked over at Jack, and he rolled his eyes and gave a bit of a smirk. "Uh, sure. Let's do it," I said.

Daniels paused to close the vertical blinds after we entered his office.

"Are we good?" I asked, getting a little nervous.

"We're good. I only need you to sign these papers to get back to work."

"You mean like actual work?"

"Yes, Caine. Actual work. I am tired of seeing you mope around here doing nothing, and there's a case that needs attention. Sign them and let's go."

As I walked from his office, Jack looked up and flipped me the bird.

"Asshole. You knew, didn't you?"

He smiled and put his feet up on his desk.

"Gimme the file," I said. "I need to review it."

****

As I continued to write in my journal over the next several weeks, expressing what I'd seen in the dreams, felt like I was communicating with *her*.

I'd picked up a few books about dreams and their meaning and hoped there would be something in them to help me understand. There was a metaphysics store close to my condominium. I stopped in to talk with a young woman behind the counter. She was thin, blonde, with royal blue streaks of color running from the crown of her head to the middle of her back, and she sat behind a large desk. I noticed a soft fragrance in the air. Jasmine?

Placed next to the desk was an oversized upholstered Queen Anne chair. The interior of the store was dark with thick, maroon-colored velvet curtains. The bookshelves were dark with cherry wood. She stood as I entered. She was tall. Her name tag was at my eye level on her left shirt pocket. *Charisse*. She extended her hand and introduced herself.

"Carter," I responded.

"And what can I do for you today, Carter?"

I explained I was looking for books on dream interpretation. Something that, perhaps, may help me better understand how the mind interprets dreams.

She walked from behind the desk with an effortless grace and led me to a small section of book titles in the back of the room. After recommending a couple of authors, she said she would let me peruse the other titles. "If you have questions, I'll be at the desk working on my thesis."

"College girl?" I asked.

"Yepper," she said. There was a sigh in her voice. "On the last leg of this journey, and hopefully on to the bigger and better things in life."

As she turned to walk away, she said she'd brewed tea earlier, and that I was welcome to try it. I turned it down, but the thought was there, and I could feel she was a kind person.

I checked the time on my watch. An hour had passed as if it were only a few minutes. I gathered three books I thought might work, paid Charisse, and left the store.

I sat in the park and read one of the books. A quote early in the book said one could control a dream by simply repeating a mantra before sleeping. It said something as simple as the word "Remember" could be enough to trigger the subconscious. I thought about how crazy something like that sounded, but *why not*? *Why shouldn't I try to talk with this girl in my head*?

Over the next several days, I consumed the other two books. One about lucid dreaming—controlling your dream as if you were awake. My mind absorbed the information like the desert absorbs rain. Every crevice within my mind burst with thoughts and ideas.

I needed someone that knew more about the topic than I did. I was just a novice in the dream world. That level of consciousness was far beyond what I could understand. I set out for the store again, needing to see Charisse.

When I arrived at the store, dark clouds had gathered overhead—an ominous black cloud shelf with crossing bolts of lightning. The rain soaked me as I ran from the car to the front door. She looked up from a book as I came in. "Mr. Caine!" she said. "Good to see you again."

I smiled and tried to wipe the dripping water from my face with my shirt sleeve. She handed me paper towels and commented on the weather.

"I had second thoughts about coming over, but I needed to talk with you about the books you sold me."

"They have opened your eyes and mind, I see."

"One could say that. Do you have the name of someone who could explain some things about dreams and consciousness to me?"

She nodded, then handed me the business card of a holistic intervention spiritualist. Martin Crespo. I knew I'd call him soon, but I had to find the time and keep it on the down-low from my partner. Jack was hardcore and wouldn't understand. I decided my best confidant– as always–would be Jimmy.

I contacted Martin through the phone number on the business card. He confirmed the comment Charisse had made to me about being booked far in advance, but there had been a cancellation just minutes earlier. I was glad not to have to wait weeks to see him.

"It happens sometimes," Martin said.

"Kind of unusual, don't you think?"

"The Universe, you will discover, can be mysterious *and* accommodating," he said with a chuckle.

"It almost feels as though you were waiting for my call," I said.

"Sometimes that happens," he said. "So, tomorrow, let's say three o'clock? Is that good for you?"

I'm a cop. We don't put much faith in coincidence or serendipity, but I accepted my good fortune and agreed to meet. The office was in Miami, at least fifty miles from my condo. Although I could safely drive short distances, it felt like too far of an excursion, and the cab fare would be expensive. And I wasn't comfortable dealing with Miami traffic.

I was still thinking about the logistics and expenses when Jimmy called. I explained what I was doing.

He was excited. "Totally cool, man. I'll take you down."

"I'll grab a cab," I said, not wanting to impose.

"Oh… no way, dude. I can be to you in thirty, and when we get back, we can go to Nick's."

"What about your store? Aren't you busy?"

"Store? Where have you been, man? I have three stores now and a fourth opening next month. I got people, dude. People!"

****

Jimmy is one crazy man. We arrived at Martin's office building twenty minutes early. I don't know what I had expected, but the building looked like a nondescript office building on any street in America.

I shook my head as Jimmy parked. Black lights and crystals were supposed to be in the window. I could have just as easily been seeing a doctor or a lawyer.

There was a small furniture and office supply store on the first floor: a lawyer and dentist's office at the back of the complex. I checked the location board at the elevator and noted Holistic Interventions was on the second floor, Suite 220, next to a tax accountant. Jimmy said he'd wait in the small coffee shop at the back of the building.

I took the elevator to the second floor and found Martin's office effortlessly. I knocked, and he opened the door. He had a broad smile, curly brown hair, and an impressive mustache. "I'm Martin," he said. "Please come in."

After we exchanged handshakes and pleasantries, and I sat across from his desk, he looked me over head to toe and finally said, "You have an interesting energy."

I joked, "I'll bet you say that to all your first-timers."

He flashed his smile again, and with a slight wink, he said, "No, Mr. Caine. You honestly have interesting energy. I felt it as I opened the door. Once I shook your hand, I better understood why you're here. I'm sure you understand what I mean."

I thought his comment intriguing. Since the shooting, when I shook a hand or touched a shoulder, I could see into the other person if I wanted to generate the energy. Sometimes, it would only be a feeling like good or bad, or sometimes I could feel the emotion or the thought itself.

When I shook Martin's hand, I didn't even think about it, but I felt calm. Over the past several weeks, my nerves had gone over the edge. My arrival at Martin's office changed my entire demeanor. Someone was directing me, and I believed it was the girl.

I sat across the desk from Martin as though I had a job interview. The desk was empty except for a legal pad and two sharpened pencils. Fresh flowers filled a vase on the credenza.

A Reiki table covered with a sheet, a pillow, and six smooth, black stones in line occupied the other side of the office. There were no pictures or photographs on the walls. A wide window allowed the light into the room through sheer coverings. Martin, it was plain to see, was a very inviting personality. I felt comfortable with him.

He said, "What can I do for you?"

"I've read some books on dreams and metaphysics and had questions. The young lady at the bookstore where I bought the books recommended you."

"Ah. Charisse," Martin said.

"That's her."

"She was one of my students. A truly gifted young woman."

"Yeah. So, I am trying to find information regarding dream interpretation."

"Anything in particular?"

"I guess. I don't know for sure. I have dreams, which is why I bought the books. I was hoping to shed some light on it, so to speak."

"You've had some interesting dreams, haven't you, Mr. Caine?"

"What do you mean by *interesting*?"

"Your dream has been with you for a long time. The same dream, but it changes, right?"

"I didn't mention that. I'm puzzled about how you'd know that."

"I don't know that; I only feel what you're projecting. Of course, there is some logic involved since you said you've been reading books about dreams."

"Good point," I said. "That makes sense."

"I assume you've let your detective side down a bit."

"How do you know I'm a detective?"

He just smiled. "I know, Mr. Caine. That's what I do."

"Yeah, this is more than a little weird for me."

"I understand. Let me assure you. I'm not here to intrude or read your mind. I don't do that."

"What do you do?" I asked. And what was I doing there?

"I receive messages, sometimes from the Universe, but mostly from your Guardian Angel. I'm what some call an Angel Reader. Some call me a Translator."

"A translator of what?"

Martin smiled. "Let me explain. Everyone has a Guardian Angel. Yours is here now. She's always with you, but now she stands on your right, just over your shoulder. My job is to tell you what she has to say."

"Uh. Yeah."

"Seriously. Relax and make yourself comfortable. Since this is your first time, I know you'll find it interesting."

Martin sat forward in his chair, rested his elbows on the desk surface, and folded his hands across his face. He took a deep breath. "I'm going to speak to her now. You may interrupt at any time with a question."

Martin covered his face with both hands as if to focus. He took another deep breath and exhaled. He lowered his hands and folded them together. "She is young. She has shoulder-length black hair, a light complexion, and brown eyes. She hoped you would find this conduit and says *your timing is perfect.*" He chuckled a little and said, "She says *you are a skeptic.*"

"I suppose I am. Most cops would be, I would think. What does my timing is perfect mean?"

"*The Universe knows what is and what will be. You have free will to make choices, and those choices can decide the outcome, but if you listen to what the*

Universe has to say, the decisions will lead you to the answers you seek."

"That's a lot to absorb."

"That's fine, she says. Your friend will teach you."

"My friend?"

"The one that brought you here," he said.

"Jimmy?"

Martin smiled, closed his eyes, and took a deep breath. "We're ready," he said.

"Her name is Sophia, and she is your Guardian Angel. She says, *as humans, we tend to enter shifts and cycles. You entered a shift last year and coming here today aligns with your next shift. According to her, there will be another shift several weeks from now. It will affect you for about four years. That shift will allow you to recreate your foundation. She means where you live, your job, economics, life, and finances. She added that everything around you will change. You will get a four-year timeframe to eliminate what you don't like, bring in what you like, and start again.*"

I felt as if I'd lost my mind while listening to Martin. It was his voice, but Sophia's words supposedly spoke through him. "I know it takes some getting accustomed to, but you'll see how it works as we progress," Martin said. "Her words are pictures. They flash before me like television or a movie screen. I then translate the images to words you'll understand."

I knew exactly what he was saying. Since the shooting at the bank and the stay in the hospital, I had the same ability. I didn't tell him about all. "I'll try to keep up."

"She says *you need to be more daring. You'll need to bring things into your heart, and there are things you'll need to let go of at once*. She's also telling me–" Martin paused at that moment and looked at me. I saw a change in his demeanor. "The dream," he said. "Your dream."

"Yeah. What about it?"

"Sophia says it's a girl. A young girl?"

"Okay. I know that."

"Right. Sorry. Yes. I'm getting mixed messages. Your Guardian Angel says it's not a dream, and right now, it's like they're both talking."

"Both?" I asked.

"Yes. Your angel *and* the girl in the dream. Wait," Martin said. "The girl is *not* a dream. She's a vision. It's like they are the same, but they are two entities. Give me a second. Let me sort this."

I sat back and watched. Martin was in a trance-like state. He mumbled something and then said, "Got it." I thought he was talking to me, but it became clear he was talking to someone I couldn't see. "She said, *you are so close. Keep searching, and the answer will present itself*."

"Close to what?" I asked. "And which one wants me to keep searching?"

"*The girl. You're close to the answer*. Something about the water? I don't know. Like I said, my communication is through pictures, like a movie. *She's in water, struggling, but knows you're coming.*"

Martin's face flushed to a rose red and then back to normal. He opened his eyes and said, "She's gone."

"Who?" I asked.

"The girl. I've never had that happen."

"What happened?"

"That was, at least I believe it was, the girl in your

dream."

"My dream? I never told you about her."

"You did not, but this is metaphysical. Anything can happen. By the way, she also asked me to tell you, right before she faded, that you will be fine and save her."

All I could muster was, "Yeah, sure."

Martin gathered his thoughts, apologized, and said, "Sophia is still here. She said it's all good, and things sometimes happen. Relax and listen."

I couldn't explain it, but the feeling of comfort I had when she spoke was like nothing I had ever experienced. I could feel Sophia. Her arms wrapped around my shoulders. I noticed an aroma of jasmine.

Sophia continued through Martin. *"You are two people. You have a double personality. Hard and quiet; generous and caring. You like to keep things inside and be in charge, but you are also compassionate and protective. This meeting should help you learn how to speak from the heart. You entered a life shift a few months ago, and the next shift–a new life–is coming soon."*

"A new life? You could say that. After getting shot and almost dying, along with my divorce, it hasn't been a great journey."

"It's beyond that," she said. *"Not to worry. I know you were shot and came very close to dying. I was there. I did everything I could to save you. You have a higher meaning in life right now. You now have a gift from me for you to use. Use it, and it will lead you to what you need. You've had thirty-four lives before this. You are now on thirty-five; if you can change, you won't have to return. Your near-death experience was*

part of the plan, and that's over."

"Wait. What? Thirty-four lives? She's saying I've lived before?"

Martin held up a finger and then his entire hand. *"You need to trust your inner voice,"* she said.

"Inner voice? Like dreams?"

Martin shook his head, still in a trance, eyes closed. "Like that, but more like visions than dreams. *You will need to filter the images and what is the conceptual realization and outcome."*

"Can you at least give me an idea of what's coming?"

"You'll know when you see it. Understand that your life is a choice, free will. The things you see and the decisions you make will create the outcome. Ultimately, it's all the same, but how you get there is up to you. You're going to be surprised. I can tell you that much. What the surprise is, it will be you."

"Will be me? What does that mean, the surprise will be me?" I asked Martin.

He shrugged. "That's what Sophia said. I don't know anything more than that, and sometimes she speaks in riddles that even I can't interpret. Oddly, when it happens, whatever it is she's referring to, you will eventually understand."

****

I could not get those words out of my head, *'the surprise will be you.'* Riddles, I figured. What can you do? I let it go.

I worked with Martin for a month. He taught me breathing methods and meditation techniques. He also taught me how to regulate my visions. Focusing was the most challenging part.

After weeks of trying not to control the vision, I became weary. I thought the effort was fruitless. I remembered Martin said to keep trying, and it would happen. He said I could control the vision to have it take me where I needed to go.

I'll remember the day that happened as well as I know my name.

Chapter Eleven

September 2017

Driving home from the gym one evening, I received an unexpected call from my Uncle Derek, my dad's brother. He lives up north, in Atlanta; we seldom see each other. As a child, I saw him during summer vacations and sometimes spent a couple of weeks at his place. Other than that, there wasn't much contact. He was the loner type, and I didn't have many conversations with him over the years. His wife had passed years ago when I was just a kid. It was difficult for him in that she died soon after the birth of their daughter, Amy. I don't know much about that except I think it had something to do with postpartum depression. After that, he raised Amy alone. It surprised me when he called.

"Have you spoken to your mom lately?" he asked.

"It's been a week. Why do you ask?"

"Dunno," he said. "It seems she's getting forgetful, but that could just be age."

"We were together last week, and other than the usual absentmindedness, she seemed fine."

"When I called, she didn't recognize my voice," said, sounding concerned. "That was odd enough, but when I identified myself, she still sounded confused."

"That's weird. Maybe you woke her from a nap?"

"Unlikely. It was around eleven in the morning. Anyhow, maybe you can stop by and chat with her. See if you notice the same."

"Got it. I'll keep an eye out. How are you doing? How's Amy? I haven't talked with either of you in what seems like forever."

"Yeah. Time moves on, doesn't it? Amy is doing well. She's graduating from nursing school. The first part of it, anyway."

"Graduating? I'm feeling old."

"You? How about this guy? It seems like yesterday I had her in diapers."

"Yeah. Fast." And then I had this idea. "What's she doing now? Amy, I mean."

"Taking a break. She needs some community hours to keep her scholarships, so she was going to volunteer at the local hospital."

"Perhaps this thing with Mom could be an opportunity for her? With her being alone, and me busy with work, someone to be with her. With that, I'd better understand what direction I need to take. I mean, it's up to Amy, but it could work with those volunteer hours. And I'd rather have Amy with her than a stranger. So would Mom."

"That's a great idea," Derek said, "but I think we should treat it as a visit and not a watching her type of thing."

I agreed, and later I learned Derek talked with Amy. Of course, Amy was thrilled. She could spend some time in sunny South Florida and get in her community service hours.

I also agreed to keep a closer eye on my mother. After all, Uncle Derek and I were all she had left. I asked him to move closer, but he said his business and health wouldn't allow him to relocate. He said he had too many local customers, and an established company.

Over the next couple of weeks, I noticed, in our conversations, that Mom's health *was* failing. I had never really seen it before, but then again, I had a lot going on. Perhaps it was age-related; honestly, with everything I had been through over the past year, she was always there for me. It was mainly forgetfulness, times, and places, but more. After a few months of staying closer than usual, I was glad Derek and I came up with Amy staying with her at the house.

Before Amy arrived, I took Mom to an early dinner to ease into the explanation. I had decided it was best to be upfront with her about our thoughts concerning her health. I didn't know how she would take it, her being such an independent type. It was essential to have someone stay with her and ensure her safety. Having room for someone wasn't a problem either. Amy would have her side of the house and be there full time; Mom would have her space as well.

"I suppose," she said, but she didn't look convinced. "Amy is such a sweet girl, but I haven't seen her in a long time."

"It's a good thing, Mom," I said. "She needs the community hours for school."

"I guess."

"Mom, it's better than the alternative. You'll still be in your house with your gardens and all your things around you. Amy will be there to take care of any emergencies and just for company."

Mom was a tough lady with a robust belief system, even if her memory was fading. After we got home, I went inside to ensure she was safe before leaving. The kitchen was well-stocked, so she did not need to drive to the store. I left feeling comfortable about her.

If she worsened, I'd consider placing her in an assisted living community where she would have full services, but we weren't at that stage yet. Before leaving, I explained I'd call her later in the evening.

That afternoon, the heat index was over a hundred degrees, with only a slight breeze. As I pulled into the driveway at my condominium, thunderclouds had formed over the Everglades. A summer storm was arriving soon. I took advantage of the closing light, knowing that soon I'd be stuck inside for the night. I sat on my balcony in my Bahama chair overlooking the Intracoastal. Unusually relaxed, I drifted into a slumber—the sunset and lightning danced across the sky.

I sighed. I focused on muting the sounds of the day and closed my eyes. For a moment, a cooler breeze washed across my face. It felt refreshing after such a hot day, but I knew the cooler air foretold the storm was coming. I felt like drifting off to sleep, and I was comfortable. The chaise lounge was soft, and it felt good to be there, and my mind drifted.

As if watching a movie without a screen, she appeared before me. It was a translucent image, like a hologram. At first, her mouth moved, but no sound. I asked again and twice more, "Who are you? What's your name?"

Her voice was as clear. She could have been standing on the balcony with me. "*You know who I am*," she whispered. "*I was the only one there for you. Please help me. You're all that I have.*"

After the first thunderclap, I almost jump out of the chair. The vision had vanished. It was dark, and my scar was on fire.

Then there was silence.

I grabbed my phone and called Jimmy. I needed someone to tell me I wasn't going crazy.

"Hey," Jimmy said. "Glad you're calling."

"What's that mean?"

"I dunno. You seemed stressed the last time we chatted."

"I was. I still am."

"What's up, brother? Are you having any pain from the shooting? Talk to Jenna lately?"

"No on both, thank God. I'm just trying to get through life right now."

"How's that?"

Jimmy had this way of letting a person talk. He would ask a question and then go silent.

"Remember, I told you about the young girl in my dream?"

"You did. She's back?"

"With a vengeance."

"Interesting. Did she tell you anything?"

"I think she's telling me everything."

"In that case, you need to listen."

That was it. That was the answer I needed. It was simple.

Listen.

****

Monday rolled around, and I started my day working on the case, chatting with Jack, and going over the details. After work, I spent the afternoon in meditation. I felt it when the girl arrived. My scar warmed, and the silence came like a vacuum. She appeared, and she spoke using pictures.

I didn't have to dream any longer to see her. I interpreted what she meant, like watching a movie on a screen. She didn't often talk with words, but through visions that seemed to float behind her.

I got accustomed to having her around. The visions were sometimes scary, but I could handle them. I understood her. It felt better once she started showing up when I wrote in the journal. It wasn't much: help me, let me go, why am I here, what's happening to me? At that point, it was pieces of sentences—utterances of words that didn't make much sense.

I took the visions for what they were worth: apparitions, extensions of the dream. What else could they mean? There was no correlation. I hadn't tied them into the events or the things I knew. Who would?

I hadn't associated the dreams with my near-death experience. But I discovered everything becomes clear once you have all the information. The pieces to the puzzle were there but hadn't come together.

Like me and Jenna and her boyfriend, once I knew about him. It was easy to understand the rest of it and why she acted as she did. Her job was to chase me off—get me to quit. Before the revelation of her affair with Edward, I thought our marriage was unraveling because I was doing it wrong.

After I understood the divorce wasn't my doing, it became my undoing. I had to face that Jenna was never in love with me. I finally understood that our marriage was retaliation against her father. She used to use me to get back at him.

The value of facing that reality was that I learned

my lesson and was grateful to be alive.

The following morning, I called in and told the boss I was taking the day off. I put on shorts, an old Miami Dolphins jersey, and my favorite ballcap. I slipped into a new pair of sandals and planned on nothing special that day. As usual, something told me to get moving and nudged me to have breakfast down at Jake's. I left the house without my regular coffee and toast.

I sat in the last seat in the last row, back to the wall, and thought about meeting Jimmy later in the day. I'd promised to stop by and, if nothing else, shoot the bull for a while. I figured I could talk him into catching a couple of waves. Even with a psychosomatic limp, I could still surf with the best of them.

As I sat in the booth at Jake's, I noted a few things in my journal and thought about how I had made it through the worst part. I considered the good things in my life. Every week I got a paycheck and the ocean at my back door for doing what I love to do. I thought about the camaraderie of my job, that one thing behind my success, although I didn't like to admit it. With police work, the connection is clearer than in other professions. It comes from when you have laid your life on the line, and it's only you and your partner. It could be on a dark street in a dangerous neighborhood or a bank robbery. You build confidence with each other, which doesn't exist in most friendships.

I was enjoying the sunshine streaming in the windowless opening at Jake's. They recently changed the inside color from a pale blue and painted the walls an intense yellow. It seemed much brighter than usual. I liked the café. The color was not my favorite; still, I liked the place and the people. They knew me. It was usually quiet, and my favorite seat—against the wall—was typically open when I arrived. They called it the Carter Caine booth. From there, I could observe everyone who walked in the restaurant or along the Boardwalk.

Lauren was the server. On this day, she wore street clothes: low-cut jeans and a red-colored cotton shirt. She tied the shirt short and showed off her latest piercing. Red glittering stones hung from a circular gold wire attached to her navel. She was young, tall, and slender. She approached me with a hesitant smile framed by her strawberry blond hair and summer tan. This contrast gave her a striking distinction against sky-blue eyes. Carrying a tray with one hand balancing a steaming cup of coffee, she swung the tray down onto the table. "Good morning, handsome."

"It seems to be a good one," I said.

"I think so," she replied, "other than my boyfriend is out of work again. You know anyone needing a welder?"

"Yeah. No. What do I know from welding? I'll put out a word, though. See what I can come up with."

"You never know," she said.

And with that thought in my head, I knew I'd have to leave her a bigger tip.

Between the blinds, the sun invaded the space with a vengeance.

"You gonna order anything today?" Lauren said from across the room.

"The usual."

She knew I liked eggs, sunny side up and burned toast. So did Tommy, the short-order cook. On her first morning working there, I ordered the egg and toast special. After a hard day's work, the toast arrived as dark as a coal digger's chin. She apologized like crazy, and I said, "Don't worry about it. I love my toast well done," and it's been that way ever since. I don't like burned toast. I could never bring myself to tell her.

"Carter Caine Special," she yelled.

Tommy looked up and grinned, saying, "Hey Carter." He usually liked to come out of the kitchen and chat with the patrons. On this day, he kept to himself.

I picked up the newspaper left by the last customer and tried to read, but the words melted into a mesh of black and gray. My thoughts returned to sleepless nights with the repeated vision of a young girl pounding on the wall. I felt the scar, and it was warm. None of it made any sense still after all this time.

I understood she was more than scared. I saw her eyes bulging, shaped like giant brown almonds. She was glaring at me; her wet black hair was flat against her pale white skin, her mouth twisted like she was calling out. Bloodied hands and the water leaks into the room, and it becomes dark, then quiet. I always awoke the same startling way; arms outstretched, covered in sweat, gasping for air. It was as if I was there with her.

At least now I thought I knew what she was saying. *Help me, let me go. Why am I here? What's happening to me?*

I didn't know whether to thank the psychiatrist for suggesting I journal about my dreams, work, and life. He said writing it down will put things into perspective and help sort things out.

"But I'm not a writer," I told him.

"You are a detective and should be able to write

your thoughts. Treat it like an investigation."

So, there I was, alone in my thoughts, my journal next to me. I was enjoying a Saturday morning, sipping my coffee as I thought about how my life had changed. I was thankful I had my health back, more or less, and it all seemed somewhat chimerical when I thought about it. Like none of this had ever happened, yet everything had happened. I still felt like it was someone else's life, someone else's dream. Jimmy calls it phantasmagorical.

"Like in a dream created by the imagination," he'd said.

I continued to write my thoughts in my journal and waited for Tommy to finish my breakfast. I was so hungry, and I had second thoughts about ordering a pork chop or a steak to go with the eggs. I looked over to Lauren. She was flipping through one of those women's magazines. I was about to call out to her when I heard footsteps against the concrete sidewalk alongside the café. I looked over to see a beautiful woman, a goddess. I am not taken aback by a beautiful woman—all the fish in the sea thing; you know—but this was different.

She walked into the restaurant wearing a wife-beater, tight jeans, and high-heeled boots. Of course, I did what any man would do. I stared at her until I remembered I had left my sunglasses on the island in my kitchen. I looked up, and she was staring at me. It was not the same kind of stare, mind you. More of a sneer, like a "Hey Jerk, my face is up here" sort of a smirk. I managed a weak smile. She curled her lip, rolled her eyes, and gave me that "Whatever" look some women seem to do so well. I didn't have anything to lose at this point.

"Hey there," I said.

She turned her head as she sat on the seat at the counter. She glanced at me over her shoulder, then turned around to look at the menu.

I didn't have a choice but to approach her. I walked over and said, "Name's Carter," as I leaned onto the seat next to her.

There was no response except a corner eye and a flip of her long black hair off her cold shoulder.

If that didn't say welcome aboard, nothing would. Right? What else could I say? I tried to think of something clever like it would forgive my staring. I was about to open my mouth and defend my stupidity when she turned toward me and cocked her head slightly to the side.

"Buy me breakfast, Carter," she said in a voice so velvet soft, it wrapped around me like a steamy and dark August night.

"Uh. Yeah. Sure," I said.

"Good. We can call it even, then."

"Even?" I said.

"Yeah. Even. Like making up for your eyes, not being able to find my eyes a few minutes back."

"Ah. Gotcha. Fair enough."

I figured she was playing hard to get and suggested moving to the booth where I had been sitting. She agreed, and as I slid in, I introduced myself again.

"Carter Caine."

"You said that earlier. I'm Lacy Brown."

The sunlight streamed across the diner floor and outlined her raven-colored hair. Then the oddest thing happened. A glow of lavender surrounded her head, billowing out like a cloud.

Lauren brought over coffee, interrupting my thoughts, and when I looked back at Lacy, the color had faded.

"That was weird."

"What?" Lacy said.

"Oh. Nothing. Never mind. I hear the Spinach Omelet is good."

She nodded and kept scanning the menu.

"Where you from?" I asked.

"Is this how it's going to be?" she said as she looked out the window as if she expected someone else to show up.

"How's what going to be?"

"Our conversation," she said, looking straight into my eyes. "You know. You ask me where I'm from. I ask you where you're from, where you went to school, and all the rest of the bullshit people do on first dates. Then the next thing I know, you're asking me to go back to your place, and I'm thinking, 'What the heck? Nice guy.' And there you are now, trying your damnedest to get into my pants. And that's what I mean by, is that how is going to be. Simple enough?"

"First date?" I repeated.

Lauren returned and reached across the table, setting two glasses of water in front of us.

"You know what I mean, big guy," she said as she motioned for another coffee.

I didn't, but I couldn't let that stop me, so I kept talking like I knew. The conversation was pleasant, and it seemed we were hitting it off. Not what I would've expected, but my Angel had said to be more daring.

Lauren stopped by with coffee refills. As she walked away, she said the food would be out soon.

Lacy and I continued the small talk while I tried to keep up with her. She had a lot of energy as if it was all bundled up inside, and she had let it out.

The food arrived, and Lauren set the plates in front of us. Lacy dove into the omelet as if she hadn't eaten in a week. She took a bite and said, "You ought to try this. It's great." She pushed her filled fork toward me.

"Yeah, no thanks," I said.

She looked down at my plate as if checking to approve of my order and said, "You always eat burned toast?"

"Long story."

"I have time."

"You would think it stupid."

"Why would you say that? And how do you know how I'd feel?"

"Just sayin what I'm sayin."

She sighed.

"Fine," I said. "The first time I came here and ordered breakfast, Lauren brought me burned toast. It was her first day on the job, and I didn't want to embarrass her, so I didn't say anything. I always order the same thing, so when I come in, she knows what I want, and this is what I get."

"Burned toast?"

"Yes. Burned toast."

"Wow."

"Wow, what?"

"Wow. As in, you are a seriously nice guy."

"I don't think so. I like the toast well-done."

"You are, and that's nonsense. No one eats burned toast."

I shrugged. "Sure." And with that, she smiled, and

I saw a spark between us.

"You don't meet many nice guys. Do you?" I said.

"I meet plenty. I just don't date any of that type."

"So, if the guy is the overly confident, assertive type, that's your style?"

"You mean asshole?" Lacy replied.

"Sure. You could take it that way."

"Then, yeah. Most of my dates in the past were assholes."

"Really?"

"Yeah. And don't worry."

"Worry?"

"Yeah. You fit right in."

"I'm an asshole now? Is that it?"

"No. You're the confident one, but a nice guy. A rare bird."

"Confident and nice. Okay."

"Hey! That's a good thing. You know. BDE and you know what they say about nice guys."

"No. What? What the hell is BDE?"

She gave me a quizzical look. "Don't worry about that. Stay nice, and maybe later I'll show you what happens to nice guys."

Who was I to argue?

Lauren stopped by with a fresh pot of coffee, dropped off the check, and gave me a wink. It seems she had noticed the vibe Lacy gave off while sitting there. We finished eating, and Lacy grabbed her napkin, wiped her mouth, and pulled a mirror from her bag. She checked her face, ran her fingers across the corners of her mouth, lifted her hair back over her shoulders, and made a ponytail with an elastic band on her wrist. I noticed she wore no makeup, yet her skin was radiant and smooth.

"You ready to go?"

"Ready?"

"You're not good at subtlety, are you? And do you always answer with just one word?" She didn't sound amused.

"No—Yeah. I'm ready. I'm ready. Let's go."

I reached for my wallet and pulled out the cash for the tab. As I folded the cash into the check, someone called my name.

The voice was familiar—too familiar. I looked up to see the last person I would ever want to see at my beach. She stood as big as life in her flowered muumuu and oversized sunglasses. She wore a matching large straw hat and had a giant beach bag hanging off her arm. Still as condescending as I remembered.

"Hey, Jenna," I said.

"Who's your friend, Carter?" she asked.

"Friend? Who? Oh, Lacy. Uh, yeah. We just met."

"Hi," Lacy said.

I avoided eye contact during my conversation with Jenna by looking out the window. A limo pulled up to the curb. I also noticed that Lacy glanced toward the car and did that lip curl thing again, but it wasn't at me this time.

"Oops. Change of plans. It looks like I gotta run."

"What?" I said, now perplexed at the change of circumstance.

"The car. It's for me. Gotta run, but thanks for breakfast!"

Lacy kissed me on the cheek, looked over at Jenna, then said, "Nice to meet you," and headed for the door. I followed her out, and as she reached the limo's rear door, she stopped and turned.

"Hey! What's your number?" she said.

I gave her my cell number, and she gave me a wink and slipped behind the black windows. As the limo rounded the corner, my phone rang.

"Now it's your turn, big guy. Call me," she said. "And good luck with the Dragon Lady. Ex-wife, I am assuming?"

"You're assuming correctly."

I walked over to Lauren and handed her the cash. She shrugged and said thanks. I turned back to Jenna, being polite, and waved goodbye. You would think that was it, right? No. Not with Jenna.

"Kinda flighty, isn't she? You were sitting here. Right?" she asked. "You sure made a mess, and your girlfriend didn't eat all her breakfast."

I shrugged, and Jenna said, "Burned toast?"

Jenna was the same Jenna I knew so well: rapid-fire questions, judgments, patronizing conversation. I didn't need or want that any longer. I was free and preferred to stay that way and not get dragged back into her world.

"Yeah, but I was leaving, so you can have the place all to yourself."

"Oh… Are you headed out to meet up with your new girlfriend?"

"She's not my girlfriend."

"Could've fooled me," she said, giggling toward her friend Marcia. "No, really, Carter. I'm glad to see you've moved on."

"Why are you here?"

She looked up and gave me the smirking face, and I thought, *What the hell is up with these women smirking? Is it me?*

"We're going to the beach?" she said. "Is there a problem with that?"

"Yeah, like the floppy hat, sandals, and your bathing suit didn't give it away. I had figured that one out."

"You're still a smartass, aren't you, Carter?" said Marcia.

"Jenna and I had an agreement, Marcia. Mind your own."

"What agreement?" Jenna said. "I don't recall an agreement."

"You at Fort Lauderdale Beach and me, Hollywood. Remember?"

"Oh, that. Meh," Jenna said with a wave of her hand. "What are the chances of us running into each other?"

"Well. We just did. Isn't that a coincidence?"

And I knew that, but it was what it was, and I was the bigger person. She knew this was the place I always stopped for breakfast. My bet was she had planned on my being here. She shouted, "Have a nice day, Carter!" as giggles overcame their conversation.

"Women," Jimmy always says. "You can't live with them, and you can't live with them, and if you put them in the trunk of your car, you'll be in trouble with the law."

Jimmy is sometimes profound.

Chapter Twelve

A big surprise was the divorce was amicable and went smoothly. I think back and understand that it was more likely because Jenna got her way. I didn't fight anything. I didn't have any fight left in me. Jenna ended up with the house, my Jeep, and whatever else my life was when we were together. The fact was I just wanted out and to move on with my life. I did, and Lacy was the first glimmer of hope I had seen in a while.

The beach was a bust, and I wasn't about to hang around while Jenna was there. I got home and tossed my keys on the counter. As I charged my phone, I noticed I had missed a call from my mother. I had hit the silence button inadvertently and didn't feel the vibration in my pocket. Her voicemail wasn't clear, and she sounded tired or confused. She stammered, or should I say mumbled something. Then her voice faded, and she hung the phone. I didn't understand why she called, but there was a concern. I dialed her up.

"Sorry I missed your call, Mom. What's up?"

"Did I call you?" she said. "I don't think I did. Did I?"

I remembered her forgetfulness. "Uh. No. I meant to say sorry that I hadn't called you earlier. Anyhow, since I have you, I was thinking about taking you shopping. You know, for your birthday."

"I would love that, Carter."

"Lunch also?"

"Sounds good."

It seemed it had always been the two of us against the world. Dad had passed over twenty-five years back, and I felt this was a big deal for Mom, and it was only us, except for Uncle Derek and Amy.

"I'll pick you up in the morning," I said.

"I'll be ready at nine if that's okay with you," she said.

"Sure. We'll get breakfast."

I hadn't felt well all week, and the weekend appeared as if it wouldn't be any different. I thought it was too much time at the gym and too little time sleeping because of the dreams that kept haunting me. A cup of strong coffee could help, I thought, and would help clear my head.

I crossed the living room and headed toward the kitchen when a knock at the door drew my attention. I was not expecting anyone. Someone had to get past Buddy, our security guard, to enter the elevators. I don't know if that is a real name, and he is a retired NYPD cop, so he may like to keep it on the down-low. A real bulldog. Nobody got around Buddy.

Then I realized it was Saturday, which meant Rosalinda, the cleaning lady. Still, I reached for my Glock, which I kept by the door, and looked through the peephole.

She stood in the doorway with a look on her face somewhere between impatient and annoyed. I deactivated the house alarm, flipped the locks, and let her in.

"*Buenos dias,* Señor Caine," she said.

"Good morning, Rosa. Come on in."

"*Gracias*, Señor Caine. You got nobody here?"

"No. We're alone."

"*Hokay, dokay*," she said and toddled into my condo. Her buckets rattled with the arsenal of cleaning fluids.

It took a moment until I realized she meant okay, or more likely, okey dokey, something I often caught myself saying. It was clear when she had attended a class recently. She had enrolled in an English Second Language course at the college. The college students volunteered and offered classes to the Hispanic population to gain extra credits. I noticed the uptick in her trying to use English rather than her native tongue. I admired her tenacity, even if it meant I sometimes had to translate the translation. She'd attempt the American lingua franca and butcher the words more often than not. At least she tried.

"Look like you need a coffee," she said as she dropped her buckets.

I agreed. "How 'bout you make some of that Café con Leche I like so much?"

"*No problema,* Señor Caine. Maybe I have some too. These place looking like a bum in it."

"Bum? Oh. Bomb."

"*Si*. I say bum. A mess. You don't pick up anything." Rosalinda pulled the coffee from the cabinet.

I agreed. "Sorry. It's been a hectic week at the office. How was your week?"

"It was beautiful," she said, tamping the coffee into the filter holder.

"Really? It sounds like you enjoyed it."

"Oh, *si*," she said. "I go to South Beach with my two lovers."

"Your two lovers?" I asked.

"Yes. It was very nice, and we have a good time."

"Ah. I see."

At that moment, she realized what she didn't mean. "*Un momento*," she said. "I mean to say, my two loves. I mean my daughter and her husband, no lovers. I am so sorry to say this."

Her face turned a crimson red. I chuckled at her error, which didn't help the situation, but explained that her mix-up is common. "No worries," I said.

After Rosalinda left the house, I reached for one of the cold beers in the refrigerator. I thought about how forgetful my mother was becoming. I assumed her age was catching up to her, and it wouldn't be long before she would have to move in with me. I sat at the kitchen table and thought about my life, career, and how I had ended up in this life. When I was a kid, I never felt as if I belonged. It was like someone had left me alone on a doorstep. As it was, I lived in a house with a nice lady and a big guy who was a police officer. I could never explain it, but I knew something was missing. I had always had that feeling if you want to call it that, and it had stayed with me all my life.

After college and a degree, I needed a good job. Public service was the obvious choice. I applied and then started a career as a Crime Scene Investigator. My first crime scene was downtown along the New River canal.

There was a Cuban restaurant on the corner. It was across from the courthouse, which served the best café con leche in town. I could get to the station, grab my gear, and make it there before the downtown crowd started. My little slice of heaven on a typically shitty day dealing with only God knows what, considering the criminal intelligence on some days.

One of my first cases introduced me to Doctor Artemis Rite. As I finished my morning coffee, my dispatcher radioed me. She said there was a floater behind Bubier Park. Dispatch uses codes rather than words, so Carmelita, the cashier, had no clue. I did. A floater is a dead person in the water. I acknowledged, in code, of course, and headed for my vehicle.

As I arrived at the scene, I saw the Medical Examiner. He knelt over a bloated body the police dive team had recently pulled from the murky water. The victim's eyes stared into nowhere, clouded and white. His mouth gaped as if his last scream froze in time through a cadaveric spasm.

"Nice way to start the day," I said as I readied my camera. "Looks like somebody's snitch ended up with the fishes."

Rite responded without looking up, his trademark Meerschaum pipe clutched between his jaws. He said, "Looks like a normal day in paradise, Carter. Another day, another body, another free ride to my office."

Rite's sarcastic sense of the macabre helped in some strange manner. It gave way to the tragic examples of how life is. The pipe he clenched within his teeth was a gift, part of a collection, and had quite the reputation. It was a gift courtesy of a serial killer Rite had helped arrest in his younger years. It's told that the killer had a talent for carving up his victims, leaving pieces around the city as a clue. The heads were never found. The surprise and the truly interesting thing about this case was the resolution.

The sick bastard used sepiolite stone, more

popularly known as Meerschaum, to replicate the victim's cranial profile, carving it into a pipe. He then, we eventually discovered, crushed the actual skull to eliminate that part of the evidence. Creating smoking pipes from this stone was common, but this killer's method was bizarre. The pipes, each a sculpted carving of a skull using the stone, arrived, every so often, by personal messenger and an anonymous note. The gifting became more frequent until Rite owned several.

The break in the case came one evening as Rite puffed away on his latest gift. He was sitting in his favorite Chesterfield Queen Anne High Back Wing Chair, reading an article from National Geographic magazine. The story was about a rare pygmy tribe that shrunk the heads of enemies conquered in battle. The tribes, it's believed, did this to tackle the enemy's spirit, to keep the enemy in the spirit world, and to prevent them from avenging their death. The tribe hung the skull around their necks for spiritual protection. When he recounted the story, he chuckled. He couldn't imagine the thought of a Meerschaum pipe protecting him from evil spirits. "That is," he told me one afternoon, "until I thought back for a moment and realized the human skull on my examination table at the morgue was a perfect replica of my pipe."

The Forensics team used the pipes for facial reconstruction and created three-dimensional models. The final product was perfect human face replicas. The detective bureau used the faces to cross-reference unsolved murder cases. Within two weeks, they had identified the victims.

After the department connected all the dots, the newspaper dubbed him, The Meerschaum killer—each sculpture a message and part of the puzzle. I like puzzles, which is one reason I became a detective.

Rite hunched over the body found in the canal and pushed the button on his recorder. "Caucasian male, about thirty years of age. Fully clothed, cataleptic rigidity, body evidence is not remarkable, no sign of foul play."

"You're holding his hand like you want to propose, doc. What's up with that?" I said, curious about his actions.

Ignoring the wisecrack, he said, "I need to have you guys check the psychiatric hospitals for recent releases. Start with the County first and work your way down."

"Releases of what, doc. You don't think this is a murder?"

He pulled the man's hand up, showing me the victim's fingernails, and said, "He was a patient. See the blue coloring of the fingernails?"

"Yes," I said, and focused my camera on the deceased man. "I figured that was the cold water."

"Not at all. The blue shows heavy use of Imipramine. Hospitals prescribe it to treat depression in psychiatric patients," Rite said. "It's an assumption but look at the clothing and the condition of his hands. A facility released him, or he escaped."

"So, you are saying this guy planned to take a bath in the New River and didn't make it out?" I asked.

"Best laid plans," the doc said.

Police work has taught me a lot of things over the years. One of the most important things is that appearances can be deceiving. Take this floater they found in the river. I discovered he had escaped from the local hospital ward. The hospital report said he suffered from delusions of grandeur—a person with schizophrenia with manic episodes of bipolar disorder. I was sure the dead man thought his day would turn out fine. It didn't, and as the doc said, we have the best-laid plans.

That brings us back to the Carter Caine plan. Of course, one never plans to get shot or divorced or be part of something they can't quite explain. My life hasn't been what I had planned. Now I was the cop that almost died in the bank robbery. Not exactly what I had planned. Best-laid plans, as they say, but once a cop, always a cop.

It had been several years since the incident at Bubier Park. I was now the Detective Sergeant for the Crimes Against Persons Unit. While it sounds like something important, it's just a fancy name. It means a place where you end up if you're dead and someone wants to know what happened. But that has all changed now. With my second life in full gear, I was ready to take on the next thing. I didn't know what the next thing was or meant, but first things first: a new woman in my life, maybe. I was going to get back to work, which made me happy, and then there was the case that gave meaning to my future.

Chapter Thirteen

I had been thinking about my Lacy Brown adventure at the beach. I had let her stew long enough, and it was time to call her. I could wait longer, but I thought it might look like I wasn't interested. Any shorter time and I could appear anxious. I thought this relationship could have a future, but I couldn't let her know my plans just yet. I dropped my keys on the kitchen counter when my phone rang. It showed as a restricted call, which usually means I will send the call to voicemail, but my gut said to answer, and I am glad I did.

"Hey lover," a sexy voice poured like soft velvet. "What's up? Are you avoiding me?"

"Why would I be doing that? Just playing hard to get."

"I like the hard part and speaking of getting…."

I knew where that was going, so I interrupted, "Cute. I'll pick you up at about seven, and we can do dinner?"

"I like that, but let's do this. How about I meet you at Briny's downtown at seven?"

I couldn't care less. Pick up, meet. Whatever Lacy wanted. It was all the same to me. Before leaving, I had a couple of drinks on the patio. Relax for what was going to be a long night. I thought, can't be too anxious, as I chilled in the soft chair overlooking the water. One time, Jimmy had said some guy named Ovid noted that love is full of anxious fears. Jimmy had a lot of friends, and I have always wondered who Ovid was. I wasn't in love, at least not yet, but I was sure there was lust in the picture. I watched the sunset and left for the restaurant an hour later. My apartment was a short walk to the restaurant, so meeting her there was great if she showed up and stayed this time. I hoped she wouldn't flit off like the day we met at breakfast.

Rosa had been in earlier, so the place was clean, sans a few dishes, which I tossed into the dishwasher. I dimmed the lights to prepare for our return and walked to the restaurant.

Arriving at Briny's, there was no place to park. The bar seating was close to full. I was glad I decided not to drive the car and happy that I had made a reservation. I planned to enjoy a nice dinner, drinks, and maybe a couple of dances. Afterward, we could head back to my place via the water taxi and spend the rest of the night together without interference from you know who. It had been a while since I had taken the time to exert this much energy into a relationship. After Jenna, it was a roller coaster ride with shallow and meaningless relationships. I tired of meeting, screwing, and then trying to remember their name the following morning. My fear and anxiety melted as I rounded the corner and saw Lacy sitting at the bar.

She held a Mojito in one hand and did her best to wave off an admiring crowd of college boys. The slit on her floral dress exposed a long, tanned, muscular leg that ran right up to a tight waist. Long raven black hair fell around a high-cheeked face and cascaded onto a pair of rounded shoulders. College boys flocked around her like bees floated around a flower petal.

I cut through them. "Need rescue?" I said, nuzzling her neck.

She turned in her seat. Her shadowed blue eyes met mine, and she wrapped her arms around my neck. "Anytime," she said.

I ordered a beer, chatted with Lacy for a moment, and then signaled Matt, the server. He directed us to a table in the corner, took our drink order, and hurried off. We talked about the day while listening to the band play a song with a Rod Stewart look-a-like.

"So, do I count this as a date?" I asked.

"If that's what you want to call it, then okay," she said as she ran her fingernails along the inside of my thigh. "Let's look at it as where we left off."

Matt arrived, handed us menus, and Lacy waved him off, looking over at me.

"You order," she said.

I suggested the swordfish in a bearnaise sauce and a bottle of wine. Lacy loved it. Our seats overlooked the South Fork River. After dinner, we held each other and watched the tourists walk along the riverfront. A tour boat shuttled some of them by the million-dollar houses lining the seawalls.

"I have an idea," I said.

"What could that be?"

"Not what you are thinking."

I signaled Matt, then asked for two glasses and another bottle of wine. He obliged. I paid the bill and hailed a water taxi. The captain pulled up against the sea wall and extended his hand to help Lacy aboard.

We moved to the back of the vessel. Lacy sat at the starboard corner and looked at the homes on the other side of the river. She tilted her head slightly as if pondering, eyes looking off into the distance. I noticed she was lost in thought, pensive. Looking at her, I felt exhilarated, blood rushing through my veins, undefeatable. I could have held that view forever with her classic beauty and the Fort Lauderdale backdrop of lights and water. She held a curiosity I had never experienced. She was delicate yet tough, animated yet gentle. I wanted to protect her, hold her, and care for her. I was about to blab; I love you, but hesitated. Then the boat captain interrupted my thoughts, thankfully.

"Where to?" he asked.

"To the end of the line and beyond, if you can manage it. We won't be getting off."

Lacy looked back at me and said, "Can you be anymore corny?"

I shrugged and tipped the captain so he wouldn't stop for other passengers.

"It looks like we have a full boat," he said.

"Full of something," Lacy said.

We sat on the bench at the back of the vessel. Lacy put her head on my chest, curled under my arms, and closed her eyes, draping her arm across me.

"That was a splendid dinner," she said.

"Glad you liked it."

"What's for dessert?" she said as she drew her polished nails across my stomach.

"I have a little something in mind."

"Little?" she said.

"For now," I said. "I'll save the big surprise for later."

"I don't know if I can wait until we get back to your place."

After the ride along the river, the captain pulled up to the seawall. We stepped out and walked the river path past a few shops and back to my place. I opened the apartment door and said, "Something to drink?"

"Sure. But I need your bathroom." I lit the candles on the patio, poured two glasses of wine, and sat on the oversized Papasan. Lacy came out of the bathroom dressed in a baby blue robe, her hair falling across her shoulders. She laid across my lap and kissed me.

"Hey, big fella," she purred. "I missed you."

I felt the blood rush through my body as I wrapped my arms around her waist and kissed her.

****

The sun peeked above the windowsill in my bedroom. She was sleeping across my legs. I stayed for a moment, not wanting to disturb her, relive the night, and savor the relationship we were experiencing. I ran my hand across Lacy's bronzed shoulder, noting it lacked a tan line. Quietly, I pulled myself away without waking her, but forgot about my numb legs as I admired the sensual curve of her body. I slid out of bed, almost falling flat on my face.

My legs returned to life with some circulation, and I hobbled to the kitchen to make coffee. I heard the shower start as the coffee pot gurgled, so I knew she was up. I considered joining her, but quite frankly, I was tired. It had been a long night.

I sat at the kitchen table, and shortly afterward, Lacy walked in. Her hair was dripping wet, and she had dressed. She leaned over, kissed me, and said, "That was a great night. Call me and let's do it again."

"You want coffee?"

She shrugged and said, "That would only make me

stay longer, and that wouldn't be a good thing."

"I think that would be a great thing."

She grabbed her bag and winked. "Ciao!" she said as she blew a kiss and walked out the door.

And just like that, she walked away. I thought about her exit at breakfast and how she so casually departs, leaving your heart happy and hurting. I hadn't felt that in a very long time.

I gathered the wine glasses left on the patio and cleaned up the melted wax from the expired candles. The yachts on the waterway headed toward the ocean. I carved some time out of this quiet morning. I walked to the kitchen and poured a cup of coffee. I heard my phone ringing in the other room but let the call go to voicemail because my rule is they always call back if it's important. It was journaling time, and I felt I needed to write.

For once, I didn't feel as if I were on trial or investigating someone. Our conversation was light, the talk refreshing. For the first time in a long time, I laughed. I was already missing Lacy. Looking back, I wished I could have opened up more and told her about the little girl haunting my dreams. I figured there would be time for that. My phone rang again, and this time I got it.

"Hello?"

"Carter?"

It was the familiar voice of a young girl. "Amy?"

"That's me!" a squeaky little voice said.

"Delightful surprise! You here? In Fort Lauderdale?"

"Almost! I stopped in Orlando to see a friend, but I will be there by Tuesday. I'm coming down for Auntie

Joanna's birthday. But I also wanted to discuss your conversation with my dad."

"I appreciate that. Do you think you can stay with her?"

"Of course. It will be good for both of us. She'll get the attention and company she needs, and I will get my community hours and spend some time with my favorite auntie.

"As long as you understand the situation."

"I do. Dad explained, and dementia is part of the job, so I'm good."

"I just worry. That's all. You are so young."

She grumbled, "Carter, you know I am over eighteen! And I'm graduating college soon."

"Oh yeah. My bad. Well, young woman, welcome to Florida! When you get close, send me a text. You can stay with me for a few days, and we will see mom and move into this arrangement gradually. Okay?"

"You could show me around town?"

"That's a plan. I have an extra room at my place for when you arrive, and then we will go to Mom's and get everything settled. She has a big place so you will have your private room. Got a pen? I'll give you my address."

"Just text me when you have the time," she said. "I can GPS it."

I called Rosalinda and asked her to come over and clean up the place. She chided, "Today? Is this for *overtim*? Is Sunday, *ju* know."

"Over time," I corrected her, trying to help her pick up the language, and explained I would make it worth her while. It wasn't my wheelhouse from a woman's perspective when it came to cleaning the place up.

Jimmy always said to me, "You gotta know what you gotta know," and I knew I wasn't the house cleaning type.

Besides catering to an eighteen-year-old, I already knew what the next day would bring. That alone is challenging enough, but there was the mom thing I had to handle. Of course, Mom's birthday would be like every other day she spent alone in that big house. She would rise from bed, slip into her housecoat and slippers, and walk to the kitchen. On her route, she'd stop to open the drapes in the living room and look up and down the quiet street in front of her house. She would open her container of coffee, the blue one with the sealable top. She'd count exactly four carefully measured spoons of decaf into the filter. Pour the water into the machine. She would remove a small saucepan from the lower drawer while holding her lower back. She'd wonder if she should put the pots and pans in a location where she wouldn't have to bend over. Afterward, she'd take a box of oatmeal from the cupboard. One bowl of oatmeal with a cinnamon dusting and two cups of coffee each morning. It was her routine for as long as I could recall.

As the coffee perked and the water heated in the saucepan, she would walk to the front door to get the morning paper. It would often land in the middle of her daisy-filled flower garden rather than her driveway. Joanna Caine followed the same routine, day in and day out, yielding the same results each morning. Her life remained unchanged since her husband died and I had moved out a few years back.

This morning, with only a few days left until her birthday, I knew she'd be thinking more about the past.

As she'd said to me before, she believed she was ready for whatever life would bring. She had said she had become accustomed to the solitude of quiet mornings and creaking floors. The old mantle clock in the living room curio cabinet was something that she appreciated. She looked to the sound of the chimes every quarter-hour. I supposed it gives comfort and something to look forward to each day.

I had this feeling it was the beginning of a new cycle in my life. I had found a new girlfriend. Amy was coming to help, and we would celebrate Mom's birthday. Now, I only needed to get back to work on the case. But first, I needed a nap. Lacy had worn me out.

Chapter Fourteen

I hadn't dozed off for over ten minutes before my cell phone buzzed across the coffee table and woke me up. I had set it to vibrate in need of a bit of quiet. I should have turned it off. I picked it up and walked onto the balcony. The sun was dazzling this morning, and my eyes narrowed as the sun peaked toward noon over the high-rise apartments across the river from my condominium. Yachts ambled under the 17th Street bridge heading toward the ocean. I thought about how I could have been sitting on one of those mega yachts. All I would have had to do was surrender to Jenna's demands. Be a good husband and work for her daddy.

"What is it?" I said, answering the call.

"You sound like crap," Jimmy said.

"Yeah. I just dozed off, and you woke me up."

Jimmy's southern accent always sounded so damned cheerful. Still, I didn't want to talk with anyone. There was too much happening at the same time. Amy was coming down for a visit, this thing with Lacy and me, my mom, and her memory loss. And then there was the case with the van, the class ring, and a dead girl's bones.

"What's crackin' kid? You dreaming about Lacy?" Jimmy said.

"Same shit, different day, and no, I wasn't. She just left."

"You know you gotta get moving. It sounds like you're in a slump," Jimmy said.

"Yeah. Easy for you to say. A lot is happening right now."

"Work? It'll come. No worries."

"Let's hope."

"Good. So, you and the girl hitting it off?"

"Lacy?"

"Yeah. That's it. You guys a thing now?"

"No. Not a thing. It was a good night, and she is a hottie!"

"That sounds serious," Jimmy said.

"Well, it could be."

"Come on, dude. Don't put it all out there yet. There's lots of fish."

"Doesn't always work that way. It's like shrimp. Sometimes you go through a dozen before finding the right one, and sometimes the right one is on top."

"Shrimp?"

As soon as the metaphor left my mouth, I knew it wouldn't work, but what choice did I have?

"You know what I mean. When you're fishing and you need a shrimp. Sometimes the best one is in your hand."

"Speaking of fish," Jimmy said, "that's why I called. Me and a couple of the guys are taking out the boat. How about you get dressed and come along? You could use a distraction."

"Not feeling like it, pal."

"Aw. Come on, CC. Let's do some fishing and later some beers at Nick's."

As great as things seemed to be moving, my life felt like slow motion. Everything around me either made sense or made no sense at all. I felt something was wrong with my mother; you just know these things. Lacy fell into my lap, literally, at a moment when I needed someone like her, and then there was the case Jack and I were working on. I should have known then like I know now. Nothing is as it seems. It's the detail that solves a case—the shit you miss the first time around. It's what is not said.

I recalled my first case where we discovered the floater. This time I'm not the one behind the camera gathering evidence. I'm the guy responsible for justice in solving a murder. The load was getting heavy, and I needed to do some things. It felt like a juggling act with everything I had in the air. I should have been happy that I had options, but these were not choices I would have preferred. I considered the problems with Jenna, the girl in my dream, my getting shot, and now Lacy.

Although Lacy appeared to be everything a man could ask for, I felt something was missing. Although she was wicked smart, I didn't want to be influenced by her beauty. Sometimes, she seemed too good to be true. As far as Jenna, I needed to let that shit go. That chapter had closed, and there was no reason to revisit. Either way, I had enough of it. It was time for a change, and I needed time to clear my head.

I chatted with Jimmy a little longer, telling him about the plan with Amy and my mother. He thought that was a great idea. I promised we'd get together soon. Later that day, I took a long walk along the Boardwalk toward a psychic shop. I'd passed it a hundred times with little thought. That day, a young girl stood by the door watching me approach.

"*Veni*," she called to me in a familiar accent. I

recognized the manner of speaking in that we had resolved a case a few years back that involved a Gypsy family who'd emigrated from Romania. The parents of the children would shout, *veni, veni*, when they got behind. It meant, come, come, and they all sounded like this woman. "You like palm read?"

I chuckled at the thought of getting my palm read, although I'd always assumed that some toothless old woman occupied the house. Seeing no one around the place, I'd wondered how she could've survived. Now I saw she was neither toothless nor old. She was seductive, with brown eyes and long, flowing black curls. Her stance pulled me toward her like a moth drawn to light.

I shrugged and said, more to myself than her, "Why?"

"Come on, mister," she said. "Only ten dollars and no wait for you."

I followed her inside, and she sat in a high-back chair behind a round table covered in a blue cloth. It wasn't unlike what I'd imagined or seen in movies, except there was no glass ball in the center. There were white candles lit all around the room. Burning incense created a ribbon of fragranced smoke, and the room, lined with heavy draperies, hid all doorways.

"Sit," she said. "I don't bite. Unless you want me to." Her smile reflected perfect white teeth. I could feel her as if she were inside of me. I was sure she knew exactly how I felt and what I thought.

As I sat in the chair across from her, she said, "Give me your hand. First, the right one, and then we read the left."

She laid her arm across the table, and I placed my

hand, palm up, in hers. Her skin was soft, and her touch was light. She traced the lines on my palm with her red-painted fingernails. They matched her lips. I tried to read her but saw nothing. I could use my abilities when I wished and suppress them as needed, but this time, it was different. I knew this, however. My scar was warming. I figured this could be interesting and let it play.

"What has happened in your life to cause lines so deep?" she asked.

For the first time, I spoke to her. "Nothing of note."

"Something, deep inside," she said. "*Tu nu somn?* You not sleep?"

I felt my scar warm. "Not well, I'm afraid."

"Yes. I can tell. It says you will have a long life but troubled."

"Troubled?"

"What happened before you were young?" she said.

"I don't understand."

She struggled with the words. I could also feel something pulling at her, blocking her thoughts. She repeated something, but I didn't understand.

"Your father. I see him. Young man."

"No. My father was older. Retired." *Warmer.*

"No. I see young. He is not here now."

"My dad was not young when he died." *Warmer.*

"I see. Before you were young," she said. "Like when you a baby. Your mother, she's not—"

Before I could respond, she released my hand. "We need to read cards."

My scar now burned, and the pit in my stomach churned. Something was coming. I felt it in my bones.

Her hands slid from mine, pulling out a deck of Tarot cards. I had seen enough. I stood to leave. My scar was on fire. I placed my hand across my forehand but felt nothing, but I knew it was time to stop. "There's been enough mystery for today."

"One card," she said.

"Maybe some other time. I've had enough for now." My scar was sending me a message. "I have to leave," I said and felt the room spin, and I steadied myself on the chair back.

"Okay. It's good. Come back, and we talk." She stood and walked around the table. She touched the crimson scar running above my eye.

"Before you go," her fingers brushed across my forehead, "let me tell you, you *will* remember. You will see what I see, and she will come to you. But I must warn you about something. *Sometimes* the truth is better left hiding in dark places."

My head was spinning, and my scar burned. After backing out of the room, I bumped the wall. I closed the door behind me and paused at a bus bench along the road. I closed my eyes and took a deep breath. I tried to assimilate what had happened. She knew something and wasn't telling me. I could feel that. I thought about her comment; *truth is better left hiding in dark places.* What did that mean?

I decided it was best to head back to my apartment and think about what the gypsy said. I could feel she saw my dream. She knew. At least, I thought she knew. It didn't matter. I knew it hadn't been some magic trick or some figment of my imagination. I recalled how Martin and my guardian angel spoke to me through images, but this was more intense.

Still, was I losing my mind? It was too much to handle, and I got some rest, but I wasn't tired enough to sleep. I got home and poured a drink, then sat on the balcony for a long while thinking about what the gypsy girl had said; *sometimes, the truth is better left hiding in dark places.*

****

I dozed off, and the next thing I knew was I heard pounding, like a fist beating a drum, and a voice, muffled, but I knew it was female. She called my name. I was in a small room, and water crept along the edges of the ceiling. There was thunder and pounding rain. I was in close quarters and couldn't stand without bumping my head.

She was in the corner. She was crying and reaching out but wasn't close enough to me. I felt it raining on me. It was pounding like on a tin roof. Water had soaked everything around us. It seeped from every crack, then gushed through the walls. I crawled toward her. I felt like I was falling, and she screamed as I touched her hand. There was a flash of light.

I jolted from the chair and realized I was still on the balcony. I grabbed the hand railing and stared twelve floors below.

Catching my breath, I went into the kitchen, drank a glass of water, and sat at the kitchen table until daylight. As the sun rose and its light crept through the window, I stood and knew one thing for sure: my work was a long way from being over. It was clear. The vision had returned with a vengeance. She had more to tell me, and it was apparent that she was not leaving. I knew it wasn't going to be easy. She was talking and was trying to tell me everything.

The memory faded when I tried to remember. I stopped and attempted to regain focus. The snippets of conversation were making some sense, but there was babble, too. I heard and saw bits of pictures, actions, sounds, and sights.

Some of it was like my session with Martin. The images presented themselves, leaving me to interpret. I was getting better at understanding her, but the answers were still not clear.

It had taken me a long time to realize what was happening, but now I believed I knew how it would end.

Chapter Fifteen

After Amy arrived as planned, I took her to lunch at the sandwich shop down the block from my condo. "So, what is the plan with Auntie?" she asked.

"Good question. I was thinking, tomorrow, we could take a cake over and do a small celebration of her birthday. Then we could talk about you staying there while visiting."

Amy nodded in agreement. "Pass me the mustard, please. That's works for me. I'll just be visiting for a bit and keeping her company."

"Truth is, she'd like that. There's not much for her in that big house."

"Good. Done and settled. Nice sandwich, by the way."

****

The following morning, I woke and called Mom. "Good morning. Did I wake you? You sound sleepy."

"Oh. Good morning, Carter," she responded. "No. I walked past the phone as it rang, and I didn't expect it. Lost in thought, I suppose. Are you coming by today?"

"Of course I am, but I'll be there tomorrow, not today. Remember, I promised to take you shopping for your birthday."

"I'd forgotten about that. You know how forgetful I can be at times. What time will you be here?"

"The mall opens at ten, so let's say I pick you up at

nine-thirty unless you'd like to go to breakfast. And I have a surprise. Amy came in yesterday."

"No. I'll just make coffee and have a little oatmeal. You said, Amy's here?"

"I did. Maybe we can have lunch together?"

I reminded her to be ready since she ran late. She assured me she'd be waiting for me long before I arrived. She also reminded *me* I didn't have to remind *her* to be on time.

I stood at the bar in my kitchen and mentally replayed the conversation. I recalled the tone of my mother's voice. Her thoughts drifted these days as if preoccupied. My years of police training taught me to listen to what people didn't say, and my mother was no exception. I could hear something in her voice, and it puzzled me. Amy came around the corner.

"Good morning!" Her smile brightened my mood. "You okay?"

"Yeah. I'm good. Just got off the phone with Mom. She's expecting us."

"Cool beans! This ought to be great. I really like her."

"She likes you, so you guys should be fine."

****

We arrived at my mother's house and walked up the brick sidewalk. I let myself in and found her sitting in a chair beside her backyard garden, still in her robe. Touching her on the shoulder, I said, "Hey. You were supposed to be ready."

She reached up and patted my hand. "I'm sorry, honey. I guess time got away from me. It's so peaceful here. Go pour yourself a coffee and I'll get dressed."

She got up and noticed Amy standing to the side.

They were excited to see each other, which gave me great relief. Mom said she'd be right back so we could go.

I stepped from the garden back into the family room. There is a picture of my dad and me sitting on the couch in the living room. I was about four years old; Dad wore a dark three-piece suit, and I sat with intent, listening to every word of a story.

"You never met him," I said.

"No. He died before I was born," Amy said. "My dad talks about him, though."

Amy strolled past the curio cabinet looking at my mom's memories. Pictures of me as a child, my dad, and outings we had sat alongside an old mantle clock and an ornate blue vase with gold trim.

"You were a cute little boy," Amy said.

"Uh. Sure. Long time ago."

"Haven't changed much. Does that clock work? I don't think the time is right."

"Probably not. It's been sitting there next to that blue vase for what seems like forever. Mom likes to keep things, as you can see."

"It seems, but a lot of older people are like that."

As I walked into the kitchen, I saw the newspaper on the table. I realized it was an old copy because the lead story was about stolen vehicles pulled from the canals by city workers. I found it odd that she would have saved that particular issue of the paper. But since I'd told her I was working on a related case, maybe she thought it was important. She seemed to save every little thing.

I shrugged it off but felt the pit of my stomach turn, and my scar tingled. I could have sworn I heard a voice whisper, "*This*."

Amy might have said something. She hadn't. Then I assumed it was mom talking to herself again—a regular occurrence. I looked at the photo of me and my dad. It hung on the wall, and I reached up to straighten the frame. "Looks like a good case, eh, Pop?" I said.

"What was that, dear?" mother said as she rounded the corner.

"Oh. Nothing, Mom. Just reflecting."

"Okay. Well, I'm ready. Amy? Are you ready?"

"You look very nice," Amy said.

We walked to the car and then drove to the mall. After shopping for a while, I saw Mom tiring. "How about we sit at the coffee shop and grab a cup?"

She agreed and ordered a small pastry. I studied her face as if she were a case file, a habit I picked up from police work. Her thoughts were far from the shopping trip and traveling further away each moment. "Any plans with your friends tonight?" I asked. "For your birthday."

"No. I think it will be a quiet night. They wanted to get together, but I called them and said no."

"It would be good for you to do something with them."

"Maybe. I'm not so sure. I'm not too sure of anything anymore."

"What the heck does that mean?"

"You know… it's been a long time since your father died… and don't say hell."

"I said heck, Mom. Did I tell you I went back to work?"

"Did you want to go back?"

"I missed the action." I shrugged. "I missed having

purpose."

"I figured you had enough action with getting shot and what's her name leaving you."

"Funny, Mom. Besides, a different kind of action and work may be just what I need. Speaking of which, did you see the story about the cars pulled from Cold Water Creek?"

"No. You mean in the paper?"

"Yeah. That's where I saw it. But I was wondering why you still had that issue of the paper."

"I don't know. It's probably been sitting around, and I just haven't cleaned up. I don't read the paper much anymore. At least not the bad news."

I glanced over to Amy who gave me a shrug that said, *let it go for now*.

I changed the subject, thinking Amy was right, better to leave it for another day. "You miss him badly? Don't you, Mom?"

"Your father? Not as much as I once did, but he was nice to have around the house most of the time. I need to talk to you. I mean, I think we need to talk."

As she sat at the table, she was wavering. It was in her eyes, far away, glassy, as if she looked right through me, and that had me worried. "You okay, Mom?"

"What's that, honey?"

"I asked if you are okay."

Amy drew Mom's attention by placing her hand on her arm. "Hey, Auntie, won't it be great to spend some time together? Maybe we could go shopping and leave ol' stick in the mud Carter behind."

Mom chuckled. "He means well, dear. But it will be nice having you around for girl talk."

"Cool! I'll grab my things from Carter's place and see you in the morning."

While Amy and I drove back to the apartment, she said, "Your mother has deteriorated quite a bit."

"I agree. It's hard to see someone disappear like that."

"That's okay. I'm here and can watch over her while you decide on her future care."

There were going to be decisions. I didn't know how serious those decisions would be. Jimmy would say, "Everything changes and don't take it personally."

I knew aging was part of life, but this was my first personal experience.

Chapter Sixteen

October 2017

Monday brought another day of investigation and with Amy there, life would be a little easier. I sent her a text before heading to lunch.

— did you get settled in? —

— I did. we're good. talk later —

Jack walked over and mentioned lunch.

"You wanna hear something crazy?" I said.

"Like?"

"I was at my mom's house over the weekend. She had a newspaper article about them creating that new park and finding the vehicles in the water. It was sitting on her kitchen table."

"Okay. That doesn't sound unusual."

"Yeah. On the surface, it doesn't, but it was unusual as far as I'm concerned. Think about it. That article came out like four months ago, and now it's turned into a missing person or murder investigation."

"So what? She's interested in your work. That seems normal to me. Didn't you ask her?"

"I did. She brushed it off."

"Maybe you should, too. Let it alone. She's a mother, for Christ's sake. It's what they do. Can we go to lunch?"

Jack waved me off, but that feeling in my gut

wouldn't leave it alone. After lunch, I got back to my desk and pulled my notes. So far, all we had was a van, a skeleton, and a ring to show the case was at least thirty years old. We also knew it was a young woman or girl and probably a runaway.

Jack arrived as I was putting the notes away. "Heard anything more about the van?"

I told him there was nothing new, even after all this time. Only a rusty bucket with bones inside.

"Yeah. Well, I don't like loose ends and neither do you. We need to classify this thing, so we know our direction, but thirty years is making any headway a long shot."

"What the hell do we do next?" I asked, knowing the answer.

Jack grinned. "I suppose a good detective would look over the file before asking such an obvious question."

"Yeah, but we're Homicide. I mean, the last time I checked. Shouldn't this go to the Vehicle Recovery Team and if they find it's not an accident, then we would get it?"

"We have one of those?" he asked, looking around the room.

"Okay, okay. Don't get your feathers up. Let's just work this until we can get back into the groove of things."

I noted the Medical Examiner's garage held the remaining pieces of the van for more extensive forensic examination. "Okay, so whether it's a murder, suicide, or simply a girl driving off the road and into the canal, the van could supply more information," I said.

Jack nodded, so I leaned forward to pick up the

phone to call Dr. Rite and knocked my coffee onto the floor. It looked like it was going to be one of those days. I cussed at my stupidity, cleaned up the mess, called Maintenance, and grabbed another cup of java. Jack was thumbing through the sports pages. He looked up but didn't offer anything. I said, "Would it kill you to lend a hand?" He shrugged and went back to reading. I redialed the phone.

"Medical Examiner's Office," the voice said on the other end of the line.

"Good morning. My name is Detective Caine with the Fort Lauderdale Police Department. May I speak with Doctor Rite?"

I continued to read the file and placed the phone on speaker. The team had discovered four vehicles in the canal before finding the suspect van. The forensics team searched all of them, and the results were all inconclusive except the van.

"Good morning, Carter," Rite said as he picked up the line. "I figured I would hear from you soon. How are you feeling? I heard you were back."

"Doing okay, Doc, but they got me back on the case where I left off. Remember the van found in the canal with the skeleton? That's still my assignment."

"It keeps us in business, I suppose, and you'll be glad to know she is still here, lying around, and awaiting your arrival," Doctor Rite said.

I had always found the man's sense of humor charming and somewhat relaxing—in an odd way. "What do we have on this thing in the canal?"

"It's hard to say at the moment."

"How hard?" I asked.

"The good news is the lab finally came back with

the DNA results. It took them long enough, but they could identify some interesting things about the remains. I still have the skull and a few other bones, but we never found a complete skeleton. The good news is, my forensics team came up with a complete facial reconstruction of what she looked like. I'll send over the pictures for your file. It should help with identifying her."

"That's great news. Unfortunately, Jack didn't come up with any missing person's reports to match the time period. Was she a child, an adolescent?"

"Well, more like a young woman, about five-foot-four-inches tall, maybe seventeen years old. Not much to go on, but some interesting things. I put it all in the report, but if you want to go over it again, feel free to stop by with a pastilito and coffee." Rite said. "Don't know if any of it will help,"

Since he'd stated the DNA showed the girl to be of Indo-European ancestry, when I asked Rite what that meant, he said, "She may have been born here, but her family tree is not. Her parents, or at least one of them, are from the other side of the globe. That may help you narrow the field.

"I suppose that could help," I said. "And if she was about seventeen, she'd have been in high school."

"Better than that," Rite said.

"How can it be better?" I asked.

"The DNA, if you follow the markers enough, indicate not only Indo-European but there's a good chance at least one of her parents immigrated here, which means there are records. Maybe both of them, for all we know."

Once I explained the findings to Jack, he was ready

to jump back into the case. "That's good info. We also have that high school ring, so we know where to look, even if we don't have a missing kid reported."

Before I knew it, the day had ended. I decided a drink was waiting for me at Bezo's, a small bar close to the office. The place was dark as I walked in. The owner, Jeremy, was there with a Scotch in his hand.

"How'd you know?" I asked.

"Sue saw you drive up and told me you were here."

"Dude. I haven't been here in quite some time."

"Almost a year. But I always remember my best customers."

I was there for about an hour when my phone rang. It was Lacy. "Hey, slim," she said. "What'r ya doing?"

"Having a couple of drinks at Bezo's."

"Starting without me?"

"Are you back from Tallahassee?"

"I am. We got the other guy to concede, so the case settled. Got back this afternoon."

"Why don't you meet me here? My treat."

She laughed. "Why don't I meet you at your place?"

"Better. See you there."

****

The sight of Lacy sitting in the lobby made my heart race. She wore a tailored, navy-blue business suit and matching blouse with an ascot. As I approached the large glass window that fronted the lobby area of my building, I stopped before entering and watched her. She flipped through a file; a brief, I figured. I don't know how long I stood there watching. Time wasn't on my mind, but she was. I watched the angle of her head as she read. How she tapped a pen on the folder as if thinking of the words before her.

Finally, I walked through the doorway and without looking up, she said, "You need to stop that."

"Stop what? I was only standing there and admiring you."

She stood as I came in and walked toward me. Lacy was tall, and we were eye to eye with the heels she wore. "Yeah. That and thinking dirty thoughts about me."

"It's what I do. You mean a lot to me."

"I do, eh? I'll bet you say that to all the girls."

"I do, but with you, I really mean it."

"Funny guy." She feigned a slap.

"Besides. You're hot stuff and I'm a lucky guy."

"Yeah. You got that right. But you're not so bad yourself."

"Ya think?"

She wrapped her arms around my neck. "I don't normally say this, but I want to."

"Say what? I was thinking something was on your mind."

"True words." She paused and reached for my hands. "I promised myself that I would have no more commitments after I left my boyfriend last year."

"That bad?"

"Worse. He was horrible and I really don't want to discuss that right now."

"No worries. I'm not asking."

"Thanks. Anyhow. I need to say something to you."

I didn't like the tone of that statement, but there we were, alone in the lobby, and it wasn't like I could tell her to hold that thought and run off. I took a deep breath. "Sure. You can say whatever you want."

I prepared for the worst. Of course, the last thing I wanted, or needed, was for some shit to go down inside my condo. With that, I didn't want to head up the elevator. Fortunately, in the lobby, there is a small café around the corner. They weren't open, but residents had access. I made some excuse that suggested we walk over there so we were not sitting in the lobby. The café was lit only from the lighting running along the walkway, so there was a quiet solitude about the place. We sat next to each other in a booth. Lacy looked into my eyes. It was like she could read my every thought.

Her eyes dropped pensively, and she clasped my hands into hers. "I like where this is going. I really love being with you. You know that, right?"

"What's not to love?"

She pulled me close, looking beyond my shoulder. "Let it go, Carter. I'm serious."

"Sorry. I don't mean to make light of it. I don't understand why, but I'm feeling the same thing." I attempted to lighten the moment. "Is this what they call love at first sight?"

Lacy rolled her eyes. "I'm not saying that, but there's something here, and I think we should explore it."

I ran my hand along her lapel, touching her slightly. "I'm all for exploring."

"Not my blouse, Carter. You know what I mean. There are still people around."

"I know, and I want them to know. Besides, I'm just trying to lighten the moment. But I can tell something else is bothering you. There's an unspoken 'but' in here somewhere. What is it?"

"I want to ask you something."

"Alright. I gotcha." I adjust my seat to face her more closely. "So what is it?"

"You will not believe this, but I was thinking about the case you're working on."

"Really? I didn't expect that response. Why would you do that?"

"I don't know. Honestly. I don't even understand why it popped into my head. Anyhow. I was also thinking you should give me a key to your place."

I played it cool and shrugged. What I wanted to do was yell out, 'Hell yeah!' but said. "That's a thought," I said. "Maybe it's time for that. Did I tell you mention you look good and smell even better?"

"Just good?"

"Let me try again. How about we go for it right here?"

She hugged me, then pulled away. "You're funny, but you look worried."

"Oh, really? Changing the subject, I see." I said with a lopsided grin.

"No silly. I'm serious." Lacy reached inside my jacket. "And you're wearing a gun."

"I always look worried. And yes, that's my service weapon. The city makes all us cops wear one. You know, bad guys and crap like that."

She nodded. "I guess with you back on active duty. I should have seen that coming. That should keep you busy and out of trouble, and it explains the worried look on your face. Anything interesting come up on that cold case?"

"Plenty, but still nothing concrete. Is that all you wanted to ask? About a key?"

"Yeah. That was it and I spent all day working up the nerve."

I chuckled. "No need to worry. I'll have one made up tomorrow."

We headed to the elevators, and I punch the button. She was quiet as we walked down the hallway to the condo. I began to second guess my decision in that she seemed calm, if not a bit detached. That all changed when the door closed behind us, and I reached for the light.

"You don't need that," she said. "I missed you," she said as she unbuttoned my shirt.

"Missed me? It hasn't been that long. Has it? Sometimes I lose track of time." I winked at her. "Is this the exploring part you mentioned earlier?" I missed her but wasn't letting on.

"Didn't you miss me?" she said as her hand slid down my pants. "Oh," she smiled. "Never mind. You don't have to answer that. I hope your gun doesn't go off before we get inside."

****

I never bothered with hitting the light switch. There was enough light coming in the windows from the full moon. I paused long enough to grab two glasses and a bottle of wine and flipped on the music. Lacy was in the shower before I could undress. I stripped off and stepped into the shower behind her. It took only a glance to see what I'd been missing. I carried her across the room and gently place her in my bed. She pulled me in close and kissed me; her hand placed firmly on the back of my head. I knew at that point she was the love of my life, and I didn't deserve one bit of her.

Afterward, we both slept for an hour. She was very

athletic, and sometimes there was an effort to keep up. She nudged me awake. "I'm hungry."

The moon had set behind the clouds, and the only light in the bedroom was from a candle. She was even more striking in the shimmering candlelight. Her long hair flowed down her back and fell across her shoulders. I could see the outline of her silhouette against the backdrop of the moonlit sky.

"You know? Me, too," I said, stretching my arms out over my head. "What do you say we hop over to Lester's and grab something to eat?"

"Better idea," she said. "I'm going to shower, and you're going to call Chang's and get a little Chinese up here."

"A threesome?"

"You're hopeless," she said, bounding from the bed and back into the shower.

I called Chang's and ordered, slipped into my gym shorts and tossed on a faded blue tee shirt with a surfer on the front. The food arrived at the same time Lacy did. I set up a table on the balcony, and we ate Chinese and tried something new—we talked.

"So, I have to know," I asked. "Exactly what do you do?"

She lowered her chopsticks. "Here? Or do you mean what kind of work do I do?"

"Not to me. I mean, what kind of work."

"I'm an attorney," she said. "You couldn't tell? What kind of cop are you?"

"I know you're an attorney. There are a lot of lawyer specialties—I know. My ex-wife's family was full of them, but they didn't all practice the same kind of law."

"True. I thought I'd told you."

"No. But it doesn't matter. I'm just asking. Making conversation."

"Not your kind of law," she said.

"I didn't think so. So, no criminal law. My guess is corporate?"

"Yeah. You're right. Let's say it's more like private practice for specific clients. Leave it at that."

"What does that mean?"

"Don't be silly. You ask a lot of questions, and you know what they say about curiosity."

"I'm not a cat," I said, wondering why I'd just gotten the dodge. Then again, I had other motives on my mind that night, and I didn't care what Lacy did for a living.

After dinner, we opened a bottle of wine and moved over to the chaise to watch the moonlit sky. We were silent for a long time. She was here, and that was all that mattered for the moment. It was comfortable, and I enjoyed being with her.

"So, catch me up. How's that case you guys are working on? Is it a murder? Missing person?

It surprised me she asked again, but figured she noticed it was on my mind. "Making progress," I said. "Today was interesting, though."

"Why?"

"In the past month or so, the DNA came back. It seems the girl's not from here. At least her parents aren't."

"DNA? That's cool. I took one of those home DNA things where you mail it off, and they send you the results that tell you about your bloodline."

"How'd that turn out for you?" I smiled and raised

my glass to her.

"Pure Italian."

I laughed. "Pure?"

"Well, damn close." She said as she stood and walked to the railing. "The surprise was that there was more French in there than I expected. You ever do one of those?"

"DNA test? No. Never tried it." I walked over and stood behind her, wrapping my arms around her waist.

She turned around and faced me and pulled her fingernails across my chest. "You should. I think it would be interesting." Using her finger, she popped me on the nose to make a point, I suppose. "I'll order a kit for you. You can get them online, do the swab, and mail it off. Before you know it, you have all your history in your hands."

"No need. My dad was Irish, and his folks came in straight from Ireland. My mom's parents were English and Welsh. Pretty simple stuff."

"I'm going to order a kit for you, anyway. I need to make sure you're not pulling my leg about being British and Irish because I'm thinking, with the way you are in the bedroom, there's some Italian in you."

"Ha. Funny. But speaking of pulling my leg."

"Stop. Be serious for once. Why did you choose to be a cop?"

"Now, who's asking a lot of questions?" I shrugged and ran my hand down past her waist. "It just seemed a natural choice. Does being a cop bother you?"

"Natural? Interesting. And no, being a cop is kinda cool, I think."

I liked that answer. I picked up the wine bottle and added a few ounces to our glasses. "My father was a cop, my grandfather as well. Guess it runs in the family."

"Retired?"

"Yeah. After thirty years, he called it in. Sadly, soon after he retired, he passed. It's just my mother and me."

"Wow. Your dad was still kinda young?"

"He was. I don't remember a lot about him. My mom said she always tried to get him to go to the doctor. He always said he felt fine, and that doctors were for wimps."

"Lemme guess," she said. "Clogged arteries?"

"Yup. Led to a heart attack," I answered. "If you ask me, I believe he died because he lost his purpose. He missed being out there. You could see it in his eyes. The only thing he had was police work and his hobbies."

She tilted her head to the side. "Hobbies?"

"He liked woodworking. He built a beautiful buffet for the house and most of the furniture. End tables, coffee tables, and such. He was talented."

"How about you?"

"Woodworking? Not this guy." I laughed again. "Nothing I build would even stand up. I never got the hang of it. I wasn't much interested in working with my hands like that. The only wood I'm thinking about right now—."

Lacy laughed. "Stop being a horny dog and talk to me. No brothers or sisters?"

"Nope. An uncle in Atlanta. My dad's side. Now *he's* like my dad with the woodworking and owns a cabinet shop. He has a daughter named Amy. Other than that, no relatives."

"Hmm. Me neither. Your mom lives here?"

"Tamarac."

"Ah," she said. "Heaven's waiting room."

I didn't answer.

"I'm sorry," she said.

"For what, the comment?" I waved my hand in the air. "Heck. It's Tamarac, and most everyone there is old. She just had her seventieth birthday, but she's in good shape except for some memory issues."

"Really?"

"You say that like it's unusual."

"No. I'm looking at the math. You're what? Around twenty-eight, twenty-nine?"

"Close. Yeah, I know. I was a late baby."

"Late? Your mom was around forty when she had you?"

"Pretty close. Somewhere around there. I've never done the math."

"That's a long time to wait to have a baby."

"Yeah. I've asked about that, but Mom would only say that's how it was, then would change the subject." I sipped the rest of my wine and placed the glass down. "I suspect I was more of an 'oops' baby. Definitely not one they planned on having."

Lacy smiled.

"What?" I said.

"I was thinking about an article I read once that said there is no such thing as an oops baby. The cited that some people believe those babies are supposed to be born."

"Supposed to be? What the hell does that mean?"

"You know. A higher purpose. They were born because they had to be born. Destined to do something."

"Destined. Sure. I think I was just born, and that was about it."

"I don't know. Funny thing about destiny. You sometimes don't realize it until the end."

Chapter Seventeen

The radio in the car, tuned to a news talk station, blasted the details of the current heatwave stretching across south Florida.

"I can't believe the heat down here," Jack said as he reached to turn down the radio's volume.

"Heat? It's October," I said. "This is glorious weather."

"I can tell you this," he groused. "The one thing I will never get used to is this freaking traffic. Just look! Can you imagine what this looks like at five o'clock?"

"You're a piece of work, partner. I think you like to complain about everything."

"Maybe so," Jack responded. "But it seems to me, city planners and construction companies are in it for the money. They're more interested in jamming as many people as possible into one square block than they are about quality of life. No regard to streets or services."

Since I was a native to the area, I couldn't argue with his logic. At one time, Fort Lauderdale was a lovely, quiet local town, but that had changed over the years. The city attracted people to year-round days of beautiful weather, albeit sometimes way too hot. I turned up the air conditioner and continued south on the interstate to exit 8 where the sign said, *Welcome to Coconut Palms.*

"So, what's the problem?" Jack asked. "Did you and your girlfriend argue last night?"

"None of your business, wise guy."

"Just sayin'," Jack responded. "Seems like you're on edge today, and I was just being polite."

"When was the last time you were polite? Oh, wait! Let me think. Oh yeah! Never?"

"What?" Jack responded by putting his hands in the air. "I'm a nice fuckin' guy."

"Yeah. Keep it up, Jack. It's a long walk back to the station."

After a few minutes of silence, I said, "Girlfriend. Yeah, she's a piece of work. Sometimes I wonder why she comes around."

"See? Told ya. I know about these things."

"We were talking a bit about the case last night and she mentioned she had done this DNA test thing. Apparently, it's all the rage. Anyhow, she wants me to do it for fun, of course, so I agreed. She's bringing over a kit."

"What the heck. Go ahead. It won't hurt and it would make her happy. You know, happy wife, happy life."

"Yeah. Not a wife. Still, the girlfriend and I want to make her happy. Anyhow, that's not the entire reason. I mean, we didn't argue. Quite the opposite–it seems we're really hitting it off."

"So, what is it?"

"I don't really understand it. For one, she's more woman than I could ever dream of having, and she's great to be around. We fit each other like a glove. It's like this relationship was supposed to happen." I glanced at him, then at the rearview mirror. "You know, it's this case. It's been bugging the crap outta me."

"Why? It's not like it's your first, and we've been doing this for a while," responded Jack. "We could solve it and we might not. Won't be the only one, pal."

"I know. I mean, something is missing. Something we're missing. I can't put my finger on it. Oh. Before I forget, Rite's team came up with a sculpture of the girl in question."

"Cool. Is it in this file?"

"Yeah. Right in front. I freaked when I saw it. So life like."

Jack opened the file. "Holy shit. She was a kid."

"Uh yeah? We know that."

"I mean she looked so young."

"That she was, and we now have a composite."

I turned left toward the main entrance for the high school, noting the large Home of the Cougars sign on the corner. The curbstone has a designated visitor parking area. I shut off the ignition and notified dispatch we'd be off the air. "Alrighty," I said as I took a deep breath and opened the car door, "let's get this shit over with."

Wiping his brow with his handkerchief, Jack said, "Gads, it's hot! It should be nice and cool now, being October and all. And have you seen the bugs down here?"

"You northern boys are always complaining about something. I'm sure they have air conditioning inside the building."

We walked up the breezeway to a set of large doors. Jack pulled one open, and the odor of paper, pencil, and the miasma of high school adolescence invaded my senses. "I think I smell dope," he said, his nose up in the air.

I rolled my eyes, raised my hands in exasperation. "Jesus, Jack! Just leave it alone and focus. We don't have the time to deal with that now."

"Yeah, but it would be fun to shake down some punk holding weed. You know, something the little delinquent can tell his friends about."

A chilly breeze welcomed us as we opened the doors to the administrative offices. We saw a sign that said "Principal's Office" in bold letters with an arrow pointing the way. It was a matter of following the signs posted on the walls. A young girl, appearing half-asleep, sat behind a low wall. She looked up at us as we entered. I noticed her name tag: Juana.

"Hello, Juana. We are here to see Principal Phillips," I said. I flipped my badge and approached the counter. "This is Detective Nelson, and I'm Detective Caine. We have an appointment."

The young girl looked at our gold badges, then picked up the phone with a noticeable amount of disdain as Principal Phillips walked out of his office. He glanced at the front desk and saw us there. "Detective Caine," he said as he walked toward us. "Please, come through the door over here on your right."

We walked through the opening and followed Phillips to his office as Jack whispered, "I don't think Juana likes us."

The principal sat in an oversized brown leather chair behind a sterile desk. I glanced at Jack's notepad, and he was writing: one black phone, one brass lamp, desk mat, three number two pencils, two pens.

Principal Phillips wore a checkered jacket with a

starched white shirt. He had tied a blue bow tie, sported a thin mustache and manicured fingernails. After he sat, he adjusted his bow tie, then peered over the top of the round-rimmed eyeglasses. "So. What can I do for you, detectives?"

I glanced toward Jack, then back to Phillips. "It's a routine investigation. We're attempting to identify a young adult. So far, we've determined she lived near Coral Springs and may have attended this high school when she was about seventeen years old."

"I see. Do you have a name?" Principal Phillips asked.

"That's the challenge and why we are here. We don't know what her name was."

"Was?" said Principal Phillips.

"Yes, Principal Phillips," I said. "*Was.*"

"Hmm. I see. So, she's no longer with us?"

"Correct. We believe she attended this high school. If so, perhaps we'll be able to identify some of her friends, and there may be a chance they still live in the area. It would be good to connect a name to the evidence we have."

"You don't know if she was a student here?"

"We found something that points to this school. That's why we started here."

"Have you contacted her parents?"

"Once we positively identify her, we will. Or we'll try. At this point, we don't know if her mother or father, or any family for that matter, is alive. To continue the investigation, we'll need a name to identify her. Without a name or identity, everything else becomes a moot point, and we'll sadly close the case as a Jane Doe."

"I see," said the principal. "You know, I have an idea that might help in your case."

"How's that?" I asked.

"Depending on the time period we're discussing, we have specific files regarding children who did not graduate. In this case, this female not only would not have graduated, but she would also have been truant. A record like that would have its special place. I mean, how often do people just disappear?"

"We estimate she'd have been a student about thirty years ago. If you have a file that old, that sounds positive. What's next?" I asked.

"So, 1986 through 1988? I'll have the files pulled for all truants. Male and female are separate, so that should narrow the search," Phillips said. He leaned forward and pressed the intercom button. "Juana, can you come in here for a moment?"

She arrived, pen and steno pad at the ready. "Yes, Principal Phillips?"

"I need you to pull the file for truant females, 1986 through 1988. It's tab filed, so it should be easy to locate. If you need my help, let me know."

Phillips leaned back in his chair and said, "Tell me something, Detective Caine. Dead for almost thirty years?" He then leaned forward with an eyebrow cocked, then tapped his finger to his lips. "That's a long time. How in the world would you identify someone after that time? DNA? Like on TV?"

"Actually, that's a good question. Through DNA, we can tell a lot of things about a person," I said. "We ran a DNA analysis on the remains we discovered, and it seems she is of Indo-European descent."

"I see. Was it like one of those things when

someone finds a body buried in the woods? A dog bringing home a bone or something like that? I saw an episode of Quincy where that happened."

"Not quite, sir. All I can tell you is we discovered remains after a routine sweep pulled a vehicle from one of our canals." "I vaguely recall the story," he said as he placed his index against his temple. "It was in the news a while back. Cold Water Creek? The city is building a park and boat ramp there."

"Yes, sir. That's it. But that's all I can say at this point. It may be an old case, but it is an ongoing investigation."

Juana walked back into the room with three files about an inch thick. "It took me a while to pull these out," she said. "There were only three, buried deep in the back."

"Thank you, Juana," Phillips said. "We don't need anything else for the moment."

I opened the manila folder and flipped through the student pictures. I came across one that resembled the composite drawing of the clay model that Dr. Rite had provided—and sat up a bit straighter.

"Sonovabitch," I said quietly. Thankfully no one heard me.

The name under the photograph was Siran Yesayan. I noted the similarity to the face and head reconstructed by the forensics team and passed it to Jack. It was frightening to see her in real life but satisfying to know we'd made progress. The specifics from Doctor Rite about body shape and size matched. According to the records, Siran was five feet and four and a half inches tall, one hundred and forty pounds. The picture showed her to be cute with straight brown hair, brown eyes, and freckles.

I felt my stress level lessen, but my scar started to tingle. Both were good signs.

Siran Yesayan looked like a perfect match to our skeleton.

After a quick scan of other documents in the folder, a couple things didn't sit right. "Can I get a copy of this file?" I asked. "It could provide additional evidence for the investigation."

"Of course," Principal Phillips said. "I wouldn't expect you to read it all here."

After we had the copies, Jack and I walked back to the car. He continued to bitch about the heat.

"Here. You drive," I said and tossed him the keys. "I want to read this over while we head back."

Jack adjusted the seat to fit his large frame, started the car, and turned the air conditioner to its highest setting. He flipped the air vents in his direction and loosened his tie. "Freakin' heat."

I ignored him. My brain felt like it was on fire. The answers were right around the corner and my scar told me we were on to something. I didn't know exactly what it was, but something itched at me.

The records from the high school revealed Siran Yesayan was an only child and lived with her father. Lucky for us, he had a minor police record for drunk and disorderly which made things easier to gather information. It was almost as if I knew him, as if I had met him, and yet, that would've been impossible.

The school records also showed the father never exhibited much interest in Siran so she ran free most of the time. He had not filed a report after she went missing but the notes from the Youth Services investigator piqued my interest. Apparently, the old man didn't file a report because he believed she ran away with some kid—whose name he couldn't remember.

The investigation didn't go anywhere, mainly because someone in the line dropped the ball and the whole thing ended up falling through the cracks. The father was a known alcoholic who, neighbors said, beat on his daughter often. It was a classic story. No one paid attention, and the Department of Youth Services filed the case away as a runaway.

Birth records showed Siran's mother died giving birth. Could we assume the father blamed the daughter for the death of his wife? By now, my scar was burning, and I believed everything we needed was there. We just had to put the puzzle pieces together.

****

We arrived back at the station. It was a long day, but I had to keep going. My mind reeled with the names found in Siran's school records. At least now we had something.

I still figured she could have been driving the van, lost control, and ended up in the water. Christ's sake, I thought, she was only seventeen. Her last known address was a house in Coral Springs, but that was useless information. Her father had died not long after she disappeared and the house was now owned by someone else, unrelated to the family. In that it appeared there were no relatives, any history or other information about her would have died with him. There was nothing hinting to Siran's existence other than names of people who'd been her classmates.

I pulled the folder from my briefcase and settled in

at my desk. The file held a report from 1987 where juvenile authorities named Siran and a few of her friends as truants.

They'd been loitering at McDonald's, eating fries, and drinking soda. Kids being kids. It was nothing serious. The officer had escorted them back to the high school, where they served detention for the next week.

Then something caught my eye. I pushed back in my chair and made myself read the report three times in case there was an error. After the third time, I realized it wasn't an error, and this case took a serious twist.

I stood and read the list of students out loud, as if doing so would make more sense. Siran Yesayan, the girl we believe we have been trying to identify. Her mates with her on that day? David Machelli, Louis Green, and Jefferson Caine.

I said, "Who in the hell is Jefferson Caine?"

I called Principal Phillips to verify if any of the three boys were associated with his high school. Of course, Juana answered, so I provided what I needed. Name verification and last known home address, if possible. I also called the station since I had to wait. My guys could provide an additional background check for the three boys.

After about an hour, Phillips called me back. "Detective. I have some information for you as requested."

"Good news, I'm hoping."

"It seems. Machelli and Green were easy to find— at least as far as their home addresses for that time. The challenge we had was finding anything on the Caine fellow. It seems his name was on the truant report, but there is no record of his attending this high school. I personally checked the records and there was nothing related to him at all."

I thanked Phillips and called one of the guys I'd put on the search. "Any luck?" I asked after waiting for several minutes.

"Two names came back; Machelli and Green."

"Local?"

"You're in luck with one, detective. Machelli's last known address is in west Broward County, a trailer park called Everglades."

"What about Green?"

"Sad story. He died in Panama during that mess with Noriega's forces. He was only eighteen.

"That sucks. What about the Caine kid?"

"Yeah. I tried that a couple of times. That's what was taking the time. Nothing came up. It's like he never existed."

"That's odd," I said. "I have his name on a report from the school file."

"What's odd is the guy has your last name. I also checked the popularity of the name. There's about four thousand in the United States and none are in Dade or Broward counties except you, of course. So, there could be another one out there, I suppose. Can you imagine two of you?"

"Thanks, smartass. I checked that also while waiting for your callback. Weird, but I can't explain it. I don't have any siblings, nor do I have any relatives with the name Jefferson. Believe me, it would have made this case a lot simpler if we had some background information on him."

I would have preferred to check Machelli out over the weekend, but that wouldn't happen. Unlike TV shows, overtime costs the city money. Since this was essentially a cold case, there wasn't much pressure to resolve it, so next week would be fine.

I headed back to the apartment, but that name, Jefferson Caine, kept popping in my head. Who the hell is this guy and what happened to him? Maybe Jack could shed some light on it. I called him at home.

"I hope this is important," he said.

"You could say that."

"What is it?"

"I was reading the files from the school."

"Okay. So?"

"We have a list of suspects, but only one is here. One suspect, you will not believe the name."

I could see Jack rolling his eyes. "Try me."

"Caine."

"What? Caine like you, Caine?"

"Yeah. Jefferson Caine. And get this. No history, no record of existence. Nothing."

"Nothing?"

"Nothing."

****

Monday couldn't arrive soon enough. I hit my office at five in the morning. I couldn't sleep, so it didn't matter whether I stared at the ceiling at home or stared at my computer screen at the station.

Jack ambled in about seven-thirty with two large coffees in a holder. "Hey, Sunshine! Got you a coffee!"

"And here I thought you were a jerk. Then again, maybe that's partly me."

"*Partly* you?" Jack asked with a grin. "How long you been here?"

"Early. Before dawn."

"What the hell brought you in so early?"

"It wasn't *that* early. I couldn't sleep, so I figured why not?"

"Yeah. The desk sergeant said it surprised him to see you here."

"It wasn't that early. I found some interesting stuff in the files. And after running the backgrounds, I'm thinking we may solve this yet."

"Great," Jack said. "Like what?"

"For starters, little Siran had three guys hanging with her. I mean, not that it's a surprise; they went to the same school, but still."

"That's interesting, but not much help—if you know what I mean."

"I know, but one of them still lives here."

"Okey-dokey," Jack said. "You said three?"

"Yeah. Three. Am I going too fast for you, Jack?"

"Nope. Too slow. What are the names?"

"David Machelli, Louis Green, and Jefferson Caine. Machelli still lives in the area. Shortly after graduation from high school, Green enlisted, then bought it in Panama during the invasion. That leaves Jefferson Caine as our second person of interest, and it seems he's disappeared from the face of the earth. The initial dives indicate there's no record that he ever existed."

"Hmm," Jack said, sipping his coffee.

"I'm sure it's just a coincidence," I said. "To my knowledge, my family doesn't have any relatives down here. I don't know anyone named Jeff or Jefferson, and I'm an only child, so it looks like that's a dead end. I have an uncle in Atlanta named Derek, but he's never lived here."

"Really?"

"Yeah. Let's focus on David Machelli and hope something comes up. If that's a dead-end, we'll go full throttle on this Caine guy."

"But you said he doesn't exist," Jack said, tossing the empty coffee cup in my trash basket.

"He doesn't exist on paper, but no one just vanishes. Let's walk and talk on our way to the car."

"Right with you. Okay, Machelli. Where is he?"

"Last known indicates he lives in a trailer out off of US 27. This ought to be a hoot."

"Hoot? US 27?"

"Goddammit, Jack! Are you going to echo everything I say today? Yeah. He lives off US Highway 27. It's called Everglades Park. He lives in the first trailer at the end of the street, next to the campground out there. It seems he's an artist, but the word is, he's an alcoholic and on disability, along with all kinds of other problems. The park manager said we couldn't miss the place. Just look for the trailer painted like the horizon. Sound to me like this one is a bit of a loser."

"You gonna drive?" Jack asked.

"Yeah."

"Okay."

"What?" I asked him.

"Nothing," Jack said, shrugging. "I thought you might want to read over the files. Make some notes. Get a plan."

"You mean you don't like my driving?"

"You said that, not me."

"Fine," I said, thinking I could probably keep this trip under eighty.

Jack tossed me the keys and got in. I turned all the air vents on me.

Chapter Eighteen

Everglades Park turned out to be an unincorporated suburb of Broward County. To the west of the trailer park was nothing but sawgrass and alligators. North and south offered nothing but open land and small housing developments scattered to the county line. A few horse pastures, farms, and the sprawling suburb of Pembroke Pines was off to the east. The population in Everglades Park was so small there was no cop shop. The Broward Sheriff's Office provided public safety.

Before we left the station, Jack and I had called the sheriff's office for backup since being in plainclothes could get you in trouble in that type of neighborhood. I did not know Machelli as a real bad guy, just a DUI, petty theft, and one assault charge. We had no plan on charging him with anything and we didn't expect any trouble. Still, in our business, there could be a surprise around every corner. Both Jack and I wore our Kevlar vests, just in case.

A BSO green and white sat at the corner as we approached the block of at the indicated address. The uniformed officer pulled in behind us as we passed. From what they knew, Machelli lived in the trailer with his girlfriend.

We drove into the trailer park and noted an array of broken-down vehicles on blocks in front of trailers. High weeds and children's toys were prevalent.

Stopping at the manager's trailer, he told me again that Machelli lived at the end of the turn in the last trailer on the right.

"You can't miss it," the park manager said. "It looks like the sunrise as you make the turn. The ugliest thing here."

"I'm doubting that," mumbled Jack.

The faded orange trailer with yellow-streaked paint sat back in the lot. Duct tape held the two front windows together—scattered toys decorated the patchy front yard, but no car. The hand-painted trailer would look like a sunrise only if you had an imagination. I knocked on the screen door, which no longer had a screen. After a few moments, the inside door opened, as far as the safety chain allowed.

Someone about four feet tall peered through the three-inch opening. I leaned over and asked, "Are your mom and dad here?"

The door slammed shut, and tiny feet pounded on the floors. I looked over at Jack, and he stood there, calm as could be, his hand under his jacket on his Glock.

I heard the chain slide, and the door opened. A large, barefooted, heavy man stood there in a soot-gray T-shirt and baggy plaid shorts. *If hair was money, this guy would live in a mansion.* "Yeah? Whaddya want?"

"Are you David Machelli?" I asked, but it was a formality. I knew he was the right guy since I had a picture of a younger version in the file.

"Yeah. That's me," he said while he scratched his protruding belly. "And I didn't do nothin'. I was here all day and all night and all week."

"Never said you did anything, sir, and that's not the

point of our visit. This is Detective Nelson. My name is Detective Caine. We only want to ask you some questions. We need some help with an old case, that's all."

I noticed Machelli's eyes shift as if trying to remember something when I said my name. "Yeah. Well. Uh. Okay, I suppose. I ain't in no trouble, am I? Right?"

"No, sir. Just a few questions," I said, "and we'll be out of here."

Machelli turned, leaving the door open, and waved us in.

The house was clean, a pleasant surprise. Machelli told the kids to play outside as he sat in a well-worn green pleather-covered recliner. Using the remote control, he switched off the television.

Jack and I sat on the couch. I opened my notebook. "We're investigating a missing person case. The girl involved is Siran Yesayan."

I watched Machelli's eyes and noticed the same shift as he seemed to struggle to remember. Then he smiled, a subtle, sad smile, and looked away. "You mean Sara. I haven't thought of her in a long time."

"Siran Yesayan, sir. Records show you went to the same high school as Miss Yesayan," Jack said. "Here's a high school picture of her."

He looked at it for a long moment but didn't touch the photo. "Yeah. That's her. I did, but back then, we called her Sara."

"Sara?" I repeated.

"It was her nickname. Man, she hated her given name, so she said we had to call her Sara. Her dad had come up with that name, a family name, or something like that. She and him didn't get along too good. So, she wanted her name to be Sara. She seemed to like that. Anyhow, yeah, there were a few of us that hung together. Me, my brother, Lou, Jeff, and that's it. Maybe that's where I know you from. You related to Jeff, by any chance?"

"No. Just a coincidence with the name," I said. "Same last name. It's common. You're saying you knew Jefferson Caine?"

"Yeah. Exactly. I knew him."

"How did you know Mr. Caine?"

"Well, for one, we went to the same school."

I tucked the information away in the notes. I had thought we were making progress, but now, I couldn't or should say I didn't want to raise other suspicions with Machelli, so we kept the question moving forward.

"Tell me, Mr. Machelli," Jack said. "What do you remember of Siran?"

Machelli sat quietly for a few moments. He seemed stuck for words, so I let him think about what he was about to say.

"Yeah. Sara," Machelli said. His defensive demeanor changed, and he relaxed in his chair. His shoulders dropped and he smiled the way someone does when they remember something good from long ago.

"So, I take it you two were friends?" I asked.

"Hell. We were more than friends. We loved each other. I mean, as much as two stupid kids know about love."

That comment got Jack's attention. He sat up straight and looked at me. I thought this could go somewhere. Jack must have seen the anticipation in my eyes, so he continued the line of questioning. "So, what happened?"

"The last time I saw her was at the hangout, by the canal. We were all together hanging, drinking, smoking, uh–"

"It's okay. You can say whatever you wish," I assured him. "Consider this a free zone, and we only want to know about Sara."

"Okay. Yeah, so we were smoking weed and pretty screwed up. But we did that all the time."

"How did you guys get there?"

"Oh. We usually drove our cars. Just getting a license and all that, so it was cool."

"Did Sara drive there herself?"

"Sara? Oh no. She came with Jeff. She didn't have a car. Besides, she was the only one that had a job, so I guess Jeff picked her up."

"Did that bother you?"

"Well, kinda yes and no."

"What does that mean?" Jack asked.

"Well. They were just friends, like the rest of us. But they had dated for a while. Then they broke up, then dated. It was on and off."

"But you said you two loved each other."

"Yeah. We did. At least I did. We were just getting to know each other. You know, at that level. I mean, we hadn't done much of anything else but kiss and hold hands. But nobody else knew about it. I mean. With Jeff and everything. He was one of the buds, so nobody wanted to get hurt."

"I see," said Jack. "So, you guys, you and Sara, I mean, were fully serious or just at that friend's stage?"

"Yeah, no, not really serious, but it was there. Like I said, at least it was for me."

"How did Jeff feel about that?" I asked.

"Oh. He didn't know. I don't think he did, anyhow."

"Did they leave together that night?" I asked.

He sighed and looked at the ground, then up at us. "See, now that's the question."

Jack leaned forward. "What do you mean?"

"Like I said, we were pretty wasted. I had a nice campfire going, drinking beer and that. It rained like hell, so we all ran up under the bridge, thinking it would stop soon. It didn't and just got worse and worse. I mean, it was like a monsoon. While we were waiting, I guess we all passed out."

"All night?" Jack asked. "Jeff and Sara didn't join you?"

"No. Jeff had a van. Last I remember, Sara and him was sitting in the front seats talking or something."

"You said he drove a van?"

"Yeah. A custom one with bench seating in the back and everything. Really nice."

I sat back and looked over at Jack. We were close and I knew there was something Machelli wasn't saying. I decided to let it ride and see where it would take us. "So, all of you were under the bridge until morning?"

"Yep. Except for Jeff and Sara. They were gone when we woke up. The van was gone. Nothing."

"Nothing?" I asked. "You mean it was gone?"

"Yeah. Nobody Nothing. There but the rest of the gang, and that was the last time I had ever talked to her or Jeff. A few weeks went by, so I figured she left town. I really don't know. I only know that she was there one day, and the next day, she and Jeff were gone.

I figured maybe she loved Jeff more than me, and they split." Then he paused, looked at me with furrowed brow, and said, "You sure you ain't related to him?"

I looked at Jack, said nothing, then looked back at Machelli. "Like I said earlier, no relation."

Jack interrupted. "What we're trying to determine is a timeline of her whereabouts. It's safe to say you knew Siran, or as you knew her, Sara, and you were friends and attended the same school."

"I think there's more to it than that, Detective," Machelli said, becoming agitated.

"How's that, Mister Machelli?"

"Well, ya see, how I figure it is those two ran off together."

"What makes you think that?" Jack asked.

"Listen. Me and Jeff both really liked Sara. She was cute. The difference was she liked me. She even said so. So, you gotta figure Jeff maybe took away her against her will. Right? At least that's what I'm thinking now that you brought it up."

"Are you saying you believe someone, maybe Jeff, kidnapped her?

"What do I know? You're the cop. Then again, maybe she was just playing me and didn't give a shit about me, and her and Jeff was in love."

"So, you think they ran off because of this?"

"No. Not exactly. See, me and Sara, uh, you know. We were close, and like one night–I almost got to third base. You know."

"Yeah. We know," Jack said. "So, you had sex."

"No. That was the thing. She got all weepy-like and said it wasn't a good idea. And then she said she was late. You know, *late*."

"Late?" Jack repeated.

"Yeah. She was worried what her dad would think, you know, 'cuz she was late."

"You've lost me," Jack said.

"Damn it," I said and sat back. "She thought she was pregnant."

"Yeah," Machelli said, nodding. "That's what she said, but I didn't believe her."

"So, what happened?" asked Jack.

"Like I said, we never did it, and so I knew it wasn't mine if she *was* pregnant."

"Any idea who the father might have been?"

"If I guessed it would be Jeff, 'cuz they were doing it, I think. Anyhow, after it was clear it wasn't me, we sort of went on like nothing was happening. We were still friends, but we never made out again. She didn't look like she was pregnant, but she wasn't a skinny chick, if you know what I mean."

"Heavy?"

"Not heavy. Well, chubby. Anyway, all that talk about Sara thinking she was pregnant happened a before they both disappeared. The night I am talking about. The night when she and Jeff got there, it was raining, was later. Thinking back, it seems to me she would have had the baby, or something, before that night like she had already had the kid like a couple of weeks. We all thought she was pregnant, but she kept it a secret from everybody. Anyhow, that night was the last time I saw her and Jeff."

"So, let's review because I am getting confused and we need to gain a better understanding of this timeline," Jack said. "You and the gang loitered regularly in this area?"

"Loiter? I guess you call it that. It was the only place we could just hang out. It was just a canal off Atlantic Avenue, and there wasn't nothing around but the bridge, woods, and stuff. We hung out, drank some beer, smoked some pot, and listened to music."

"And that night, all of you passed out. Right?" I asked, checking my notes.

"Yeah. It was a crazy night; we were drunker than ever, and I mean wasted. It had been a long week of school bullshit. I suppose we passed out for a while when it was raining."

"And in the morning, the van, Jeff, and Sara were gone," I said.

Machelli nodded. "That was the last time I saw both of them."

"What about the baby?" Jack asked.

"What baby?" Machelli asked.

"You said she believed she was pregnant. Was she?"

"I said we all thought she was pregnant. She never said anything, and we never saw a baby. I dunno. Maybe she had it removed?"

"You mean an abortion?" I asked.

"Yeah. Maybe that." He shrugged. "Wasn't illegal but she probably wouldn't be bragging about it, either. She was pretty private."

"Do you think that's what happened?" Jack asked.

"I dunno. What I said is all I know. That's it," Machelli said.

"Gotcha. So, we think she was pregnant. Not sure. Never saw a baby, and after that night, you just left?"

"Well, yeah! What clse? I mean, I went to Sara's the next day, but her old man said he hadn't seen her.

He didn't seem too broke up about it, either. He was a piece of work, that sonovabitch.

"Then I went over to Jeff's and his mom's place. They didn't live far from the hangout but said she hadn't seen him, either. I never saw his van around, either. After a couple of days, I went back to Jeff's, and his mom said he was missing, and she'd called the police. I never saw it in the papers and everything, but nobody never found either one of them."

"I see," Jack said while scribbling notes on his pad.

"So, tell me, Detective Caine," Machelli said, sitting straighter in his chair. "You from around here?"

Chapter Nineteen

I had kept a constant communication open with Amy. Not much was going on with my mom except for the occasional memory lapses. It was the same routine day in and day out with the two of them. In the morning, after coffee, they would take a walk through the neighborhood. Chat with a few of the neighbors, and then head home. Mom worked in her garden, Amy read her study books and took notes. Each evening they would have dinner, chat, a little television and go off to bed. A couple of weeks after Amy moved in, I received a text from her.

—*call me when u can* —

I called, expecting to hear her cheerful voice again, but that didn't happen. Amy was sobbing. "Carter. My dad died last night." Her words were choppy between deep breaths.

"What happened?"

"It's all so stupid. It was one of those freak accidents you hear about on the news. Dad was on his way home from Atlanta. He'd gone down the day before for a meeting. On the way back, a front came through with nasty snow. I know he drives I75 up and back, and my guess is he took a wrong turn. He ended up on Highway 41, the road that borders the Chattahoochee River. I dunno. He could have been looking for gas. Either way, it looks like he lost control of the car, and it slid down an embankment. The car flipped into the river. Some people stopped to help and said it looked like he couldn't get the door open before the car sank as the river swept him and the car out of reach. Rescue guys got there, but it was too late. At least, that's what they told me."

"That's terrible. Pack some things and we can leave in the morning if you like."

"No. That's fine. I think I'll fly up. There will be a million things to do, and then I'll need to plan a funeral."

"Okay. If that works for you. Have you told my mom?"

"No. That's just it. I don't know how she will take it. She's been a little off lately and I can understand why you are concerned. I was about to call you, but this happened."

"I get it. All of that can wait. I'll be over in a few."

I called my captain to give him the news and asked for time off. Since Jack was in court on a case he'd worked while I was on medical leave, Daniels promised to let him know.

I drove to Mom's house to explain the situation.

"I don't understand," she said.

She, of course, was upset that Derek had died. I tried to calm her the best I could and explained I'd arrange for a direct flight, but my mother refused to get on a jet.

"Fine. I'll drive you," I said. "The boss gave me the time. Besides, Derek was my uncle and Amy needs our help with this."

We left Saturday morning and arrived in Atlanta a little before midnight. I drove to his home and Amy greeted us. We'd stay there.

My uncle had many friends in the area. The house was full of flowers, cards, and neighbors had brought food. We sat in the living room and reminisced about him and his business until my mother announced she needed to sleep. Amy said goodnight and headed off to our bedroom. It was close to two in the morning by then.

I was restless and couldn't sleep. All the recent events were wearing on me. I had a lot to deal with Derek's accident, our current case, and my mom's failing health. It was mounting up. I took a walk around the neighborhood. It was quiet out, everyone else sleeping. I found a peace listening to the tap of my footsteps echo off the houses. The case was still up in the air with no solid leads or evidence. We were guessing at that had happened, but I felt we'd make progress soon.

Mom was failing more rapidly than I had expected. On the drive up, she asked me twice about getting to the mall. I had to remind her we are on our way to Atlanta for Derek, not to the mall for shopping. She would doze off and when she awoke, she'd ask again.

The night was chilly, and there were still traces of snow on the ground. I thought of how peaceful it was as I sat on a small bench in a park. My scar warmed, and I knew what was next. There was a flash of light, and water rained down before me.

"*Now is the time,*" the voice said. "*You are too close to give up on me. I'm waiting for you to fix this.*"

I don't remember anything after that.

Sometime later, I woke in my bed. I stared at the ceiling, wondering how I'd gotten back to the house.

****

We sat in front of a closed casket at the church after the services. The funeral director staged Derek's picture on a pedestal at the front of the room. The services were nothing out of the ordinary, and Amy said a few words about her dad. I held onto Mom, who now looked even more fragile. All the losses were piling up.

Leaving the church, I picked up a small remembrance card and placed it in my shirt pocket. After the funeral, Mom and I returned to the house to check on Amy. She was going to be okay and there wasn't anything else we could do for her. Her church family was going to make sure she had anything she needed. Mom and I sat in the parlor area of the house and chatted while the guests left. Thankfully, she seemed a bit more coherent.

"Are you okay, Mom? Sleep well? Are you hungry? We'll get through this. It will be fine." I was rambling. I knew it. What else can one say when someone loses someone close?

"It's not that, Carter. I'm not worried. I'm sad and a little tired, but I'm okay."

"I'm thinking about driving straight through, if you're good with that. We should make it home by tomorrow. It's about nine hours, and we can stop on the way back so you can rest."

"Ridiculous. I can nap in the car, and you can keep driving if you are up to it. You have a lot of work to get back to."

"Nothing that can't wait, Mom. Nothing that can't wait."

Amy walked in from the hallway and quietly motioned for me to follow her. I made an excuse to my

217

mother about needing to use the bathroom or something. "Everything okay?" I asked once we were alone.

"Yeah. The last of his friends are gone."

"Good. You can get some rest and we will head out."

"I'm glad you guys were here, but I wanted to say something about auntie. I noticed her during the ceremony. She was drifting and the look on her face was like she didn't understand why she was here. I've seen it before in the Alzheimer's patients we managed."

"Yeah. On the drive up, I saw a bit of that. I've made an appointment with her physician and see her next week. I should have a better idea of what to do. She appears to be declining faster than I expected."

"Actually, it's been longer than you know. Most people don't recognize the signs, but with me being around patients, I saw it as soon as I moved in with her. But that's not all."

"How's that?"

"When I was there. You know. At her house. I'd hear her talking."

"She does that sometimes," I said.

"I know, but this was different. She would have a conversation like someone was with her. She was in her bedroom and asking questions to the person. 'Why are you here? Who sent you over?' I'd knock on the door, and she be quiet, then open the door like nothing was going on. I'd say, 'I thought you called me' and she would shrug and tell me it was nothing. It was weird, and I figured it was part of her decline."

"Well, that makes it more important we get to her doctor."

"Carter. There was something else."

I could see it scared Amy which was odd. Her demeanor is normally very cool and collected. "It's okay," I said. "You can tell me."

She shuffled her feet and looked at the floor. "I think she's seeing things that aren't there."

"That's odd. Like what?"

"She was in the kitchen one afternoon making tea. I walked in and she asked if I wanted some. I said, no thanks."

"She said, 'Okay. Sara and I are going to have some, but you can join us if you change your mind.'"

"Sara?"

"She pointed to the kitchen table and repeated, 'Sara.' Is that a friend of hers?"

"No. It's not," I said. "But I think I know what's happening."

****

Mom and I left in the morning. She seemed her normal self. As I drove, my mind kept churning. This new friend of hers was a big tell, and I was afraid of what it meant. I didn't want to think it, but it was too surreal to let go. Not only that, but the questions also it raised, frankly, scared the hell out of me.

She dozed off during the drive, which I appreciated, but woke a couple of hours later. "Are we almost home?" she asked.

"Still quite a way to go, Mom."

"Do you want to stop for coffee? Are you hungry?"

"I'm good. Are you?"

"Yes. Fine." I paused for a moment. My scar was warm. I knew I had to ask. She was gazing out the window. "Mom. Can I ask you about Sara?"

"Sara?"

"Yeah. Do you know a Sara?"

"I do. How do you know her?"

"I don't know her, Mom. I was asking you."

"Well. She visits me."

"What does that mean?"

"I don't know. She visits. Comes over. We talk."

I didn't push the conversation. I knew it wouldn't do any good to badger an old woman that was already confused and had lost her brother-in-law. I also knew I couldn't sleep, so stopping at a hotel would be useless. The case Jack and I were working on wasn't going anywhere, but something was ticking in my head, keeping me awake. I had missed something, and I knew it. I didn't know what "it" was, but every lead that we'd investigated had come to a dead-end.

David Machelli checked out without a problem or a connection. He was oblivious to anything that may have happened that night the van ended up in the water. That poor guy had more to worry about than a van with bones in it. Lou Green was not a suspect because he was KIA during that mess in Panama. Then, there was the disappearing Jefferson Caine. I also knew we needed facts. Only facts solve a case, not a dream, a little girl, or a missing person.

I had so many unanswered questions. If his van and girlfriend were in the creek, where did Jeff go? Was it an accident? Had they both been inside, and he got swept away? Had they lost their baby and ended their lives? Had there even been a baby? Maybe they are all dead?

I drove on as my mother slept deeply in the seat next to me.

****

It was late when I arrived at her house and got my mother situated inside her home. Before I left for my place across town, I made sure she was comfortable. I arrived at my apartment just as Lacy called. I shut the door behind me and dropped my go bag on the floor. Then I headed for the kitchen.

"You back?"

"Yeah. Just dropped off my mother, and it's time to hit the bed."

"Are you okay? Need help getting tucked in?"

I'd missed her, but I wasn't up for any company. "Not tonight, but thanks for the offer. As tempting as that is, I'm exhausted and need some sleep. Call you tomorrow."

I stripped, got into the shower, then fell into bed. I stared at the ceiling fan for what seemed an hour and dozed off. *Don't forget me.*

It was a whisper, but I heard it like a voice in the room. I turned, but there was nothing. Again, I listened as if someone was in the room. *Don't forget me.*

I knew it was her. "Not now. Please. Not now." I pulled the pillow over my head.

When I woke again, the morning sun crept over the balcony, and I turned to see the clock, which said six o'clock. I jumped into the shower, dressed, grabbed a coffee from downstairs, and headed for the office by seven.

Chapter Twenty

November 2017

"How was it?" Jack asked when he walked in.

"It was a funeral and a long-assed drive."

"Yeah, well, no one ever wants to bury someone. How's your mom?"

"Not any better. Amy and I are thinking Alzheimer's, but I don't know. I'm making an appointment with her primary care physician so we can get some answers."

"I got it, and I'm sorry about all that. Tough times and just another problem. Right?"

"Yeah. I'll get through it."

"Wanna get coffee?"

"Excellent idea, and I guess that it's probably the best idea you'll have the entire day."

"You're an asshole," Jack said. "Anyone ever tell you that?"

"Yep. You do. All the time."

"Asshole."

"You said that already. You're repeating yourself, partner. You heading downstairs now, or would you like to continue to critique my personality?"

We stopped at the café on the first floor and sat in a booth to chat about the case. "Anything open up while I was gone?" I asked.

"Nothing much more than what we know. Siran, or Sara like everyone called her, was pregnant at one time, it seems, from one of the guys, although there is no child. Right? My guess is, it wasn't Machelli, so that leaves the Panama kid, Green, or Jefferson 'Houdini' Caine. Green is dead, and we can't find this Jefferson fellow."

"Something tells me it wasn't Green, or Machelli would have talked about him more," I said. "He seemed the jealous type and probably hot-tempered–or was back then. With that, I'd pick him to be the one that may have slapped the girl around, but only a maybe on the pregnancy."

"I hadn't considered that angle," Jack said. "That's a good probability."

"Maybe, but I got the feeling he felt unconcerned. I mean, wouldn't you be at least a little concerned if I said your girlfriend was pregnant?"

"I believe Machelli," Jack said. "He believed she was pregnant and talked about it. He was upfront. He said there was nothing there."

"Okay. But I still think he's hiding something, but if you say so, we can take your angle that you believe he was honest with us. Then Jeff would be the likely suspect, considering he and Sara vanished. We also have to consider the vehicle in the canal will probably come back to him."

"Yeah. Sure if they can salvage the VIN. But I get the feeling you're thinking about something else."

"Eh. Something's chewing on me."

"What? Chewing? Like a flea?"

"No. I was talking with Jimmy during the drive back. He was helping me stay awake that last couple hundred miles. You know Jimmy, right?"

"Yeah. The surfer guy."

"Well, he said to me that sometimes the shortest answer is the most obvious one."

"What that the hell does that mean?"

"He called it Occam's razor. You ever hear about that?"

"No. Who the hell is this Occam dude?"

"He's a guy from like the fifteenth century. Think about it like this: there are a couple of explanations for this problem. In this case, the one that requires the smallest number of assumptions is usually correct. So, the more assumptions we have to make, the more unlikely the explanation."

"Aha. Keep it simple, stupid, right? So, where does that leave us?"

"I have an idea," I said.

****

We returned to our office, and I went to the whiteboard and wrote the assumptions in black marker:

The van was in the canal and probably belonged to Jeff.

We have a dead body. Skeleton. Possible homicide. Sara.

We have a possible motive. Baby? Father?

Jack interrupted. "Are we sure she was pregnant? I mean, are we sure she had the kid?"

"What do you mean? Machelli said she was pregnant."

Jack sat up in his chair and held his hand out. "No. He said he thought she was pregnant. He never saw a baby, remember? Even with that, when did we start trusting suspects?"

"Good point," I said, tapping the marker on my forehead. "It was Machelli that brought that up and he said he never saw the baby."

Jack shook his head. "So, you're saying we're pretty sure she was pregnant–or at least Machelli was. If aborted, we wouldn't be looking for a baby. That would make a difference. Right?

"Yepper," I said. "But I have some information that will change your mind."

"Here we go. You keeping secrets?"

I chuckled. "No. This morning has been hectic, and my mind is racing. I thought you had read the report from Doctor Rite. It came over late last night. He said it appears she'd given birth at one time. I saw it on my computer early this morning when I remoted into the office."

"You need a life, Caine. And that's not fair to play me. You're withholding evidence."

"I was getting there. Don't get your panties in a wad. He said he could tell she had given birth from her bones."

"From the bones? No shit. How would he know that?"

"I called him and asked the same question. He said that normally he wouldn't have checked, but since we mentioned the possibility of a pregnancy, he would look again."

"And I'm guessing he did," Jack said.

"He said it was faint because of the age of the bones and water damage. He would have missed it, except he was looking for it after we mentioned she may have been pregnant. It was just a hunch he had, and if the victim had been pregnant and given birth and not aborted, there would be physical evidence. He told me there were a series of shotgun pellet-sized pockmarks along the inside of the pelvic bone. During childbirth, Rite said, it tears ligaments. The bone impressions are a permanent record of the trauma."

Jack whistled. "That changes the picture."

"Exactly. It does, but it only means a baby was delivered. It doesn't mean it's still alive. But there could be a baby out there," I said, pointing at the board. "Call me crazy, but something tells me Machelli knows that."

"So, let's assume there is a baby," Jack said. "Now that baby's an adult. Somewhere out in the world. I got a feeling that if we find the baby, we can end this thing. Hot damn, our job just got a little more interesting."

****

Jack and I contacted Machelli again to discuss the baby. I heard the surprise in his voice. It could have been fear, but he cooperated.

"Did you know for sure that she was pregnant?" I asked.

"Nah," Machelli said. "Like I told you before, Sara was a little chubby. Always had been so nobody woulda thought nothing. But she was worried about being pregnant."

"Did she look pregnant when you saw her last?"

"How many times are you asking me the same question? I said no, before. Nobody knew she was pregnant. She coulda had it the month before or when she ran off. I dunno."

Machelli was getting agitated; I heard it in his voice. There wasn't much of anything else he could have contributed, so I thanked him and hung up the phone. I called the medical examiner's office. Rite said there was no timetable for the birth other than confirming Sara had given birth.

"I assume the baby survived. It may not have. Did anyone report finding a stillborn? Sometimes girls panic and throw them away. Or they did thirty years ago. But, if the baby survived, you could assume it went up for adoption," Rite explained.

"Got it," I said. "I know it's a long shot, but I am going to check the hospitals. Thanks, Doc. I owe you a Cuban coffee."

I gathered a list of hospitals and then narrowed the search to those that were open from 1985 and beyond. That left three hospitals in the area and only one had a maternity ward. Jack and I went to visit, and after several hours of running through records, it was a dead end.

"What now?" Jack asked.

"Dunno," I said, annoyed yet again. "While I was looking for hospitals, I also tried to create a list of neighborhood clinics."

"What did you find?"

"Nothing."

"There's got to be something," Jack said.

"There is, and you'll never guess what."

"Okay. I'm game."

"Remember when Machelli mentioned Sara was late and this Jeff guy had brought her?"

"Yeah?"

"He said she had a job."

"Okay. Lots of kids work during high school. What did she do? Was she a cashier, like most teenagers?"

"No. That's the interesting part. Sara had a head on

her shoulders."

"She was smart, you're saying?"

"Yeah. I was going over the notes from Machelli. I'd noted that she had a job and put a question mark beside it. I didn't think much about it because, like you said, she was probably a cashier. Not very memorable. I was wrong."

"What was she?"

"Little Miss Sara was a veterinarian's assistant. What do you think about that?"

"She worked for a doctor?" Jack asked, his eyes lighting up.

"Exactly," I said.

Chapter Twenty-One

I posted a map on my office wall to draw a radius surrounding Sara's house. After several hours of research, I discovered three veterinarian offices. All the offices were less than ten years old. The timeline didn't match, so I called the offices and asked the next logical question.

"Are you aware of any veterinarian clinics that would have been in the area around the late 1980s?"

The last office I called was Doctor Sharon Wisenbaum. Her answer surprised me. She was personally aware of an office during that timeframe. "My mom was a veterinarian, Doctor Laura Wisenbaum," she explained. "She had a practice off Sunrise Boulevard for a long time. Back then, she was the only local vet for the area."

"That's promising," I said.

"Why are you asking?"

"We're looking for a veterinarian that might identify a young woman. Our lead show she worked as a veterinary assistant. If there's any chance we could review employment records from that time, it could be helpful."

"I can certainly check with her if you like. Perhaps that would work for you."

"Yes. She can call me directly, or we can call her."

"I know my mother. She wouldn't mind if you

called her. She retired to the Keys several years ago. My father and her own a home in Ocean Reef."

"Let me email your office, with a formal request," I said. "You can respond with her information."

****

The following afternoon, I contacted Doctor Wisenbaum at her home in Key Largo. The challenge was she lived in a high-end property at the north end of the island. Still, I had decided that a face-to-face interview might be less intimidating, and the doctor obliged. The drive to Ocean Reef was a long way from my office, so Jack and I made a day of it.

After arriving in Florida City, we turned left past the Last Chance Saloon and onto Card Sound Road. "Have you been to Ocean Reef before?" I asked him.

"Not this guy. But I've been down this road to Alabama Jack's."

"We can stop there afterward for lunch," I said. "It's the only place to eat around here, to be honest, unless you want to drive over to the other side of Key Largo.

"What? They don't have restaurants where we're going?"

I chuckled at the thought. "They do. Just not our type of restaurants. It's a private club and your money is no good at Ocean Reef.

"You're kidding me, right?"

"A few years back, I was fishing with Herb and his sidekick Willy, and this guy named Horton. Herb is a cousin of some relation. We were running low on fuel. He thought his friend Willy had checked the tank, and Willy thought Herb had checked. Anyhow, we figured it would be a good idea since we were right off Ocean

Reef Club to hop over and grab a few gallons. We came through the channel, and there were all these yachts, and I mean *yachts*. Mind you, Herb's boat is no dinky skiff. It's a forty-two-foot Sportfish, but some of the craft along the waterways had to be over a hundred feet long."

"Big boats!"

"Yeah. So, we pulled up to the marina, and the dockmaster came out. *What's up, guys*? he asked. Herb yelled over that we were low on fuel. The guy smiled and said, *Wish I could help, but the fuel is for members only.*

"How can that be?" I asked him.

"Private club," he said. "Believe it or not, the Club doesn't take cash. It seems people there have so much money they don't even use cash."

"Well, that's bullshit if I've ever heard it," Jack said.

"Kinda is," I said. "It seems they tie purchases to a member number, and they get billed for purchases of just about anything. With that, no one carries cash around with them."

"How do you know that?"

"Your not going to believe it."

"Try me."

"We're about to pull away and some guy pulls up in a golf cart. It seems he was the Chief of Public Safety at Ocean Reef."

"Chief?"

"Yeah. They have a public safety group. So, this man asks the Dock Master about us. He then waved Herb over."

"For what?"

"He told Herb that he would foot the bill to get us enough fuel to make it over to the closet marina."

"No shit?"

"Yup. Nice guy. Of course, Herb mailed him a check when we got back. Lunch at AJ's good for you?"

"Perfect. That was nice of him. Alabama Jack's sounds great."

"Order the conch fritters. They are awesome."

As we passed Alabama Jack's, Card Sound Bridge rose before us. Rising to the top of the bridge, the water below was calm and an emerald shade of green. There were boats anchored below off the main channel, fishing. The view of the bay was peaceful.

The road ahead was a winding trail of asphalt and mangrove, with the occasional small bridge to cross. People fished the sides of the road where the water was close enough. We arrived at a three-way stop sign and turned left.

"What's to the right?" Jack asked.

"An abandoned NIKE missile site, and not much else. If you follow the road far enough, the rest of the Keys, Key Largo, and US1."

We rounded the last corner and saw the Ocean Reef community and saw the main gate ahead. It was an imposing structure. "Looks like we're not getting in easily," I said as we pulled up to the guardhouse.

I rolled down my window and presented my police badge. The name tag on the officer in the window said Al.

"Hi, Al," I said. "We're here to see Doctor Laura Wisenbaum. She expects us. We have an appointment."

He politely asked us to wait a moment while he called the owners. I could overhear the conversation announcing Jack and I had arrived. Then Al said something to the person on the other end of the line and handed me a map with the route highlighted. He explained where to go.

Inside the neighborhood, we saw trees and lush landscaping with well-attended orchids lining the main street, a championship golf course, and giant yachts on the right. We passed the fountain with a bronzed panther and continued to the intersection. Across a bridge, past a marina, we turned onto Exuma Road. Dr. Wisenbaum met us on the porch of her home.

Once inside, we sat in a room overlooking the Atlantic Ocean. "Lovely home," I said. "Thank you for inviting us down. Have you lived here long?"

"My husband and I built our home here about ten years ago. He'd retired from his practice. He was a cardiothoracic surgeon, but his genuine passion was golfing and fishing. Anyhow, he enjoyed his time here, but he passed away a couple of years ago. It's my pleasure to have you here. I hope I can help you."

"I spoke with your daughter. As you know, we're trying to get some information on a potential employee that worked for you. Her name was Siran or Sara Yesayan."

"Got it," Doctor Wisenbaum said. "That's what my daughter said when she called. To be honest, it's been a long time since I saw Sara. Such a sweet girl. Troubled, but a sweet girl. She worked with us at the clinic and loved working with the animals. Is she in some kind of trouble?"

"Not trouble," I said. "Unfortunately, she may have been a victim of a crime. We discovered her remains in a submerged vehicle."

"Oh! That's awful. You mean she died a while back?"

"Yes ma'am. Something like thirty years ago."

"Oh my," Dr. Wisenbaum said. "She was a child then. I thought you meant something more recent."

"No, ma'am. She was a teen, and that leads me to my next question."

"Of course, go ahead."

"Well, the medical examiner says she'd given birth at one time. While we can't do much for Sara, but we can try to locate her child. The child would be her only kin."

"For one, it's so admirable of you to want to locate her child. But this also explains why she simply stopped coming to work."

"Yes, ma'am. That would explain it. Can you tell us anything else about her?"

"I knew about the baby," Wisenbaum said.

"Oh. So, you knew she was pregnant?" I asked.

"I did, but not until sometime later. I knew Sara's father had a difficult time getting work and had to settle for odd jobs and such."

"Why is that?" Jack asked.

"I believe he was from another country. Not American. I remember Sara saying he was Armenian or something like that. Either way, Sara had no one. Her mother had died. I don't recall the details, so she had no one to care for her or the baby. Well, except for her boyfriend, but he was just a boy himself."

"That's interesting. My partner and I checked every record we could find but couldn't discover where she'd given birth. It was like she had the baby and then the baby never existed."

"Oh, that baby existed. He was adorable, and she was completely overwhelmed. That's what puzzled me with her not coming back to work."

"How's that?"

"Working for us was her only income. We'd be inside the office, and you could hear her boyfriend's van pull up. It was loud, and he had customized it with all kinds of things."

"How's that?"

"I was outside, in front of the building one afternoon, and he drove up with Sara. She opened the back of the van and wanted to show me the work her boyfriend had completed. It was something else. The boy had set up the back where you could use it as a camper. There were cabinets, a sink, a place to sit, and the bed folded up into the side. It was well done, and Sara said that the boyfriend did all the carpentry work himself."

"He seemed a nice young man and talented. I asked where he learned how to do all that work, and he said his dad taught him. Anyhow, he dropped her off every afternoon. She would work until about seven pm and then he'd pick her up."

"He drove a van?"

"Yes. However, it wasn't like every other van on the road. That van was truly unique."

I glanced at Jack as he scrambled to take notes on the conversation.

Dr. Wisenbaum then said, "Detective."

Maybe it was the tone, or perhaps it was the timing. Either way, I heard something in that one word. I looked back at the doctor as Jack stopped writing.

"Yes, ma'am?" I said.

Dr. Wisenbaum sat forward in her chair and gazed out the window toward the ocean for a moment. Then she turned back and looked at us.

"I have a confession to make."

Chapter Twenty-Two

"Confession?" I repeated.

"I suppose. Indeed, I didn't know about the pregnancy until the last moment, but there's more. You see. I was driving home one evening, and I passed the office. I noticed the lights were on, so I turned the car around. There was a vehicle in the parking lot."

"What time was this?"

"Oh, I'm thinking, ten or eleven o'clock. I wasn't paying attention, and I was in a bit of a quandary seeing the lights on. I'd been out to dinner with friends, and I lost track of time."

"I see. So, there was a vehicle parked in the front of the building?"

"Not the front, but the back of the building, where all the employees enter. I pulled my car around and thought someone might have left the lights on. As I approached the door, I heard Sara. She sounded like she was in pain."

"Did you call the police?"

"Honestly, once I heard Sara, I didn't think of anything other than her being hurt, so I unlocked the door and went in."

"Where was she? What was happening?" I asked.

"You're not going to believe this, but she was in the back of the office. I saw her on the stainless-steel surgical table we use when performing surgery on pets.

I'm sure you've seen one."

"Yes. I've seen those tables before."

"Anyhow. She had covered herself with a sheet, and a young man was standing next to her."

"The boyfriend?"

"No. That's what was surprising. I'd seen the boy with Sara before, and occasionally, he dropped her off at work."

"So, you knew him?"

"I knew of him. I don't know his name."

"But you're saying it wasn't the boyfriend."

"No. I'm almost positive it wasn't her boyfriend. This boy was shorter, and I recall, had a lot of hair. And the car in the lot wasn't the beautiful van."

"What does that mean? A lot of hair."

"I mean, he was about the same age as Sara but had beard growth like a man, with thick, black hair. It was all over, like a grown man. If I had to guess, I'd say he was of Italian descent. Either way, it's not the boy I wanted to tell you about."

"Go ahead."

"Sara was on the table and she was distressed. That's when I realized she was pregnant and about to deliver, which was a surprise. I mean, she didn't look pregnant. I had no idea."

"Wait. So let me get this straight. She was in your office on an examination table with a guy and had just delivered a newborn?"

"No. What I'm telling you is that Sara was *about* to deliver. She was in labor and about to have a baby."

"I see. And the male that was there?"

"Yes. By her side and trying his best, it seemed, to help her, although it was apparent that he was way over his head."

"Did anyone mention his name?"

"I heard her say his name once. If I remember correctly, I believe she called him Dave or Dan. It started with a D; I remember that much."

"No last name?"

"She didn't say, and there wasn't time for an introduction. I focused on that poor girl. She was in labor with hard contractions and about to have a baby. She was scared to death and needed medical attention. I wanted to call an ambulance, but she refused. She was terrified the authorities would take the baby since she was a minor."

"So, what did you do?"

"I treated it like any other emergency. I'm a doctor first, so I had an obligation to help her. It wasn't serious enough for a hospital. The fact is, the boy had done a good job of helping her already. Sara was smart enough to know how to make sure everything was sterile."

"How did all that end?"

"As I said, Sara was afraid of Child Care Services and wanted to keep it all quiet. I had to respect her wishes, so I did everything I could to make sure she was safe from a medical point of view. She remained at my hospital for the rest of the night, and I checked in on her the following morning."

"I'm assuming she was fine?" I asked.

"I suppose. It was a shock when I returned the following morning. No one would have known something had occurred the night before. The place was spotless, and Sara was gone."

"Did she contact you later?"

"I called her home number and got her father. He

was useless. No. Sadly, I never heard from her again. I don't know what happened to her or the baby boy. I have thought of her often over the years."

"Are you positive the male was not her boyfriend?"

"For all I know, he could have been the father of the child or a friend. Sara never spoke a name when she worked here other than she would mention my boyfriend this or that. I wasn't that involved in her life. Either way, Sara didn't say anything, but a lot was happening. I assumed the guy was the father. Why else would he be there?"

Jack folded his notebook and looked over at me. "Well, pal? What now?"

I pulled out the photos we'd been carrying around from the school records. Jack had done a composite of the three boys who were known to be Sara's friends and I showed it to the veterinarian.

"Would you look at these pictures, please? Tell me if any of them resembles the young man with Sara that night."

Wisenbaum adjusted her glasses and looked at the pictures. She pointed to the one I thought she would. "This looks like him."

"You're sure?" I asked, knowing she was.

She nodded. "Absolutely." She handed the sheet back to me. "Am I in trouble?" she asked quietly.

My scar was burning. We'd been searching for this information to help us with this case. The doctor's involvement was circumstantial and probably well past the statute of limitations, anyway. She didn't provide anything but a significant lead to follow and gave us some of the answers we needed.

"No. Perhaps under a different circumstance, you

might have had a problem. But it seems you were helping, not hindering. With that, you did a good thing by helping a young woman get through a trying time. Don't you agree, Jack?"

He nodded. "Can you tell us anything more about the boy that was there?"

"I'm sorry officers, I don't remember anything else. Once I was sure she was stable and comfortable, I went home for some sleep."

I had no interest in involving the doctor in our investigation. She was a bystander, although she was certainly part of the process. I believed Wisenbaum's only crime was being in the wrong place at the wrong time. She saw a situation and handled it according to her oath as a doctor. No harm, no foul, as Jimmy would say.

We said our goodbyes to the good doctor and the breathtaking views and got back in the car.

As we approached our car, I asked Jack to drive.

"We going to that restaurant down the street?"

"Yeah. My phone vibrated while talking to Wisenbaum. It was a call from Amy. I need to talk to her."

"She's back in town? I thought she returned to Atlanta after her dad died."

"My mother had a doctor's appointment today. I didn't dare ask for more time off so Amy said she'd come down to take her for me. I need to hear what he said."

"No worries," Jack said. "Just point when I need to turn."

I dialed Amy. "Hey. What's up?" I asked after she answered.

"The doctor just called with the results."

"It is Alzheimer's?"

"No. Remember when he said he wanted to do a brain scan?"

"Yeah. I thought that was strange, but he's the doctor."

"Yeah. Well. The results came back. Auntie has a serious issue. There are signs of a tumor. But listen, please. Don't freak out on me. She is functioning fine for now and has no idea."

"That doesn't make me feel better."

"I know it doesn't, but if you suddenly show up and she's not expecting you, she's gonna freak. So, finish your day, do whatever you need to do. He wants to admit her for more tests tomorrow."

"Gotcha. Let's talk this evening."

I dropped the phone onto the seat and relegated my thoughts to the roadside passing by. Jack and I didn't talk again until he parked the car to get lunch.

****

There was a slight breeze across the open-air patio at AJ's. We sat in the plastic chairs and the server took our order.

"What do you think?" I asked.

"I think this place is a dive," Jack said. "Look!" he said, pointing. "There's a damn bird on the fence staring at us. And there's a cat walking around."

I chuckled. "Welcome to the Keys. It is, but a dive with history and good food. I was referring to the case. What do you think of what happened?"

"It looks like we're heading to the Everglades trailer park again, if you're asking me," Jack said. "Why are you acting like that phone call didn't affect you?"

"I'm not."

"You are, so tell me what's up. Your mom?"

"Yeah. That was Amy, and she said the doctor believes there's a brain tumor."

"Jesus! That's serious."

"It could be. We don't know, but there is absolutely nothing I can do right now. So, we are going to have lunch, talk about the case, and get my mind off of all the other crap."

"I gotcha, partner," Jack said. "Let's start over. Are we heading to the Everglades trailer park again?"

"Yeah. No shit. Of course we are, but not today. I can't believe Machelli didn't mention any of that."

"He's like the rest of them. They tell you what you want to hear, but don't tell everything. They'll leave out anything they think will lay the blame on them."

"So, do you think he's the father?" I asked before I took a long sip of my iced tea.

"Of course he is. Who the hell would be the guy to deliver a baby unless they were the father?"

"Maybe he was just a friend doing what a friend would do," I said.

"That's ridiculous. No. It's more than ridiculous. It's bullshit and a goddamned lie. You would have to be one helluva friend to do that kinda stuff. Besides, you heard the doctor. She said the boy in the van, not Machelli, was always dropping her off and picking her up."

"I dunno. It seems obvious, but who is the guy that always dropped her off and picked her up?" I said.

"He's the boyfriend. Are you just not paying attention, Caine? He's the guy that had the van, you know, the van found in the water with the skeleton?"

"You know what I believe, Jack? I believe the hairy fucker has a lot to explain on this one."

"Damn straight he does, and it ought to be interesting to watch him squirm, to say the least."

"So? What's next?"

"I think we need to scare the shit outta him. We could ask for a DNA test. That should get him to think twice about lying again. It shouldn't take long to get results."

"Yeah, or we could just ask him to tell us the truth this time," I said.

"Ask? Like he's going to admit it? Why are you against a DNA test?"

"I'm not," I said, swallowing a bite of cracker. "No. I meant to ask Machelli about delivering the baby. Then mention the DNA and ask if he'd agree to the test. I can assure you that if he agrees and tells us he doesn't have a problem giving us a sample, he's not the father. Taking the test and getting the evidence is easy."

Jack cocked his head to the side. "Why do you say that? Easy? Don't they stick you with a needle or something?"

"Because I've done it, and it's quick and dirty. No needle. A swab inside your mouth and it's done."

"You've taken it?" Jack said as the conch fritters arrived. "A DNA test? Why would you do that? Put your DNA out in the cyber world?"

I shrugged. "It was Lacy's idea. They did it at her office for kicks, and she wanted me to do it. By the way, the fritters are hot, so don't pop the whole thing in your mouth."

"I won't. You got results? Is being a jerk genetic?"

"What do you mean, jerk? I just warned you about the fritters. Anyhow, no results yet."

"Alright. You want to do this today?" Jack asked. "The thing with Machelli?"

"No. Not today. He's not going anywhere, and he doesn't know we're coming back to talk. I need to wrap my head around all this. I need to think about it."

"We could go after we finish lunch, you know," Jack said. "All we need to do is detour through Florida City, then head up US27 to the trailer park."

"Great thought, but I promise the traffic is going to suck on the Turnpike, and I need to think this through first. I don't want any mistakes, and I want to make sure we don't miss anything."

"Come on," Jack kept urging. "We could be there by four this afternoon."

"That could happen, but it's been a long day, and I need to process this shit. There's something that isn't adding up and I need to think about it before we talk to Machelli again. Besides. I need to follow up with Amy this evening and take care of my mother."

"Fine with me then," Jack said. "You're paying for lunch."

Chapter Twenty-Three

I arrived at my condo that afternoon as the sun was leaving a golden hue across the Fort Lauderdale skyline. I called Amy, and we discussed options. She'd made the arrangements with the hospital, and we would take mom over the following afternoon. I would head over to the house and sit with mom, explain the options, and go from there. I then called Lacy, and she agreed to come over. "Just a couple of drinks and I'll order a pizza," I said. "Sound good?"

"Perfect. Can I stop and pick up the pizza? Does that work?"

It did, and that left me time to shower and jump into my shorts and a soft tee shirt. When she arrived, I already had everything set up on the balcony so we could sit down and eat it while it was hot.

The surrounding evening was quiet, but filled with conversation about what Jack and I had discovered.

"So, she'd been pregnant?" Lacy asked.

"Yes, and that confirmed what Rite told me."

"And you believe there is a person out there. A boy?"

"Well. At this point, a man, since it was like thirty years ago."

"Oh. So, your age or close?"

"Yeah. I suppose you're right. I didn't really think of that."

"Some cop you are, Carter Caine."

"This case has been driving me insane, honestly."

"How so? It's a case, and you have lots of those. Why this one?"

"Dunno. Can't put my finger on it."

"Then let's play a game."

"Game?" I asked, wondering where she was going.

"Sure. I'll start. Tell me what you know about the case."

"Van found at the bottom of Cold Water Creek. There's a partial skeleton inside."

"Got that."

"The skeleton is that of a teenaged girl, identified as Siran Yesayan, AKA Sara."

"And you discovered she'd been pregnant. Right?" Lacy said.

"Right. But we didn't find any record of birth."

"What does that mean?" she asked.

"If a hospital or any medical facility delivers a baby, there's a recorded birth certificate with the county and state. Rite told us she'd been pregnant, so we knew. We could only assume she had the baby. We researched birth records under her name, but there was no record of that."

"How did you discover she had a baby? I mean, she could have aborted it. Right?"

"True. However, she didn't. We found out what had happened, believe it or not, by accident."

"By accident? Is that a police term?"

"Yes. A law enforcement term. Believe it or not, we cops can't see into the future."

"What happened? So, she had the baby?"

"Correct. She worked in a vet's office."

"How would you know that?"

"We didn't know where she worked, but we knew she worked. If you work, you pay tax and social security. A business must file with the state for taxes. That translates to the employee's contributions, which means a social security number. That meant Siran Yesayan paid taxes. The rest was simple."

"So, what does that have to do with the baby?"

"She delivered the baby at her veterinarian's office, where she worked."

"So, no records?"

"Exactly. Like doing it yourself—but safer. Now we're looking for a ghost."

"Where do you go from here?" Lacy asked.

"Right now? Off to bed. The wine is making me sleepy. Tomorrow, Jack and I will head back to one of the suspects, David Machelli. He has some explaining to do.

"Wait. How are you going to get him to confess?"

"I don't expect a confession. We just want the truth, so we can understand what happened."

"So, you're going to ask him to do a DNA test?"

"We'll mention it and see if it stirs anything."

"I see. Speaking of DNA test, your results came back."

"Really? Like I told you, English and Irish."

"Sure. If that's what you want to believe."

"Either way. I have a couple of things to do in the morning."

"Like what? Maybe I can help?"

"Not this time. It's my mother. The doctor suspects a brain tumor, not Alzheimer's as we thought."

"That's horrible. I don't know which one is

worse."

"Yeah. Point taken. It also kinda explains the memory lapses, visions, talking to herself and such. Anyhow, I'm going to chat with her in the morning and explain what needs to be done. Then Amy and I will take her to the hospital for admission so they can run more tests."

"I can do anything you need."

"I know you can, but we're good right now. As soon as I get her admitted, Jack and I will talk with Machelli again."

Chapter Twenty-Four

We arrived unannounced at David Machelli's trailer. The familiar pounding of little feet met us at the door. "Is your dad home?" I asked.

Machelli was standing behind the door. "Yeah. I'm here, Detective. Come in."

The trailer was clean but in the same mess as when we'd left from the earlier visit. The children were running through the house.

"Sorry about the heat," he said. "The air conditioner died last night."

"I get it," I said.

We sat on the couch across from Machelli. He'd made himself comfortable in his recliner and turned the TV off so we could speak. He told the kids to go outside and play.

"David. Sorry to be here again," I said. "We have a couple of other questions, if you don't mind."

"Do I need a lawyer this time?"

"No. No lawyer, although if you wish, you can have one," I said.

"I got nothing to hide."

"Got it. Let's get started," Jack said. "During our last visit, you mentioned Sara was late, indicating she was pregnant."

"No. She was pregnant. I knew that."

"What else did you know?"

Machelli diverted his eyes and shifted in the chair. I felt it happening. My scar was burning, which was a sure indicator something was going on. I tried to ignore it, but it was getting more and more intense.

Jack looked over. "You okay?"

"Yeah. It's hot in here. That's all."

Jack turned his attention to Machelli. "What else do you know? You have the opportunity to tell us, so I'd talk if I were you."

"She was pregnant," Machelli said.

"We know. You said that. But what happened?"

"First, I want immunity."

"Immunity from what?"

"I dunno. Whatever you guys are cooking up."

"Listen," Jack said. "We are trying to find out what happened. That's it."

"Well. Okay. First. I didn't do nutin' wrong. I was in bed. It was late. Sara called my house and said she needed my help. I didn't understand why she'd be calling me, but she was kinda mixed up, I guess. Anyhow, I got dressed, made up some story for my parents, and went to her house. When I got there, I she was like cramping."

"Contractions?"

"Yeah. Those things. She told me the baby was coming. I'm like, what the hell am I supposed to do? She said she had a plan. So, I helped her get in my car, and she told me to drive her to her work. We got there, but on the way, I asked her why she didn't call Jeff because it sure as hell wasn't my baby. She told me Jeff's dad was like a cop or something, and Jeff would demand she go to the hospital. Mr. Goodie two-shoes that guy. That dude always wanted to do the right thing."

"So, you helped deliver the baby?"

"Not really, yeah, sort of. I got the stuff Sara said to get like water, towels, a sheet on the metal table thing. I thought it was weird that I was doing doctor shit, but it was what it was. She was my friend and needed help. She was scared. Her mother died after Sara was born."

"So, you would say she kind of delivered the baby herself?"

"Yeah. Sorta. I mean, I helped. You know. I had these gloves on and the baby just slipped out of her. Uh, you know. I sort of caught it, but it was all gooey and slippery. Then I heard a noise, and the boss lady came in the room."

"Dr. Wisenbaum," I said.

"Yeah. I mean, I didn't know who she was until Sara said something. The baby had just slipped out like nothing, and then Sara pointed at the knife. She said she was going to cut the biblical cord, whatever that is."

"Umbilical cord," I said. "It's called an umbilical cord."

"Yeah. That. Anyways, I was reaching for the knife when the door opened, and Dr. Wisenbaum walked in. Man! I thought we were in big trouble."

"And then what happened?" I asked.

"The doctor jumped in and took over. That was it. Then we cleaned up. The doctor wanted us to go to the hospital, and Sara said no. She didn't want a hospital involved. The doc was really kind and helped her, told her to stay for the night. I stayed with her."

"So, the next morning, you took her and the baby home?" Jack said.

"Yeah. Sara was tough. I helped to clean up the place, and that was it. What else? There wasn't nothing I could do, so I left. And then, like I told you before, I went to her house and she was gone."

"I'm confused," I said as I rubbed my scar.

"Yeah?" Machelli responded.

"This isn't making sense. During the last interview, you said you and Sara were close, and one night, you got to third base. Then you mentioned she was worried about what her dad would think because she was late. Then you told me you didn't believe her because you used protection. You said she didn't look like she was pregnant, and I am quoting you. You said, *She wasn't a skinny chick, if you know what I mean.*"

"Yeah. She was chubby," Machelli said. "I mean, not fat, just larger."

"You mentioned that the last time you saw her and Jeff was at the canal off Atlantic Avenue," I said. "And that night, all of you passed out. Right?"

"Yeah. It was a crazy night, and I guess we passed out for a while when it was raining. And in the morning, the van, Jeff, and Sara were gone. That was the last time I saw any of them."

"The problem with that is your timeline, Machelli."

"What do you mean?"

"What I'm saying is that I understand that you went to Sara's house the next day to check on her. The problem I'm having is your hanging at the bridge comment. I think you woke up the next morning after hanging at the bridge and saw they were gone. So, then you went to her house, and the old man said he hadn't seen her. Does that sum it up Mr. Machelli?"

"Well, you gotta understand, Detective Caine. That

was a long time ago, but yeah, the baby was around a month old, I guess," Machelli said.

"Okay. Got it," I said. "I'm saying that you and Sara delivered the baby, and she took him home to her father's house. I understand that. Then sometime later, maybe a couple of weeks or several, you and the gang were at Cold Water Creek, hanging out."

"Okay. Yeah. That night at the creek was about a month after she had the kid. I get it, and that was probably more like it now that I'm thinking about it," Machelli said.

"Right. So perhaps that was the night she, or maybe Jeff, confronted you," I said. "Then all of you had a hand in figuring out what to do with the baby."

"Well, not exactly. But kinda. Sara wanted to give the little guy up for adoption, but me and Jeff said she should raise the kid and we would help."

"Okay. Now we are getting somewhere."

"Yeah," Machelli said. "So, the talk gets heated, and I just gave it up. It wasn't going nowhere. She was really stubborn. When she looked at me and said, 'It's not your baby'. She had a fire in her eyes that I will never forget. I walked back over under the bridge and popped a beer.

"Jeff and Sara got louder and louder. Then it started raining. It really came down that night. Those guys were out there having at it in the pouring rain. I gave up, laid back, and passed out like the rest of them. I figured those two would get it done without me."

"And that's when you woke up the next morning and they were gone?"

"Yep. The van, Jeff, and Sara were gone. That's the last time I saw any of them. I went to Sara's house the next day, but her old man said he hadn't seen her or the baby. Now that's a true story. Then I went over to Jeff's and his mom and dad said they hadn't seen him either. I figured they'd started over somewhere else, the three of them. I swear. That's everything."

"I get it, Dave," I said. "You were there to help and got wrapped up in it."

"Yeah. I guess. She was my friend, and it hurt me, but I miss her still. Even though it was a long time ago."

"Got it. If we have any more questions, we'll call."

****

Jack and I headed for the car. I saw Machelli watching us as we left the street in front of his trailer.

"All I got to say is, what the hell! What does that mean she was gone?" Jack asked me as we drove away from the trailer park.

"I guess it means just what he said. He went there to check on her and she was gone," I said. "Remember, her father didn't even report her missing until the school sent the authorities over to check on her. The conclusion that they'd run off wasn't a bad one."

"You know that van's been in the creek since that night," Jack said.

"No doubt," I said. "I just don't understand how the girl was inside of it and where the hell was this Jeff character. Or the baby."

As we pulled onto the highway, a blinding pain shot through my head. I pulled off the road and grabbed my head with both hands. It felt like lightning bolts were running through it.

"What the hell was that?" Jack asked.

"Man, I don't know. It hurt like hell, though. Do

255

me a favor, will ya?"

"Of course," he said, looking like he'd seen a ghost. "What?"

"You drive."

We changed seats. I pushed mine back a bit and fell asleep. Jack drove me to my condo. That was when everything went sideways.

The next thing I knew, I was hovering. Floating in the air. Observing things around me. It was a full moon night, with a few stars, and I saw a long strip of black water lined with enormous trees, vines hanging and stretching into the depths. The water glittered, and the moon sat low on the horizon behind the trees. To the other side of me, a bridge.

In the distance, across what seemed like a meadow, I saw a car. Its headlights reflected off a van parked near the water. It was foggy, and everything felt dense and muffled. Two figures stood facing each other, arms moving about as if they were in a heated argument.

I knew I was dreaming about my conversation with Machelli. I was standing close to them now. They were shadows, and I tried to listen to the conversation, but it was useless. The ground beneath became soft, muddy. I sank. Everything around me spun, and the water rose. A young girl with fiery red eyes hovered before me. The wind blew around her hair as streaks of lightning crossed behind her. She reached toward me with a swiping motion. I spun and rose from the earth.

I looked down to see a sedan arrive. A figure moved toward the van. I moved in a circle as everything spun around me. I saw a car, a van, the girl. Faces and places and things I'd never experienced before. My head had a shrieking pain, and my eyes bulged from their sockets. I outstretched my arms, my hands were on fire, and then the image of the girl, her arm the shape of a lightning bolt, shoved down my throat and yanked my heart out of my chest. It beat in her hands as blood fell into the water and I gasped for what felt like my last breath.

Bam. Bam. Bam. Bam. I slammed into the ground and gasping.

"Whoa! Buddy. You okay?" Jack said.

"Uh. Yeah. Fine. I had a dream—I."

"Yeah. You don't seem fine. You're sweating like crazy. Let me pull over."

"No. I'm good. Really. Just drop me at the condo."

Chapter Twenty-Five

Fully clothed, I found myself in bed. I sat up, wondering how I got there. I didn't recall the drive after that or Jack dropping me off. I vaguely remembered getting in my front door after interviewing Machelli.

Habits and routines are a funny thing, and regardless of mental state, we often do the same things with no conscious thought. This wasn't any different.

I got up and drank some water in the kitchen and walked back into my bedroom, mostly just to follow my steps. Had I secured my weapon? It wasn't on me. I wore the same clothes as the day before, which I didn't expect. I noticed my wallet wasn't in my pants I checked the nightstand.

When I opened the drawer, I sighed with relief. Apparently, I'd stuck to my routine and placed everything there. I then noticed the remembrance card from my uncle's funeral next to my service revolver. Uncle Derek was family, but I didn't know him that well. I'd forgotten about the card being there. I pulled it from the drawer and looked it over, thinking I'd give it to my mom the next time I saw her.

There was a lovely poem with a picture of my uncle, and a name engraved along the bottom. *J. Derek Caine*. I took a picture of the card using my phone and texted Lacy.

She called me back. "What's up with this? Why are

you sending me a picture of a remembrance card?"

"Look at the name," I said.

"At what? He was your uncle. Your father's younger brother, right?" she said.

"Yeah. And I hate to say this. I think I found my suspect."

"How do you figure that? He was your *uncle*."

"Look at the remembrance card. It has his name."

"Sure. J. Derek Caine. So, it's your last name, and he was your uncle. That makes him a suspect? What was his first name?" she asked.

"Dunno. It's the letter J. The only name I ever heard was Derek, and I thought that was his first name."

"And?"

"Are you thinking of a J as in Jefferson or Jeff, or maybe Jeffrey?" Lacy asked.

I took a deep breath. "Exactly. My non-existent suspect."

"Holy shit," Lacy replied.

So, there it was: I thought I finally had the answer. Jefferson was the last suspect and possibly the person and owner of the van. The van that had become Sara's tomb.

We were still on the phone, but both of us were silent. Finally, Lacy asked, "What are you going to do?"

I sat on the floor next to the bed with the memorial card in one hand. I stared at it. "How the hell should I know?"

"You're a cop, and it's your job to know. Am I wrong?"

"No. I got that. Thanks. I was thinking more on the lines of having to confront my mother. I'll talk with

Jack tomorrow. He'll know how to handle this."

"Gimme a break, Carter. There is no handling this. It seems damn clear. Your uncle killed this girl."

"It certainly feels like he did. But he's dead, too. And when I talk with my mother, it will probably kill her. And there's more," I said.

"Dead is dead. How is it more?" she asked.

"You're forgetting there was a baby."

"A baby? You're right. I forgot that."

"Yeah."

"So quick math says this baby, if it exists, would be about maybe thirty?"

"Yep. So not a baby now."

"Yep. So, the next question is, where is this person? He's Sara's next of kin. Her only kin. Does he even know who his mother and father were?"

"More important. Who is this person?"

Carter sighed. "That's the million-dollar question."

"True," said Lacy, "but you must consider he may not know his past. He was a baby when it all happened, probably put up for adoption since her dad was useless, and the last thing he would have wanted would be to raise a baby."

"Maybe we search adoption records from that time? I can't imagine how many there would be."

Lacy's laugh was shaky. "A lot. Either way, you need some answers. If your uncle was involved, my guess is your mother would know. How is she doing?"

"She took being admitted to the hospital like a trooper. She's a tough lady. Amy said the doctors ran the tests and we will know more in the morning."

"Are you going to the hospital to see her?"

"Of course. Tomorrow for sure."

"That's serious stuff, Carter."

"No kidding," I said. "She's only in her seventies. Her issues have been happening for a while. Before my uncle passed, he'd called and mentioned it. I've noticed things, too."

"Well, maybe you need a good night's sleep, then tomorrow will be a little easier," she said. "I'm really sorry this case has turned in this direction, but it will be okay. I know it will."

Lacy was right. Something was still wrong with my scenario. How could my uncle be involved? I reviewed all the facts, one by one.

We solved cases based on facts and evidence. Stuff like science and DNA and–I realized at that moment— my DNA. Lacy asked me to do that stupid test. At least, I thought it was stupid. I sent her a text.

—*did you get those DNA results for me?*—

—*yes . Haven't opened.*—

–*good. Bring it over when you can.*—

–*worried about a DNA result with all this going on?*—she typed back.

–*gotta hunch. Remember, I'm the cop in this picture*—

–*coming over now*—

While I waited, I got to my feet and grabbed a quick shower and put on clean clothes. I brewed a fresh pot of coffee and sat on the balcony in the sun.

What if there's a DNA match of some sort? Did I want to know? Preposterous. How in the world would my DNA have anything to do with this case? The thought of it terrified me. My mind ran wild with what-if scenarios. Looking back and considering the matched names and age, it seemed a possibility, but people have the same last name—it happens.

Twenty minutes later, there was a knock on my door. I opened it up and pulled her inside. "Hey," she said with a smile. "You okay?"

"Do you have it?" I noticed her perfume.

"Yes, Mr. Impatient. Can I have a kiss?"

"Uh, sure." I pecked her cheek and took the results out of her hand.

She rolled her eyes and sat down. I tore open the envelope.

"What's it say?" she asked.

I scanned the document, all graphs and charts, with a narrative. They impressed me. It spoke of nationality, and wellness, categories for illnesses. It was exciting and more information than I had anticipated.

The last page delivered the information I needed– and feared.

Lacy must have read my face. "Carter? What is it?"

"What?" I replied, unable to pull my eyes away from the words I'd just read.

"Do you see something in there?"

"I do."

"Does it make sense?"

"No." I hesitated. "I mean, yes. It does." I finally turned to look at her. "You will not believe this."

She put her hand on my wrist and tried to smile, but I could see the pain in her eyes. "Tell me."

"I don't know if I believe this."

The answer was too real to be true. It was too convenient. The answer, my questions, everything I needed was there. I struggled to believe it. No one would believe it.

"This can't be true," I whispered. My scar told me

differently. It burned like fire.

Lacy stood and wrapped her arms around me. "Spit it out, Carter."

"Remember I told you I was English and Irish? No doubt and nothing else?"

"I do."

"Well. It seems I am not."

"Many people get surprised—haven't you seen the commercials? They think they're German and turns out they're Irish, or whatever. What are you?"

"My DNA shows it's from the same region in northern Europe as Sara."

"What?" Lacy stammered.

"Sara. Or rather, Siran. The young girl in the van. We share the same mitochondrial DNA."

"Well, that's impossible. It would mean you're related."

The burning in my scar subsided. I nodded. "Hmmm. Maybe *you* should be the cop."

Chapter Twenty-Six

December 2017

After Lacy went home, I crawled into bed and stared at the ceiling fan for the next several hours. When I couldn't stand it any longer, I called Jack and my captain and told them I needed to take care of some personal business. I called Jimmy and asked to meet him at his shop.

He wasn't a cop, and that was the point. The last thing I needed was law enforcement involvement. This fresh evidence could be something dire, and it all pointed to my mother and my uncle Derek.

"What do you think?" I asked him after he looked over the information.

"Let me tell you," he said, running a hand through his sun-streaked hair. "A DNA match is some serious shit. If I wasn't looking at the science, I wouldn't think this was possible. This situation could have some serious consequence."

"Yeah. Tell me about it. How am I going to confront my mother?"

"The tougher part is that she's your grandmother, it seems."

"Well, that's a good point, but hell, either way, this is trouble. I feel like I've entered some kind of alternate universe."

Jimmy nodded and handed me back the report. "Yeah. Well, you know what? You have choices. There are always choices."

"Choices?"

"Yeah. Ignore this DNA stuff. Burn it. Bury the truth and move on with the case as unsolved. I mean, only you, me, and Lacy know about this."

"That's one option, but you know I can't do that."

"Well, I don't see why not. If you're Sara's son, you're her only living relative, right? You know the truth about what happened. There's no sense in keeping at this."

"How's that?" I said, sipping at the last of my now-cold coffee.

"Let's say your grandmother and your uncle, who I suppose is actually your father, are guilty of what—letting Sara die? Or maybe it was an accident they were hiding."

"Yeah. And?"

"Your dad is dead, and your grandma? Well? You said her dementia is a problem. If she can't remember, can she help defend herself? Will she even know what's happening?"

"So, you're saying everyone involved is dead, and there is no justice to be served because I'm the only victim at this point."

"Yeah. Like I've said before," Jimmy said with a grin, "it's like you're a genius or something."

I left the surf shop, still not knowing what I was going to do. But I felt lighter. Jimmy had always given me good advice. His words were wise, and he brought up some good points. I thought about the consequences and decided that honesty was the best course. I headed to the hospital.

Chapter Twenty-Seven

Mom was in her bed and asleep. I decided to let her rest while I went to grab a cup a coffee. As I turned, Amy walked in. "Oh! You're here. Great."

"How's my mother?"

"She, uh, is doing okay. I had a chance to speak with the doctor."

"Good news? Better news, maybe?"

"I'm afraid not, Carter." She shuffled her feet and looked to the floor. "Let's go outside and talk."

There was a small garden area off the main floor. We sat on the bench and Amy continued telling me the situation. "Auntie has what is called a brain herniation."

"Like a hernia on the brain?"

"Sort of. A brain herniation, or a cerebral herniation, occurs when brain tissue, blood, and cerebrospinal fluid shift from their normal position inside the skull. Usually caused by swelling from a tumor."

I leaned back on the bench. "This doesn't sound good."

"It's not. But it explains a lot of her recent issues."

"What's next?"

"The doctor said they will set her up for a procedure to drain any excess fluids from the brain. They have her on medication now to reduce the swelling."

"Does she understand what's happening?"

"Surprisingly, she does and appears to be accepting it."

"Accepting? Does she understand this could be fatal?"

"She does and believe it or not, she actually said that."

"I need to talk with her."

Stepping back into the room, she stirred. I touched her shoulder, and she looked up. Her eyes were moist and bloodshot. I sat across from her and took her hand. "How are you feeling?"

"I knew you would discover it, eventually. It took a while, and I still can't believe this is happening."

Her response puzzled me. "What are you talking about, Mom?"

She chuckled ever so slightly and patted my hand. "You are such a smart boy."

"Not that smart. Talk to me."

"Your father–I mean, your grandfather–was an incredible investigator. Some called him brilliant. When you chose law enforcement for your career, I knew it was only a matter of time. You're not only like your grandfather, but you also take a criminal investigation to an entirely different level. I'm so sorry, honey. It wasn't supposed to be like this."

"You understand the predicament, right?" I asked, placing my hand over hers. "You do realize where this could go?"

"Yes, and whatever I need to do, I will. But truth be told, it was the right thing to do at the time. That poor girl was dead and your father, Jefferson, was terribly upset at the events. He honestly didn't mean to kill her. They argued in the rain and when he went to take her arm and get her out of the rain, she pulled away to violently that she fell and hit her head. He tried to help. I mean, he was responsible for her death, and looking back, we did a stupid thing to cover it up. I should say, I did a stupid thing. Your grandfather wanted us to come clean, but he also wanted to protect us. We should have involved him before pushing the van into the water. He would have known what to do." Tears ran unchecked down her face.

I had to swallow twice before I could speak. "Mom. You don't have to tell me all this."

"No, Carter. It's time. Record it or take notes or do whatever you need to do. You're an officer of the law and it's time for justice. For Sara, for Jefferson, and for you."

"Listen. I don't understand why, but I get it. Somehow, I'm at peace and ready to move on. I need to sort this out, but maybe I can keep you out of it. It will take some creativity, but I think I can."

"You're just like your grandfather. I can tell you he said almost the same thing that night."

"I know Jefferson Caine was your son and my father. At this point, no one knows the details of what happened except you. There are some things to resolve, and I really don't know the details, but it appears that the dead girl is, in all probability, my mother."

"Yes, Carter. She was your mother and your father truly loved her. It was an accident. She really slipped and hit her head. He came here, and we went back to check on her, but she was cold and lifeless."

"I get it. So, here's what you need to do. Tell me that Jefferson acted on his own. He pushed the van into the water because he thought his girlfriend was dead and didn't want to get in trouble. Then he came home that night, and it was too late to save her."

"But the baby. I mean *you*. We went to Sara's house and got you. We couldn't leave you there alone. Isn't that kidnapping?"

"Technically, it is, but the baby was Jefferson's son. I'm hoping I can convince the State Attorney's Office to take into account your current condition and consider that you were only doing what you thought was the right thing as a mother, Besides, from what we have discovered, Sara's father wasn't fit to raise a child."

"Her father? You know about her father?"

"I know a lot now, Mom. We interviewed Jefferson's friends. Well, the only friend that was still alive, David Machelli. He told us about Sara and her father. He thinks they all ran away."

"I see," she said, looking at me sadly. "So, what do I need to do?"

"Right now, you need to stay here and not talk to anyone."

"There's more you need to know."

I braced myself. How much more could there be? "Okay. Go ahead."

"Your father died a long time ago."

"It wasn't that long ago. We were at the funeral, remember?"

"You mean Derek?"

"Yeah. We drove up. Had a service."

"Oh. I see. You thought Derek was your father."

"Isn't he my father?"

"No," she said, very clearly. "Jefferson, our son,

was your father. Derek was your grandfather's brother."

"I'm confused. I thought J.D. Caine was originally Jefferson D. Caine, and you changed his name to J. Derek Caine."

"No. Just a coincidence. You father's name was Jefferson D. Caine."

"So where is he?"

"That's complicated."

"It can't be any more complicated than what we talking about right now."

She sighed and turned more toward me. "You understand your grandfather used his contacts to remove any trace of Jefferson. Right?

"Yeah. I get that."

"Jefferson had a difficult time with that, the loss of Sara, his life changes. It was too much, I suppose. Soon afterward, he went into a deep depression. We tried to help him, but it was of no use. Long story short, he killed himself."

"Try that again."

"Understand. There was no trace of Jefferson's life left. Your grandfather had erased all signs of him. With that, everyone assumed he had run away, and we simply kept up the lie, but to Jefferson, his life was over."

"But there was a baby—me."

"That's what I meant by complicated. Jefferson and I, along with the newborn, I mean you, went to Atlanta to stay with Derek. We needed to create a timeline and Jefferson needed to disappear."

"Didn't Derek ask questions?"

"Sure, he did, but we crafted a story about Jefferson getting a girl pregnant, her family, and all that—we just left out all the bad things we did. Since the story was kinda true I guess it sounded authentic enough and Derek accepted it and us."

"I get that. You protected Derek from any prosecution."

"Exactly. The problem was Jefferson couldn't get past the trauma and I couldn't blame him. He was young and simply didn't know how to handle what happened. He truly loved Sara and I believe she loved him but in the heat of the moment, one can do stupid things, even to the people they love the most."

"That explains a lot, but what happened to Jefferson?"

"Like I mentioned, he wasn't equipped to handle the stress. He found some pills in the medicine cabinet. They were for Derek, an old prescription for when he had hurt himself in an accident in his wood shop. He'd forgotten they were there."

"Pain pills."

"Yes. Anyhow, we didn't know but Jefferson had found them and started taking them. He was sleeping a lot and we cast it off as depression and teenager. We figured he'd get over it. He didn't. One night, after we all had gone to bed, I suppose he decided it was time. When we awoke the next morning, he was dead. The empty bottle on the nightstand. Anyhow, your grandfather stepped in again and fixed it. That's when I came back, we explained you as *our* new baby."

"Oh boy. I didn't expect that."

"No one did."

"So, Jefferson has to be buried someplace."

"Like I said, your grandfather stepped in. He had a vast array of contacts. One was a crematorium."

"So, you had Jefferson cremated?"

"Yes. You know that blue vase on the top shelf of the curio cabinet?"

"The one with the gold trim next to the clock?"

Chapter Twenty-Eight

January 2018

It was all I could take; we solved a murder case. My grandmother was dying in a hospital. Siran Yesayan, my mother, could now rest in peace. Great. Another point for Carter Caine, another case solved, but at what cost?

I didn't have the heart to explain Dr. Rite's theory of catalepsy to my mother. For one, she wouldn't understand it, and more important, it would end up making a bad situation worse. Since it couldn't be proven one way or the other, I also kept it out of the case file.

Like with every story, there should be a happy ending. Mine was bittersweet. By the time all the evidence was submitted, and the courts got their act together, which took more than a year, Joanna Caine, my grandmother, had passed.

The State can prosecute posthumously but they decided not to do so. I was also relieved that the State Attorney's office was lenient because she was dead and they considered her state of mind, age, along with time passed. Not that it was okay to kill someone, but it she thought she was protecting her son and believed the girl was dead. Side note: I believe Sara was alive in the van. In that Jefferson was also dead, there was no one to prosecute. Of course, I had to sit through all the proceedings, devastating as they were and, confusing to many people, in that I could only say so much. I certainly didn't include any testimony about visions, dreams, or any such thing.

A year of this and I was in terrible shape. All the therapy I went through, and the psychoanalyzing, the spiritual advisers, all were moot points. I knew my days in law enforcement were over and I was again at a point where that proverbial curveball is headed for the batter with two outs and three runners on base. This moment could not be my game over. It was time for a new life.

Back at the condo the final and grueling day with courts and the State's Attorney office, I was exhausted. Jimmy would say, "Stick a fork in me. I'm done."

I was. Done.

The sun was setting, and a cool breeze wafted through the sliding glass doors off the balcony. I laid back in the lounger intending to watch the sun slowly drop beyond the horizon. As is did, I felt a touch on my shoulder.

She was back—Sara.

I hadn't had a dream since my grandmother confessed. It had been somewhere around a year and nothing. Complete quiet. I thought it was over and for once, I was at peace. Yeah. Lucky me, right? Remember the curve ball.

It was different this time. It was almost real. I felt the touch or at least I thought I did. I turned. Nothing. *Jesus Christ, I don't need this again.*

I closed my eyes for a second and when I opened them, she sat in the chair across from me. Not as a ghost, not an apparition, but a true to life looking person—a young girl with soft brown hair across her shoulders, beautiful brown eyes, and an olive complexion.

"*I'm Sara,*" she said.

I sat up. "I know. You're my mother."

"*Yes. I was and will be for always.*"

"I'm so sorry for what happened."

She chuckled. "*It wasn't you. And I know it was an accident.*"

"You are kind to consider that."

"*Carter. There are worse things than death. You will learn that one day.*"

I watched her quietly. You could feel the peace around her. I could tell she was gentle and kind. "I'm sorry I never knew you."

"*You did and you will. I'm not going anywhere.*"

"What does that mean?"

"*It means I am here with you always. Just over your shoulder and watching out for you.*"

It was my turn to chuckle. "Like my Guardian Angel?"

"*Yes. I've been in your dreams, but we met in that office. Remember?*"

"Martin? I remember."

"*You knew then.*"

"I did. You've been with me always. My childhood, the time I was shot, in the hospital, and my marriage."

"*I was and I am. As a child I gave you the only gift I could to get you through life. To help you find me and the truth.*"

"My ability to see what others can't?"

"*Yes. Carry that with you through your life. Learn*

to use it for good."

"I think I am done being cop."

"You don't need that to be a good person and to save others. You will do that on your own."

"My own? I have never been that altruistic."

"You saved me, didn't you?"

"That's not fair. You kinda guided me."

"No. That was you. I was only there waiting for you to find the path. You did."

"At what cost though?"

"You brought justice, and you brought peace. Humans make their choices. You had nothing to do with all that. I ended up where I am because of choice. It's how it works."

"So, none of this destiny bullshit?"

"Not destiny. Your life is planned by something greater, but you have a choice as to which road you will take. There are many paths."

"I can see that. So how will I know the right path?"

"That's just it. You won't. The choice is what gives you purpose."

"Oddly that makes sense although talking to a ghost makes no sense at all."

"Silly man. I'm not a ghost. I am your spirit. I live in your heart and soul. I am with you now and always. Just listen when you need guidance. It will come. For now, I will rest and let you make those choices we spoke of."

And as quietly as she appeared she was gone.

When I awoke it was morning. I was still on the balcony but I knew three things: I needed to change me, call Lacy, and see my therapist.

I called Lacy and apologized for neglecting her.

We made a date for later in the evening.

My next call was to my therapist. I had to confess everything; tell the whole story. I did and was surprised at the response. Sara said we have choices.

I chose to tell my story to the world if they wanted to hear it.

It seems they did.

Chapter Twenty-Nine

My therapist said my best bet would be to put it on paper. 'Write it down,' she said. 'In doing so, it can put things into perspective. Make things clearer. Change your view.' The truth of the matter was that it was time for me to make a change. A big change.

I didn't know if she was right, so, "Malarkey," I told her.

My brain said bullshit, but I needed to turn a new leaf and get away from my previous life. It took a year of soul searching and some more therapy. Lacy stuck with me through the entire torment. I finally gave in and wrote what I knew; everything that had occurred throughout the investigation, the trial, and the resolution. Reliving the horror was a lot to take, but she was right; I felt better. It was like a confession, and I also learned a few things about myself along the way. I realized I wasn't the man I should be. I could've been a better husband to Jenna and not the self-consumed jerk. Jenna wasn't perfect, but neither was I. I could've been more patient. I'm still working on that part of my life.

By the time I put the story on paper, there were over 100,000 words. As promised, I took the manuscript to my therapist. She read it front to back and said she was terrified, exhilarated, and totally caught up in the story. She suggested I edit the material and let her reread it. Of course, I did. It's bizarre how you repeat yourself while writing. Either way, I took the manuscript to her once again and said my next step would be to work on getting an agent.

Again, I said to her malarkey but meant, well, you know. As mentioned, I am trying to be more patient and not the same guy I was.

After a professional edit, more suggestions, more writing, it took about a year to finish it, but it was worth it. I sent the manuscript to Charles Dillaman, an agent I knew from a court case a few years back, for his opinion. Two days later, Dillaman called and said he loved it and he had submitted the manuscript to a place called penguin.

I had no idea what that meant and replied, "Like a bird?"

He laughed and explained it was the name of a book publisher. They want to publish my story. I laughed and said "Malarkey" but meant... well, you know.

****

Dillaman and I flew to New York to meet with the bigwigs. In the meeting, they offered me six figures for a book deal. They said there could be an option for a movie, and if so, it could be lucrative. Of course, I accepted their offer, and inside a year's time, the book came out. Within weeks, it hit the New York Times bestseller list, which surprised me. I figured someone screwed up something. I mean, I thought it was a good story, but a best seller?

Regardless of what I believed, it was a hit, and then my agent said Warner Brothers wanted to make it a movie. Who was I to argue?

After the book and the movie, I didn't need to

worry about a paycheck. I discovered that money doesn't bring peace of mind, so Jimmy suggested I move south.

"South?" I said. "Like Mexico?"

He said, "No, dumbass. Like the Keys." Didn't you say you had a second cousin from a third marriage related to someone in your family and lived in Islamorada? You also said you have been going there to fish, so it seems to me you need to move there and get out of town. Call your cousin what's his-name and let him hook you up.

He was referring to Herb. He's like one of those second cousins, twice removed from a previous marriage where no one can remember all the details. Our relationship came through Herb's wife, and he was something like her second or third husband, and I think she was a cousin to my dad or, I should say, my grandfather.

I then explained to Jimmy that moving south had been on my mind. I had spoken to Herb during the trial. He had read in the newspaper what had happened. During our conversation, he told me about his latest adventure. He has a buddy, an eccentric Cuban dude by the name of Willy. He said Willy had this insane idea to go to Cuba on a rescue mission.

I said, "Rescue people, you mean?"

He told me no, not people, but it was a long story and he couldn't talk about the details on the phone. He also mentioned he knew of a great sailboat coming on the market. I asked him to look into it, and if it was a deal, make an offer. He did, so there was also a sailboat waiting for me to arrive. It was nothing fancy; a pre-owned Hunter 45DS. This boat would be more than enough for Lacy and me when she followed.

Herb had found it on the local government website. It was for sale because the authorities apprehended the guy that owned. He was smuggling drugs from South America. After checking it out, Herb made the offer and said she was good to go and in excellent condition. That reminded me of what Jimmy had said long before all this became a thing; The Keys are a sunny place with some shady people.

Considering I had nothing left where I was except Lacy, the finding of the boat became the impetus behind my decision to move south to what some folks called Paradise. She and I met at my place, and she helped me sort out what I was leaving behind. Let's say the dumpster was full. She had some loose ends to tie up and she would follow. That gave me hope and something to look forward to. Our plans included a Caribbean cruise on the new sailboat, a stop here and there, and perhaps some naked swimming on a reef somewhere off the coast of the Turks and Caicos.

Chapter Thirty

February 2022

It was a long drive from Fort Lauderdale and through Miami traffic. There had been the usual fender-benders that tied up the expressway. It was Friday, and I had been sitting in gridlock for almost six hours. I needed a break, but I was nervous someone would recognize me, so I didn't want to stop. I had just cleared the turnpike and made it through Florida City. The road leading to the Keys passes The Last Chance Saloon. A place to grab a burger and a beer just before the turn to Ocean Reef and the Stretch. The pub was still there and a shining beacon at this point.

I was starving and needed to stretch my legs. A cold beer wasn't a bad idea as well. A place like Last Chance could be perfect, and besides, it would be another thirty or forty minutes before I got to Key Largo, depending on how bad the Stretch was going to be with all the mainlanders heading down for the weekend. Either way, I was hungry and needed a bathroom.

My eyes adjusted from the sun as I stepped through the doors of the Last Chance Saloon. I am not kidding. It's called the Last Chance Saloon, and it has a shadow graffiti of Sasquatch on the wall. Other than that, it's a nondescript, tan building at the end of Florida City.

The smell of old liquor, greasy food, and stale tobacco rose to meet me as I entered. I noticed the click of billiards to my right side. A man dressed in the clothes of an hourly worker leaned across the pool table under dim lighting. The bartender was loading the bar for the night. A server sat at the far end of the bar, flipping through a magazine—a life-sized plastic skeleton dressed as a pirate displayed at one end of the bar. Around me were the usual quips on posters with parrots about Paradise, Sunsets, water scenes. I pulled onto a barstool, and the bartender nodded toward me.

"Beer?" he asked. I nodded in return because men rarely state the obvious. "Where are you headed?" He slid a bottle toward me.

"South," I said.

"That's a long way."

"Islamorada."

"Vacation?"

I smiled and thought about that word. *Was this the end, or was it the beginning of a new chapter in my life?* I thought. No matter. Either way, it was a start. Perhaps an escape, a change, or a chance. I left behind most everything except a duffle bag of cash, some clothes, and all the shit that still rattled around in my head. I thought that being off the grid for an extended time might be what I needed.

"Why do you ask?" I said.

"No reason. Just talk. Most people headed south are running from or running to something, and you don't look like the vacation type."

"What the hell does that mean?"

"Nothing other than what I said, dude. You do look familiar, though," the bartender said.

"Do I now?"

"Yeah. Like I have seen you someplace."

"He's the guy on the book cover, Pete," said the server, looking up from the magazine. "There's an ad here about his book."

"What?" Pete said as he walked over to the server. "Damn, Gloria, you're right," Pete said as he held the magazine up and aligned the picture with my face.

"Yeah. That's me. Thanks," I said.

"So, you a writer?"

"Of course, he's a writer," Gloria said. "His face is on the book."

"What's it about?" Pete asked.

"Fucking crazy shit," Gloria added. "Is this a true story?"

"What do you know?" Pete said. "You ain't read the book."

"The article in this magazine is about this guy," Gloria quipped. "It's talking about the book."

I felt uneasy and wanted to leave. Notoriety was not on the menu, and I hoped to keep a low profile. It's hard to do when you write a book about your life and become a bestseller.

"Here ya go, Pete," I said as I stood, and I tossed a twenty-dollar bill on the bar.

"Whoa! Not so fast, writer guy. Carter, right? We haven't had anyone famous here for a long time, so stick around a bit."

"I really should move along," I said.

"Baloney. I'll make you a burger and get you another beer. That's story sounds crazy. Is it real?"

"Only the parts I didn't make up," I said.

"No shit. So, you're a cop?"

"Was a cop. Not anymore."

"Of course, not anymore, you moron," said Gloria. "He's a writer, and they made a movie about this."

"Is that right?" Pete said.

"Yeah, that's right," I confirmed with my new fans. I wasn't thrilled about the discovery but had become accustomed to being recognized. Between the news, the book, the solved case, this guy became a reluctant local celebrity. It was fun at first, and then the questions came, then the doubt, then the agents and producers wanting to make it a movie. Now the movie was out, and everyone knew Carter Caine. At least they thought they knew me.

"I've always wanted to be a writer," Pete said.

"Seems everyone does," I remarked.

"Got any advice?"

"Sure. Screw up your life. Realize there is no hope. Lose everyone you love, then write whatever you want. Just don't let it go to your head and try to publish it."

"Ain't that the point?"

"Yeah, but seriously, be prepared to screw up your life."

"Jesus, man. You got a book, a movie, and probably a shitload of cash. Right?"

"That part's not lying," I said. "It's the rest of it that will kill you."

"Like what?"

"You got a couple of hours? I'll tell you the story."

"I got it, man. Billy, my barback, he's the one playing pool, can finish what I'm doing."

The burger arrived as Pete, and I walked to a booth. We sat, and I looked at him.

"It's simple, really," I said. "But sometimes, it's

dumb luck. Sometimes it's just good police work. Sometimes the dead walk right back into your fucked-up life and tell you everything, whether you want to hear it or not."

A word about the author...

Steven LaBree, a Miami native with an insatiable curiosity worked with newspaper, law enforcement, healthcare, and technology before deciding to leave corporate life and pursue writing full time. Through those experiences, he creates stories of mystery, human frailty, and the reality of truth. He builds an imaginary journey reflecting human nature and the perfectly imperfect, using fallible, quirky, and honest characters. He loves to keep you on the edge of your seat with twists and turns served with a little paranormal on the side. www.stevenlabree.com

Thank you for purchasing
this publication of The Wild Rose Press, Inc.

For questions or more information
contact us at
info@thewildrosepress.com.

The Wild Rose Press, Inc.
www.thewildrosepress.com

Lightning Source UK Ltd.
Milton Keynes UK
UKHW020829060223
416538UK00016B/1835

9 781509 246908